THE

# ITALIAN
# PRISONER

# THE
# ITALIAN
# PRISONER

*A Novel*

Elisa M. Speranza

BURGUNDY BEND

The Italian Prisoner

Published by Burgundy Bend Press

BURGUNDY BEND

Learn more at: www.elisamariesperanza.com

Cover art by Deedra Ludwig

Library of Congress Control Number: 2021953440

ISBN (hardcover): 9781662924125
ISBN (paperback): 9781662924132
eISBN: 9781662924149

*In memory of my sister Laura,*
*and all the souls of the faithful departed.*

*For Jon*

# TABLE OF CONTENTS

# ONE

*New Orleans—March 1943*

Rose looked around the church, hoping not to run into the pastor or anyone else she knew. The early morning light shining through the stained-glass windows made little prisms of color on the pews; the cloying smell of incense transported Rose to comforting childhood times. She needed that today. The church custodian moved silently around the altar, focused on his dusting and polishing. An older woman knelt up front, dressed in black and murmuring prayers in Sicilian as she worked her rosary beads. Rose craned her neck from her seat in the back but couldn't identify her.

Rose wasn't where she should be on a Friday morning: working at the family grocery store. Instead, she was headed to a job interview at the Higgins Shipyard. She'd told her parents she was going to a blood drive. The lie was just a venial sin, she rationalized. For the war effort.

She felt through her blouse for her scapular, a drawing of the Virgin Mary on a small brown felt rectangle, tied to a ribbon she wore around her neck. She knew her big brother Giovanni and older sister Laura were wearing theirs too, wherever they were; the thought brought Rose some solace. Giovanni had enlisted right after Pearl Harbor and now worked as a mechanic somewhere in the Pacific. Meanwhile, Laura was an Army nurse stationed in North Africa, which seemed impossibly romantic to Rose. Like something out of *Casablanca*.

She prayed God would keep them safe, then added a request that the job interview would go well. Asking forgiveness for the lie to her parents could wait until her next confession.

Rose never thought she'd have a chance to work at the shipyard; her small frame wasn't built for manual labor. But her cousin Rocco recently enlisted, and he'd recommended she take his place as a bookkeeper. She felt ready, excited for the chance to do her part. And at eighteen, she was desperate to get out from under her parents' thumb, at least five days a week.

Rose looked at her watch. Her best friend Marie, who worked as a welder at the shipyard, had said the streetcar ride to Higgins would take about forty-five minutes. She couldn't risk being late. As she got up to leave, so did the old woman up front. Rose felt her heart race—it was Mrs. Serio. Immaculate Conception was the "Italian church," and all Rose's Sicilian neighbors worshipped here. Rose bent her head as she blessed herself and genuflected in the aisle, but when she looked up, Mrs. Serio was coming right at her.

"Rose! I never see you here on a weekday," Mrs. Serio said in a loud whisper. Her English was accented with Palermo, like so many others in the neighborhood. Like Rose's own parents. "Is everything alright?"

"*Buongiorno*, Mrs. Serio. Yes, everything is fine. I…" Rose felt hot suddenly, her mind fumbling for a plausible excuse for being there. "I just stopped in before work to light a candle for my brother. We haven't heard from him in so long." Another lie. They'd had a postcard from Giovanni just last week, palm trees on the front, postmarked Manila. *I miss Ma's cooking. The food is terrible—otherwise still in one piece.* No information on his

2

whereabouts or condition. Even so, they'd clung to the message. Proof of life.

"You never know these days," Mrs. Serio said, leaning on her cane. "I'll add him to my prayer list."

"*Grazie*," Rose said. "What about Stefano? Any news?" Rose had been in school with Mrs. Serio's grandson, who'd enlisted around the same time as Giovanni.

"Only that he's in North Africa somewhere. God keep him," Mrs. Serio said, blessing herself.

"That's where my sister is," Rose said. "Hopefully they won't cross paths—Laura's working in the field hospital."

They walked toward the exit, Mrs. Serio limping along. "God bless her too. Such a brave girl."

Rose held open the heavy cypress door and let in the blazing sunlight. She was touched that Mrs. Serio called Laura brave. Her own mother didn't see it that way. Rose helped the older woman down the wide granite front steps of the church.

"Sorry I'm so slow—my leg, it hurts with the sugar diabetes," Mrs. Serio said, turning toward home.

Rose pointed in the opposite direction. "I'm going this way—need to run an errand." She didn't want to give Mrs. Serio an opening to start a litany of ailments. She needed to catch the streetcar soon or she'd be late for the interview. "*Arrivederci!*"

Mrs. Serio waved her cane and walked off. Rose hoped she wouldn't turn up at the store and expose the lie to her parents. Of course, Rose would have to confess it eventually—if her prayers were answered and Higgins offered her the job. Besides, Marie's advice rang in her head: *One step at a time. Don't worry before you need to.*

She hurried down Ursulines Avenue, trying not to make eye contact with anyone as she made her way out of the thick of the French Quarter. Purple and pink bougainvillea spilled over wrought iron balconies on brick and stucco buildings, and she could smell jasmine wafting from behind narrow gates that led to hidden courtyards. These streets looked the same as they had for centuries—they were all Rose had ever known. Until today, she thought.

She passed the newsstand on the corner. The headlines read, *13 JAP SHIPS SUNK BY ONE YANK SUB* and *ROMMEL DRIVEN BACK TO STARTING POINT*. She paid much more attention to the papers these days. As she passed her favorite bakery, Brocato's, she noticed the blue service star in the window had turned to gold since she last walked this way: a loved one lost in the war. She blessed herself. In the door of her own family's store, two stars hung on a banner—one for Giovanni, one for Laura. Each night she prayed they would stay blue. She checked her watch again and quickened her pace. It was warm for March and the heat prickled her skin. She worried she'd be sweaty by the time she got to Higgins, but she couldn't be late.

Rose stepped down from the streetcar at the City Park stop. The massive Higgins factory loomed ahead, rising from the edge of Bayou St. John's murky waters. The grounds were much tidier than she'd pictured, with swaying palm trees and well-tended flower beds; a few fancy-looking cars sat parked in the small lot. Higgins couldn't be more different from the crumbling charm of the French Quarter. The building's sleek, curved façade looked like a giant boat with round porthole windows. A huge wooden replica of a ship's steering wheel hung on the wall above the front entrance. An enormous American flag flew over everything.

At the main door, a guard in a glass booth checked Rose's name against his list before letting her pass inside. There, a receptionist with a teased-up blond hairdo sat behind a tall oak desk. She wore a brown-and-white checked dress with a tight bodice, and coral-colored lipstick—like a chic working woman from the movies.

Rose smiled up at her, feeling like a schoolgirl in her white blouse and navy-blue skirt.

"Can I help you?"

"Good morning," Rose said, speaking loudly. A rhythmic, muffled hammering sound came from behind the wall. "I'm Rose Marino. Here for an appointment with Mr. Sullivan."

The receptionist raised one penciled-in eyebrow. "Just a moment, hon," she said, holding up a red-nailed finger. She picked up a black telephone handset on her desk and dialed three numbers. "A Miss Marino for Mr. Sullivan," she said into the receiver. "Uh-huh. OK." She hung up. "He's finishing up a meeting, but he'll be down for you shortly. You can have a seat over there." She pointed to a chartreuse-colored sofa in an alcove near the front door.

"Is there a ladies' room I can use?" Rose asked.

"First door on the left."

"Thank you," Rose said, glad for the chance to pull herself together.

There were four stalls in the restroom; a large mirror spanned a long row of immaculate white sinks. A poster on the wall showed a pair of red lips with a big X over them. LOOSE LIPS SINK SHIPS! Rose shuddered, thinking about Giovanni or Laura on one of those ships.

She inspected herself in the mirror, now wishing she'd worn more makeup. Her olive-toned skin looked sallow in the fluorescent light. She took a round silver compact from her purse, blotted out the shine from the humidity, then reapplied pink lipstick, and dabbed her cheeks to add some color. Turning to the side, she re-pinned a loose brown curl into the neatly knotted bun. She stood up as straight as she could, hoping she looked professional enough. Old enough. She'd worn the small gold stud earrings her deceased grandmother had sewn into the lining of her coat for the voyage from Sicily to America as a young woman.

Rose tried to channel her *nonna*'s bravery for the interview to come. Marie had helped her prepare. Still, they couldn't have possibly anticipated every question.

Back in the reception area, Rose sat on the sofa and picked up the company magazine, *Eureka,* from a stack on the coffee table. She leafed through the pages—photographs of Higgins boats landing on beaches in Morocco and the Philippines, advertisements to work harder. She flinched at a cartoon of Mussolini looking like a menacing monster, an Italian flag clutched in his hand—just like the one her father insisted on flying over the entrance to his grocery store. Since Italy was part of the Axis, the government had required her parents to register as "enemy aliens" when the war broke out. She knew her father disdained Mussolini, but that didn't stop the FBI from taking away his short-wave radio and his camera. Some people refused to do business with Italians after that, and he'd lost a few long-time customers.

"Here's Mr. Sullivan now, Miss Marino," the receptionist called.

Rose put down the magazine and stood, smoothing her skirt as Mr. Sullivan walked toward her. He was stocky, with a round, freckled face, and wore a tan suit. His brown tie was slightly askew, and his reddish curly hair looked uncombed. Still, his kind smile put Rose a little more at ease.

"Miss Marino?" he asked, enveloping her tiny hand with his sweaty mitt. He smelled like cigarettes and cologne. "Michael Sullivan, pleased to meet you. Follow me." An Irish brogue gave his voice a musical lilt.

The thumping and grinding noises got louder as they walked down the corridor. Through a long rectangular window in the wall, Rose glimpsed the factory floor: row after row of giant wooden hulls and scaffolding so high it seemed to disappear into the ceiling. It surprised her to see so many women, Black and white people working side by side. A giant sign hanging from the rafters read, *THE GUY WHO RELAXES IS HELPING THE AXIS*.

Mr. Sullivan ushered her into a windowless office. Even with the door shut, the room still hummed with vibrations. "Sorry for the noise. We're working full steam ahead on a new order from the Navy. Oh, forget I said that." He made a zipper motion across his lips.

Rose nodded, remembering the poster in the bathroom. Yet another hung here showing blue and black stylized gears: *WORK WITH CARE!*

Mr. Sullivan opened a manila file folder and took out a sheaf of papers. On top, Rose spotted the application she'd filled out in her best Catholic school penmanship. Cousin Rocco had managed to slip it to her at the store without her father seeing.

"Let's see," Mr. Sullivan said, putting on a pair of tortoiseshell reading glasses. "Miss. . . Marino. Rocco's cousin. So, you're Eye-talian too, I take it?"

Rose felt her heart thump—she and Marie hadn't thought of this one.

"Yes, sir. My parents came over from Sicily as children, but they're becoming citizens now. My father and Rocco's father are brothers. I was born here, of course." Rocco's father was back in Sicily, but she kept that information to herself.

Mr. Sullivan held up a hand. "It's OK. I'm an immigrant myself, as you can probably tell." He smiled and Rose relaxed a bit. "Of course, the Irish are on *our* side...but we have lots of Eye-talian people here, like your cousin. Good workers."

She felt a small wave of relief.

He looked down at the paperwork. "You've got a certificate from the Soulé school, I see. Did you take bookkeeping there?"

"I did," Rose said. "I enjoyed it very much. Shorthand and typing too." Her high school principal Sister Mary Arnold had put her in for a scholarship to the one-year business program. Rose's mother had objected, of course, saying they needed her at the store, and that Rose would be better off finding a good husband. But Rose's father intervened—a rare occurrence—saying she should go, that it wouldn't cost them anything. Besides, he'd said, they could use her help with the books. Rose had been excited to stretch her mind, to imagine working outside the store, though she hadn't shared that part with her parents.

Mr. Sullivan pointed to a line on the application. "Current job—in your family grocery? Do you think you'll be able to make the leap to working in a big factory like this?"

As if on cue, a loud BANG from the shop floor made her jump.

"Ah, the sound of victory," Mr. Sullivan said. "You get used to it. As I was saying."

"Oh, yes, sir." Rose nodded; she and Marie had practiced this question. "I use some of my training now, helping my father run the business. Inventory, bookkeeping, and reports for the Ration Board."

"Rocco said you were a smart girl."

Rose felt herself blush. When she was a child, Rose was always told she was the "pretty one," Laura the "smart one." Neither took this as flattery.

Mr. Sullivan closed the file and removed his glasses. His brown eyes were a little bloodshot. "So, tell me. Why do you want to work at Higgins?"

Rose sat up as straight as she could. She wanted so much to give the right answer. "To help in the war effort. My sister's an Army nurse and my brother's in the Pacific—I want to do my part, beyond collecting scrap metal and grease. My friend's a welder here, and between her and Rocco I've heard a little about Higgins. Not too much, of course. They're always mindful of security. But they've both encouraged me, sir. I want to make a difference."

The corners of his mouth turned up in a slight smile, and she knew her rehearsed answer had hit the mark.

"You're right about what we do here," he said. "I can't tell you too much until you're an official employee, but it certainly is important work. Vital, in fact."

"I've seen the boats in the newsreels. Very impressive." His words had buoyed her hopes. *Vital. Until you're an official employee.*

"Indeed. Any questions for me?"

Marie had insisted she ask about pay, but in truth the topic made Rose uncomfortable. She took a deep breath. "Um, well, I'm just wondering about the pay and the hours?"

"Of course. Seventy-five cents an hour to start. Eight to five, half hour for lunch, Monday through Friday."

Rose knew Rocco made over a dollar an hour but didn't want to push it. She'd been working at the store since she was old enough to see over the counter and her parents had never paid her a dime. "Sounds fine, thank you."

He tapped his pencil on the table. "Now, when are you available to start?"

She was startled. Was he offering her the job? "When would you need me?"

"Yesterday. Rocco's only been gone a week and already I'm drowning in paperwork. I've got plenty of other applications, mind you, but the job is yours if you can make a fast decision."

She almost didn't believe what she was hearing. She'd never imagined things would move so quickly. But of course, they would. The factory was running at full throttle. "I...I'll have to ask my parents' permission," she blurted, suddenly feeling childish and embarrassed.

He put her file on top of a stack of others, offering a strained smile. "Your cousin's a fine lad. Out of respect for him, I can give you until Monday morning. But you'll have to let me know then or I'll move on. The war won't wait, Miss Marino."

9

"Of course," she said, trying to sound confident. "I'll talk to them right away." Meanwhile, her mind raced. She'd never thought this far ahead, focusing her attentions only on the interview and concocting a plausible lie for having to miss work at the store.

Mr. Sullivan stood, and she rose to her feet as well. "I hope you'll decide to join us, Miss Marino. Our men are counting on us. Every day we lose costs lives. Never forget that." He extended his hand.

She shook it—firmly this time. She thought of Giovanni and Laura, then pushed the images away. "I won't. And thank you, sir. I'll call you first thing Monday either way."


The streetcar rocked gently back and forth, slowly making its way downtown. An older Black man sat alone in the rear while a woman near the front tried to keep her tow-headed toddler occupied with a toy bear. Rose had the double seat to herself and welcomed the solitude so she could sort out her thoughts. She leaned her head toward the open window; the breeze was fresher here by the bayou than in the crowded Quarter. She watched people going about their business—a woman sweeping the sidewalk in front of a shop; two men in gray coveralls bent over a fire hydrant while water ran into the street.

She thought back to a year before, when her sister enlisted, and the family upheaval that followed. Laura, two years older than Rose, had been working at Charity then; the Army came to the hospital to recruit. When her sister announced her decision at the dinner table, Rose burst into tears. Their father remained silent, but their mother exploded: *Always trying to prove something! You think you're better than us? You're not. I forbid it.* But it was too late. Laura had already signed the paperwork. Rose still saw her sister's unflinching face, heard her voice, its firm resolve. *I want to serve, just like Giovanni.* Their mother had scoffed. *You're not Giovanni. Nowhere close.* Her mother had stood, knocking back her chair and leaving the rest of them at the table. Worse, she refused to go to the dock with Rose and her father to see Laura off.

Now Rose had her own decision to announce, and her mother's spiteful words rang in her head. But so did her sister's bravery. Rose wondered about her own motivations; did she think she was too good to work in the store? No, she told herself. The job at Higgins was just for the duration of the war. To do her part. Still, she had to be truthful—there would be other benefits. She'd be using her brain at the factory, meeting new people, finally free from the monotony of selling groceries. Her parents had poured years into the store. Was it wrong to want to reach for something more for herself?

As she walked from the streetcar toward home, she took notice of other women, some dressed for work in shops and offices. She pictured herself at the shipyard: wearing sharp suits—like Rosalind Russell in *His Girl Friday.* Even with the rationing, it would be nice to buy clothes with her own money, rather than always having to ask her parents. Of course, she'd share some of her earnings with the family. But most of her paycheck would go into the red Community Coffee can she kept hidden under her sister's bed, where she'd slowly accumulated coins and dollar bills from birthday and holiday money over the years. The can was a savings account for her secret dream: having her own place one day.

She took a right onto St. Philip Street toward the river, allowing herself to pause a moment in front of her favorite house: a tiny cottage on the corner of Burgundy, painted white with a bright yellow door and matching gingerbread trim. She'd tried to peek inside many times, but the lace curtains were always drawn. The house couldn't hold more than a few rooms; in her imagination, she'd decorated them with tasteful, modern furnishings—no plastic on the sofa, no dusty lace doilies on the tables. Until now, such fantasies seemed out of reach; the only women she knew who lived alone were widows and spinsters. But working at Higgins could change things. A few days ago, the job at the factory was only a remote possibility. Now she felt certain she needed to be there, that her whole life—her *real* life—depended on it.

Of course, none of her hopes would matter to her parents. *Non diventare troppo testardo,* they'd say. *Don't get too big-headed.*

At last, she reached home. She stared at the back of the building her family rented, its peeling greenish paint, the rickety balcony overhanging the courtyard. How worn and run-down it all looked compared to the factory. She felt a tug at her heart: she loved her family but the thought of being trapped here her whole life made her want to scream.

She ducked in the rear door, trying not to make any noise on her way up the back stairs to the apartment on the second floor. As she changed into the old skirt and blouse she wore most days—hand-me-downs from her sister—she prayed for divine assistance. How to admit the lie to her parents? How to gain their permission to take the job when she knew it would only disrupt what was left of the order of things with Giovanni and Laura away? The longer she waited, she knew, the worse she would feel. And Mr. Sullivan was right: the war wouldn't wait.

Tonight, she decided. At dinner. Like Laura.

# TWO

Rose tried to be extra helpful in the kitchen that evening. She set the table—too big with just the three of them there and the two places left open as if Giovanni and Laura would be back any time. Meanwhile, her mother softly hummed a tune as she cooked. As always, the postcard from Giovanni had lightened her mood. It sat propped up on the living room credenza, next to a photograph of him in uniform and a votive candle her mother kept perpetually lit. There was no such shrine for Laura.

Her mother added sausages to the cast iron pan and the small kitchen filled with the mouthwatering aroma of onions, peppers, and garlic sizzling in olive oil. "Rose, let some of this smoke out," her mother directed. "And call your father up."

Rose opened the window at the top of the stairs. Her father sat in the courtyard below, a cigar in one hand, the newspaper in the other. She chased away a pang of guilt at the thought of leaving him to the daily routine in the store. Most days were boring. Still, she cherished the easy relationship she had with her father.

"Papa, supper's almost ready."

"Be right up," he shouted.

Back in the kitchen her mother transferred the food from the skillet to a big yellow ceramic bowl and placed it on the beige

Formica table. She stood a few inches taller than Rose, thin like her daughter, but with a sharper chin. Rose had seen photographs of her mother as a glamorous young woman. Looking at her now, Rose wondered what became of that girl. Strands of gray shot through her dark hair; she wore no makeup, and perspiration from the hot stove beaded her forehead. Her mother didn't even bother taking off her apron before sitting down to eat.

Her father came in and switched on the small wooden radio in the corner to the Italian music program, then sat down, tucked a napkin into his collar, and rolled up the sleeves of his white shirt, just as he did every night.

"Smells good," he said.

Rose tried to steady her shaking hand as she poured three short glasses of red wine. She shooed away the anxiety. She'd been rehearsing the conversation all afternoon as she worked downstairs in the store.

Rose's mother sat down, blessed herself quickly and muttered grace. "Bless us, oh Lord, and these thy gifts, which we are about to receive, from thy bounty, through Christ our Lord. And please protect our Giovanni."

"And Laura," Rose said.

"And Laura," her mother repeated. "Amen."

Rose and her father said, "Amen," and blessed themselves. Rose steeled herself to tell them her news when the radio announcer interrupted the music.

*The American submarine Triton, with 60 sailors onboard, has been presumed lost in the waters off Papua New Guinea in the South Pacific. Reports say the enemy destroyer Akikaze was in the area hunting American subs, and the Triton was reported overdue from patrol. In other news. . .*

Her father reached over, turned off the radio, then speared a sausage from the bowl with his fork. Her mother spooned peppers and onions onto his plate. Nobody spoke, but Rose knew they all

14

had the same thought. Navy ships sometimes transported Army troops among the islands. *Please, God, not Giovanni.* Every time they heard a report of casualties, Rose felt her heart stop for a moment.

She took a sip of wine, letting its warmth slide down her throat, as she mustered her courage. "Did cousin Rocco ship out already?"

"I think so." Her father shifted in his chair to make room for his belly. "They sent him to Fort Bragg, but he didn't know whether he'd be sent to the Pacific or to Europe after training."

Rose looked down at her plate, cutting the sausage with the side of her fork. "You know how he worked in the accounting department at Higgins?"

"Right," her father said. Her mother just nodded.

"Well, he recommended me to take his place." She took a mouthful of food, not making eye contact with either of her parents.

"Take his place?" Her father set down his fork and looked at Rose's mother. "You mean working at Higgins?"

"Yes."

"What?" her mother said, pointing her chin at Rose. "The shipyard? That's impossible. Where did he get such a crazy idea?"

Rose needed to stay calm. "I don't think it's so crazy. I have the accounting certificate from Soulé. I could do Rocco's job—he works in the office."

Her mother dropped her fork on her plate with a clang. "Why you want to go working all the way up there? That's no place for a girl." She sat back in her chair and shook her head. "First your sister, now you."

Rose resisted the urge to defend Laura. Her sister was a lost cause; she needed to save her arguments for herself. "Lots of women work there. Now that the men are gone, the factory needs them. You know Marie's been there for a few months. She's making good money."

"You're not Marie," her mother interrupted. It was a well-worn theme: Marie's widowed mother waitressed at a diner; the Leonardis never seemed to have enough money. Rose's mother used it as a cudgel to remind her children how grateful they should be: two parents, a family business, plenty of food on the table. Guilt and shame—her mother's favorite weapons. "If Marie jumped into the Mississippi, would you jump after her? No." She waved her hand dismissively, as if Marie were standing there.

"Ma, nobody's talking about jumping in the river." Rose tried to keep the anger out of her voice, knowing it would only fuel her mother's opposition. "The factory needs all the help they can get. They're making boats for the troops."

"Frank, talk some sense into her."

Her father kept chewing his food, hunched over his plate. "She has a point, Fil."

Rose tried to stay calm.

Her mother folded her arms across her chest, narrowing her eyes at him. "And what about the store? You think she can leave me trapped in there all week?"

Rose was ready for this objection. "Couldn't Carmine take my place?" Rocco's older brother Carmine helped in the store on Saturdays already, having been rejected from the service due to his poor eyesight. *The poor kid,* Rose's parents called him, even though he was twenty-five.

"*Pfft.* We'd have to *pay* Carmine," her mother said. "And he's not the sharpest knife in the drawer, all due respect."

"It's not as if working in the store takes a lot of smarts," Rose blurted. The words were no sooner out of her mouth than she regretted them. Her father looked wounded. "What I mean is, Carmine can certainly handle things."

"*Basta.* Enough." Her mother picked up her fork again. "Stop talking about it—it's not going to happen. Just one of your little pipe dreams."

16

Rose concentrated on the tablecloth. She could feel her face getting hot. She ought to have been used to her mother's condescension. As teenagers, she and Laura had banded together when their mother started in with her relentless nagging and criticism. They never understood why, only that they couldn't do anything about it. But Laura wasn't here now. She was off living her own life, and Rose had had enough. "It's not a pipe dream, Ma. I interviewed there this morning and they've offered me the job."

Her father's brown eyes widened under his bushy brows. "You…what? This morning?" He put down his fork and knife and ran a hand through his hair. "What about the blood drive?"

"I wasn't at the blood drive; I was at Higgins. I'm sorry for lying, but I knew you wouldn't want me to go." The words came out in a rush.

Rose's mother slammed her hand on the table. "Bad enough you want to do this crazy thing, but now you're lying to us too?"

"Rocco recommended me, and I filled out an application. I never thought they'd call, let alone offer me the job. But they did. And I really want to do my part."

"Absolutely not. We need you here," her mother said, as if that settled it. "Frank, tell her."

"Papa?" Rose had low expectations; her father rarely went against her mother. "It's just temporary, until the men come home."

Her father took a sip of his wine. "I know you want to do good, *cara,* but I don't know. It's a lot to ask."

"I'd share my earnings with the family, of course," Rose said, making a mental note not to tell them exactly how much she'd be paid. Her coffee can wouldn't fill itself. "And I can still work Saturdays, helping with the inventory and books like always, and—"

Her father held up his hand and Rose stopped talking. He then finished chewing and took another sip of wine. "Carmine could use the work, Fil," he said. "And if Rose is going to be making money, she could help with the expenses around here."

Her mother tapped the side of her head. "*Pazzo*, both of you. Crazy." She stood and took her plate to the sink, then stormed out of the kitchen and slammed the bedroom door.

"Thank you, Papa," Rose said quietly.

"I haven't said yes yet. Your mother and I will have to discuss it. I'm not wild about you traveling all the way up to Mid-City and back alone, working with all those men every day. Strangers. But I'll think about it."

*Quit while you're ahead*, Rose told herself. But Mr. Sullivan had been clear. "I need to tell them by Monday morning."

Her father took off his napkin and stood up. "Enough for tonight. I'm going back down to the courtyard," he said. "We'll talk more tomorrow."

Rose swallowed the rest of her words and started washing the dishes in the big white ceramic sink. She caught a reflection of herself in the window; several locks of hair had come loose from her bun, and she tucked them back in with a soapy finger. Through the glass, she could see the glowing tip of her father's cigar below as he sat in the dark courtyard.

The next morning, before the store opened, Rose occupied her thoughts by rearranging the produce section. She moved the older vegetables to the front and was picking dead leaves off the lettuce when she heard shouting on the sidewalk.

"What's going on out there?" her cousin Carmine asked as he came in from the storeroom. Frayed brown suspenders held up the gray pants sagging around his waist. Heavyset with rounded shoulders, he had a prominent nose and thick glasses that made him look bug-eyed.

Rose turned the radio down. The shouting was still there. Her father's voice and another man's. "I don't know," she said, immediately alarmed. Her father wasn't one to yell.

Carmine rubbed his hands together and walked toward the front of the store; Rose followed behind. From the open doorway, they could see her father standing on the sidewalk in his green apron, hands on his hips. A small crowd of neighbors had gathered across the street.

"My boy was *killed*, Frank—by *your* people over there, in league with those filthy Krauts." It was Mr. Prescott, a big Uptown hotel owner. His blue-and-white seersucker pants strained at the stomach, and his white linen shirt was wrinkled and had come untucked in the back. Rose didn't particularly like him; the man never missed a chance to remind people he'd been king of Carnival.

Her father put a hand over his heart. "I'm sorry for your loss."

Mr. Prescott's pink face glistened with sweat, his jowls shaking. Rose worried he might have a stroke right there on the sidewalk. "I've known you a long time, Frank. But I can't do business with the enemy."

Rose's father, now red-faced himself, took a half step back. "The enemy? You see these stars?" He pointed to the service banner hanging inside the front door—one blue star for Giovanni and one for Laura. Rose cringed; her father's Sicilian accent always sounded thicker whenever he got agitated. "My son's over there fighting the Japs, serving this country—OUR country. My daughter too."

Mr. Prescott cut him off. "And still, you have the nerve to fly *that*." He pointed to the green, white, and red Italian flag hanging limply over the entrance. "It's an insult."

Rose's father squared his shoulders, fists clenched by his sides. She had never seen him hit anyone, but now she feared the two men were going to come to blows. She couldn't stand the thought of her father getting hurt.

She pushed against Carmine, forcing him to step outside. "Whoa, Uncle Frank, is everything all right?" Carmine asked, blinking behind his thick glasses.

"Stay out of this," Rose's father told him.

"You people ought to go back where you came from," Mr. Prescott sneered and walked away, flipping his hand dismissively. "We'd all be better off."

Her father forced a smile. "OK, folks," he said, waving his hands at the neighbors. "It's all over. Just a little business disagreement. Nothing to worry about."

The neighbors—most of them Sicilian too—slowly disbanded, mumbling to each other. Rose knew they'd heard the last insult Mr. Prescott flung at her father, yet nobody stepped up in his defense.

Carmine started straightening out the wrought iron tables on the sidewalk, brushing crumbs from the chairs with a rag. Rose reached for her father's elbow. "Are you OK, Papa? He had no right to say those things."

Her father's face still glowed red. "I'm sorry you had to see that, *cara*. As hard as we work, as much as we've sacrificed. This war. *Managena*," he cursed and mopped his brow with a white handkerchief. "But the man's lost his son."

"That's not your fault, Papa." Rose was moved by her father's compassion, even after he'd been insulted and threatened. She took pride in her Sicilian heritage; still, she'd never thought of herself as anything but American. She'd heard stories from relatives about the old days and getting called dirty WOPs and dagoes. Hearing it firsthand felt different—chilling and scary. She wondered how many more people there were like Mr. Prescott, thinking the worst of them for no reason. And she worried it would hurt the grocery business to which her father had devoted his life.

Her father put his arm around her shoulders, gave her a side hug and kissed the top of her head. He looked up at the flag and closed his eyes. "Carmine, get the ladder."

Carmine brought a stepladder out from the storeroom. "Spot me," Rose's father said as he put his hand on Carmine's shoulder and climbed up. He worked the flag from its bracket. "Roll it neatly," he said, handing it down to Rose. He stepped down slowly, breathing hard.

"Always be proud of your Sicilian blood. We've done nothing wrong, but now we must be Americans first. Understand?"

Rose nodded and felt tears stinging her eyes. He touched her gently under the chin. "Look at me. You take that Higgins job."

# THREE

**One year later—March 1944**

Rose tapped her adding machine and entered figures into neat columns in the ledger book. Parts, equipment, ships under construction, schedule estimates. She loved the clean, quiet work of bookkeeping and the comforting certainty of numbers. Production had ramped up since the Allies invaded the Marshall Islands. It felt like the tide was turning, though she knew that might be wishful thinking. At least these mundane numbers added up to more Allied victories, she told herself. Giovanni and Laura would want her to stay positive. It wasn't always easy.

She looked at her watch—a delicate gold-plated bracelet with a roman numeral clock face she'd bought with her own money. It was past time to go get the mail.

Downstairs, she found the door to the mail room open. "Good morning, Irma," she said. The clerk greeted Rose with a smile; a lemon-yellow scarf tied around her head brightened up her otherwise drab gray uniform. Irma handed Rose a small stack of letters from Mr. Sullivan's box. "Here you go."

Rose had been pleased to find Irma working at Higgins. When Rose was a little girl, Irma would sometimes come to the store with her husband Melvin to deliver butter and eggs. She'd always been so kind and friendly. Rose's father called Melvin "one of the good ones." Rose never understood what he meant until she grew older; now that she'd been working at Higgins, such opinions made her uncomfortable. Everyone was working together toward victory. Irma and Melvin's own son was in the war, fighting just like Giovanni.

"Thanks." Rose flipped through the envelopes—mostly routine correspondence for her boss. At the bottom of the stack, she paused: a thin blue envelope addressed to her, written in her big sister's handwriting. A black stamp in the lower left-hand corner read, *Passed by Army Examiner,* with the censor's initials scribbled underneath. Her heart sped up.

"Everything OK?" Irma asked.

"Oh, yes. Sorry," Rose said. "It's from my sister. Mr. Sullivan gave me permission to have her send letters here." Laura wrote regularly to the family about the day-to-day of Army life: the terrible food, the cramped and dirty tents, the funny characters, like her best friend, Frances, and the other nurses. But Rose knew Laura would share more if their mother wasn't reading the letters, and so she'd written to her sister, suggesting Higgins.

"Mind if I sit here for a minute to read?" she asked.

Irma handed Rose a slim silver letter opener. "You take all the time you need. Your sister was always such a nice girl. Very studious." She went back to sorting the piles of mail on her counter.

Rose was touched that Irma remembered. She sat on a high stool in the corner of the mail room, then carefully slit open the top of the onionskin envelope and unfolded the letter.

*February 15, 1944*
*Italy*

*Dear Rose:*

*They're showing Thunder Birds at the canteen tonight. I love Gene Tierney, but I've seen it twice already, so I stayed behind. It's great to be able to write these letters "for your eyes only" (well, you and the censors). It's quiet right now, though the tent is flapping in the wind. It's so cold, and the kerosene heater doesn't help much. My hands are freezing all the time (excuse the poor penmanship).*

*Guess what? A couple of weeks ago, our outfit came ashore on one of your Higgins boats. While we waited out in the water for the all-clear, a red alert sounded. We heard the German planes and saw the flashes in the sky from the big guns. We worried we wouldn't make it, but your mighty boats did the job, and we landed at dawn. Tell Mr. Higgins we're grateful! We must've been a sight rolling off the ramp in our jeeps, trying to hold all our gear above the water. Crazy when I think about it now, but you never know what you can do until you have no choice.*

*I wouldn't wish this war on anyone. Still, sometimes I feel like I was supposed to leave home and come here. In nursing school, they told us we'd be emptying bedpans for years, but now I'm assisting in surgery. The other night, we worked for a long time on this one young soldier. A bullet to the stomach. We lost the generator, so I had to hold a lantern while the doctor operated. My arms ached,* but I kept thinking, *if I put this* lamp down, even for a minute, this boy might die. *God forbid, if Giovanni was wounded and another nurse halfway around the world didn't hold the light for him. We did our best, but the shrapnel had done too much damage. Somebody's son, somebody's brother, somebody's sweetheart. Gone. All we could do was pray for him.*

*I can't say where we are, but someone nicknamed it "a half-acre of hell." Brutal as it is, thank God for folks like Frances. Her fiancé is fighting in the Pacific. Sometimes she gets letters from him. It's how I know a little about what Giovanni's going through. The doctors mostly treat us well, though a couple of them act like we're here to serve them. They forget we're officers too! Our head nurse, Captain McCarthy, is tough but has a good heart. She's always warning us not to "fraternize" with the enlisted men. It's like having Sister Mary Arnold with us.*

*We <u>are</u>, however, allowed to date other officers. One doctor has become a special friend. He grew up in Boston and his parents are from Italy like Mama and Papa (though not Sicily). I won't lie, it's been nice to have someone tell me I'm pretty, even in this mess. The other night after a long shift, we took a walk to a little secluded beach just outside the camp. It was pitch dark and there were a million stars. He taught me how to pick out some constellations— Cygnus the swan and Pegasus the winged horse. To think they'd always been there, shining over New Orleans. I just couldn't see them!*

*Have you heard from Giovanni? I pray for him every day. Please write soon and let me know what's happening at home, and how things are going at work. I hope you and Marie are having a little fun, and that Mama hasn't got you locked up all the time.*

*Well, I can hear the other girls coming back from the movie and it'll be lights-out soon. I miss you so much. Whenever I feel lonely or scared, I close my eyes and picture our little bedroom, Mama and Papa bickering in the kitchen, Mama cooking her chicken parmigiana, Giovanni stealing tastes before it's even out of the pan. I can almost smell the garlic from here.*

*Abbracci,*
*Your loving sister, Laura*

Back upstairs at her desk, Rose tried to focus but had a hard time keeping the letter off her mind. She worried for her sister so near the front lines. They'd grown up close. Laura's life was so different now. Rose felt like she could never have that kind of courage. And this doctor boyfriend. What if he took Laura away to live up north? Rose couldn't bear the thought.

Suddenly, Mr. Sullivan burst through the door, a lit cigarette dangling from the corner of his mouth. He looked more like an unmade bed than usual today. "Morning, Rose. The bosses are after me again," he said, shuffling through the papers on his desk. "Where did I put that bloody inventory?"

"Here it is," Rose said, handing him a folder. "I fixed a few of the numbers." With each new order, he became increasingly frazzled. She wanted to make things easier for him; he'd been kind to her and made her feel important.

"Ah, what would we do without ya?" He took a drag from the cigarette and exhaled the acrid smoke toward the ceiling. "Say, you heard about Janie's husband?"

"Janie in the warehouse? No, I hadn't heard." Rose put her hand over her mouth.

"Afraid so. She got the telegram yesterday. Monte Cassino."

The bloody battle had been all over the news and Rose felt the tears well up in her eyes. She didn't know Janie well, had never even met her husband. But he was gone now, never to return. Every time she heard of a loss it was as if she'd been punched in the gut. She touched her scapular, offering up a prayer for Janie, and feeling guilty for hoping that if people had to die, Giovanni and Laura would not be among them.

"Poor thing. She's got wee ones at home too." Mr. Sullivan shook his head and stubbed out his cigarette in the already-overflowing ashtray on his desk. "Seems like someone's getting bad news every day. I just pray it won't be me." Rose knew his younger brother served in the merchant marine, dodging German U-boats out in the Atlantic.

He leafed through the inventory report. "I'd be out there myself if it weren't for my bum feet. The tide's turning now, though, thanks to our boats."

"I hope so," Rose said. She'd heard on the radio that the Russians had marched into Romania and Hungary, forcing the Germans out. "I got a letter from my sister today. She and the other nurses landed on a beach in a Higgins boat."

"God keep her," Mr. Sullivan said. He made a note in the margin of the report. "Rose, can you tell me what you mean here? It looks like you're projecting triple the number of rivets we've been ordering—is that right?"

"Yes, sir," Rose said. "If we can get those in ahead of time, we won't hold up the line. I think we're going to need them at the rate we're going."

"Clever girl." Mr. Sullivan nodded, standing up. "All right then. I'm going to get these numbers to the boss. No disrespect to your cousin, but you're doing the work of three men in here. We're going to miss you once the boys come back."

After he left, Rose opened the window on his side of the office to let the cigarette smoke out. She looked down at the big live oak tree by the bayou, its silvery-green leaves rustling in the breeze, and City Park's lush canopy beyond that. *Once the boys come back.* She couldn't root for the boys *not* to come back; she felt disloyal even thinking it. But Higgins had opened a whole new world for her—meaningful work, money in her pocketbook and in her secret coffee can under the bed. Independence. She thought about her own place all the time: somewhere she could be herself, walk around barefoot in her nightgown if she wanted. No fusty heirlooms from the old country. Nobody telling her what to do, when to come and go.

The whistle blew, pulling her from the thought. She gathered her lunch bag and headed downstairs to meet Marie. Walking along the edge of the factory floor, she joined the workers making their way to the exits for the break—men in hard hats, fedoras, and newsboy caps, women in headscarves. The shipyard employed more women than men now. At first it had felt strange, working side by side with men and with people who didn't look like her— even some people in wheelchairs. But she didn't think about it much anymore. They were all Americans, wanting the same thing.

Most of the women on the floor wore shapeless coveralls and protective gear, so even in her modest white blouse and knee-length gray skirt, Rose caught a few long stares and low whistles. She kept her head down and quickened her pace. She hated the feeling of the men's hot stares following her backside.

Outside, she met Marie at their usual spot by the dairy truck, where they both bought small bottles of milk. Marie wore light-green coveralls cinched at the waist with a leather belt, her auburn hair tied up in a black snood. She worked on the assembly line as a welder, fastening the metal hinges that allowed a Higgins boat's bow ramp to swing open so troops could land directly on the beaches. Tall, muscular, and busty, Marie towered over Rose. Sometimes people called them Mutt and Jeff, after the comic strip. When they were in the fourth grade, the nuns had arranged their homeroom desks in alphabetical order. Marie Leonardi sat directly in front of Rose Marino; they'd been inseparable ever since.

"Any word from Lou?" Rose asked. She knew Marie worried about her boyfriend—practically fiancé—fighting in Europe. The last time Rose had seen Lou, just before he shipped out, she'd spied him chatting up a pretty blond at the French Market. She knew Lou had a bit of a reputation but had never said anything to Marie about it. No sense hurting her feelings, not while he was out fighting.

"No. I saw his mother at Mass yesterday, and she hasn't heard from him either," Marie said. She pressed her lips together. "Let's not talk about it." It was often like this, talking about the war. They'd put the painful thoughts away like clothes in a drawer, only to take them out later before putting them away again so they could go on with their lives.

"I'm sure he's OK," Rose said, even though it might not be true. She thought of Janie in the warehouse but knew better than to mention anything.

"Let's sit outside—it's so nice out," Marie said.

They walked to the bayou, where small clusters of workers sat scattered across the lawn eating lunch in the sunshine. Out in the water, six half-built boats floated next to each other, being tested for buoyancy. A stately white egret perched on one of the boats. The air smelled faintly of cut grass and diesel fuel. Rose spread a small brown blanket, and Marie plopped down next to her.

Rose opened the white deli paper on her lap, careful not to spill olive salad from the muffaletta sandwich on her skirt. "Hey—I've got news."

Marie smiled, showing the dimples in her round face. "*You* with news? Do tell." She unwrapped a meatball sandwich, dripping a little red gravy onto her coveralls.

Rose loved her friend fiercely at that moment for her predictable response. "I got a letter from Laura this morning."

"This morning? You mean here?"

"Yes—I got permission."

"That's pretty devious for Saint Laura," Marie laughed. She'd always teased Rose's sister about being such a Goody Two-shoes. "How's she doing?"

"She couldn't say where she is, but it sounds rough. She even landed in a Higgins boat under heavy fire." Rose bit into the sesame-seeded bread filled with salty salami and cheese. The sandwich made her mouth water, and she felt a pang of guilt, wondering what Laura had eaten today.

"I can't even imagine," Marie said.

"Me neither." But Rose did imagine—all the time. She pictured Laura in her mind's eye, tending to wounded soldiers. Laura would be good at that. She was so kind-hearted and focused. As a girl, she was always rescuing injured animals: baby birds, kittens. Once, she'd even hid a possum from their parents until she could nurse it back to health. "But the good news is, she's got a boyfriend."

"Spill it."

"A doctor, from up north somewhere. Sounds kind of serious."

"Laura? She never had so much as a date in high school. I wonder if she'll marry him."

Rose took a sip of milk. So like Marie to jump ahead to marriage. "Who knows? I just want her home safe, with or without a husband."

"Such an adventure she's on!" Marie said. "Scary, though. All that fighting and death. The things I bet she's seen on the operating table. I couldn't do it."

Rose pushed the image of bombs and bullets out of her mind. *A half-acre of hell.* The young soldier with shrapnel in his belly. All of it. Back into the drawer.

"Working here's enough of an adventure for me," Marie said through a mouthful of sandwich. "And once Louie's back: *finito,* no more." She waved her hand at the factory.

Rose thought about what Mr. Sullivan had said that morning. "Hey, do you think they'll really just kick us out of here when the men come back?"

"Who cares? After the war, Lou will take care of me. He's got a good job waiting for him at the docks. I'll be pushing a baby carriage down Decatur Street in no time, after things get back to normal. We just need to find you a husband too."

31

The vision made Rose's throat tighten. Even though she and Marie had talked about their weddings since they were little girls, she couldn't really picture being a wife and mother. Not yet. People were always saying how things would go back to "normal" afterward, but the war was all Rose had known since high school. She was seventeen when the Japanese bombed Pearl Harbor. She didn't know what normal meant any more. What she *did* know was that she loved working in the office, being away from her parents' store, and having some control over her own life.

"I can see it now," Rose said. "You'll bring your brats to see their *Zia* Rose on Sundays."

"I'll do that. I'm naming my second girl after you."

"What about the first?"

"She's going to be named for Olivia de Havilland. Me and Louie are going to have beautiful, movie star kids." Marie patted the back of her head, batting her eyelashes.

"You and your movies, Marie," Rose laughed. "Maybe Mr. Sullivan will let me keep my job. They'll always need bookkeepers, right?"

"Get yourself a husband and you won't have to worry about a job."

Rose sighed. "You sound like my mother."

"Hah! That'll be the day. Maybe we'll find a sailor for you at the dance. I hear there'll be Navy men in port." The church was sponsoring a dance in the high school gymnasium the Saturday after next. "It'll be nice to jitterbug with some real men for a change, not just each other."

The whistle blew. "We'll see about that," Rose said, gathering up her lunch things. They dropped their empty milk bottles in the rack next to the dairy truck. Rose walked back inside and upstairs to her office. She envied Marie's way of making everything seem so simple. Movie star babies. Carriages on Decatur Street. Dancing with sailors. Meanwhile, Rose's own plans always seemed much more complicated.

Rose slid her timecard into the punch clock and joined the throng of workers swarming out of the shipyard gates. Marie's shift started and ended earlier than hers, so Rose rode the streetcar home on her own. Out the window, storefronts and shotgun houses glowed in the waning sunlight. People sat on front stoops, reading newspapers or visiting with neighbors. At moments like this, the city looked so peaceful. Except for the sign hanging over the driver's head (*We're All Pulling Together!*), Rose could almost forget there was a war on.

She closed her eyes, imagining Laura and her doctor holding hands as they looked at the stars, the battle raging around them like in the movies. Rose got goosebumps just thinking about it. She could tell Laura was trying to play the romance down, but her sister wouldn't be excited about just any man. Back home, Laura hadn't had much time for boys. She'd always been driven, graduating at the top of her high school class, then going directly into nursing school. Giovanni had never been a good student; instead, he got by on his easy-going personality and good looks. Rose had always felt like she'd never measure up to them. Still, they inspired her to work harder, especially now.

She got off the streetcar and walked down Rampart Street toward home. She paused to admire the little white cottage on the corner of Burgundy, wishing she could push open the front gate and relax on the lovely porch with its sky-blue beadboard ceiling. Someday.

At last, she reached the side gate between the store and the neighboring house. Across Dauphine Street, Mrs. Fabucci was hanging laundry out on her second-floor balcony—her husband's underwear next to her baby's diapers and her own patched nightgown. The baby squalled from somewhere inside and Mrs. Fabucci ducked through the window.

The neighborhood looked the same as always, but Rose felt something splitting inside herself. At Higgins she was Rose, the clever bookkeeper. Beyond this gate, she was her parents' second daughter. The baby. Once again, Mr. Sullivan's words echoed. *After the boys come home.* Her stomach tightened at the thought of going back to working at the store every day, of finding some nice Sicilian boy to marry, of their children playing out in the courtyard—just as she and her brother and sister had. Maybe Marie dreamed of such things, but Rose didn't, not anymore. She lifted the latch and stepped into the alley. The metal gate clanked as it shut behind her.

# FOUR

Rose stood on the stepladder and reached up to touch a red mesh bag of onions twirling from a ceiling hook. Taking the stub of a pencil from behind her ear, she made a note on a small pad of paper: *onions, 12.* The stuffy storeroom smelled of vegetables and burlap. Her brother's dog, Jake, a mutt with a mottled coat and one mangled ear, dozed in the corner. She could hear her father singing along with Louis Prima on the radio as he worked at the meat counter. She checked her watch; a few minutes more and they'd open. Then her Saturday would no longer be her own.

She craned her neck. Large green-and-gold cans of San Marzano tomatoes stood at attention above a shelf of olive oil bottles. She lost count, began again, only to lose focus once more. Her mind was elsewhere, thinking about her *real* work: the big meeting Mr. Sullivan had coming up this week with his bosses. She hoped the report she'd prepared would be good enough, that she hadn't made any mistakes in her calculations. Everything they did at Higgins was "critical to the war effort," Mr. Sullivan was always saying. Errors meant lost lives. But today she wasn't at the factory, she reminded herself. Her only task was to complete the inventory the store owed to the Ration Board. Onions. Tomatoes. Meat. Cheese.

Rose made notations on her pad. "Time to order more tomatoes, Jake," she said to the dog. He raised his head and looked at her, then went back to sleep. "You're no help." She remembered when her brother brought Jake home as a scruffy-looking puppy. Giovanni with his big, soft heart, begging their parents to keep the stray. Their mother had been dead set against it, but that day their father won the battle. "*Let the boy have something he can take care of,*" her father had said. Rose knew Jake tolerated her only because she fed him; what he really wanted was for Giovanni to walk through the door. He'd been gone over two years now, Laura almost as long. Some days it felt like forever. She was grateful to be so busy; her work at Higgins meant less time to dwell on her worst fears.

The bells over the front door jingled, signaling the first customer of the day. Business had been steady since her father took down the Italian flag. Even Mr. Prescott had started ordering from them again now that Italy had surrendered and switched to the Allies' side.

"Rose, can you come out?" her father called. "Your mother's at the market, and I'm in the middle of cutting meat."

Rose groaned and stepped down from the ladder. She was in no mood to wait on customers. As she walked into the store, she saw her father up to his elbows in a bloody side of beef at the meat counter against the rear wall, singing along to *C'e la Luna*. Her father had a good voice, but Rose hated this song: a young girl getting married off by her parents to the butcher, the musician, or the vegetable man. She stuck out her tongue at him. "Papa, *please.*"

He waved his knife. "What? It's Mr. Prima."

"Why can't Carmine come in? I'm busy back there," she whispered. Through the big front window, she could see her cousin outside sweeping the front walk.

"You know why," he said quietly. "You're better with the customers."

36

She sighed deeply but reached for her apron on a wall peg and walked toward the deli counter where Mrs. Fazio waited. Rose stepped onto a little footstool so she could see over the top of the large wooden case, its glass front displaying salami, prosciutto, giant rounds of fontina and provolone. "Good morning, Mrs. Fazio."

"*Buongiorno*, Rose. *Che bella*, you're looking lovelier every day. Frank, you'd better keep a shotgun handy, no?" Mrs. Fazio called to Rose's father. "Rose will be fighting off the boys like flies when they come back."

Rose glanced at her father, who kept his head down, focused on the meat. *When the boys come back.* She felt like every time she turned around, someone was saying it.

"Maybe my Richie, huh? Whaddya think, Rose?" Mrs. Fazio asked with a sly wink. Rose felt her chest tighten. She had no interest in Richie Fazio, a big *cafone* of a boy, and not very bright. Still, she didn't want to be rude. The Fazios were important customers. They ran the funeral home and often placed large orders to cater repasts.

"How old are you now, anyway?"

"Nineteen last September," Rose said, ignoring the other part of the question. "What can I get for you today?" She tried not to stare at the large mole on Mrs. Fazio's neck.

"I'll take a half pound of the *capicola*, dear. And slice it thin, the way I like it." She pulled a glass jar of Aunt Inez' olive salad off the pyramid display next to the counter. "And one of these too. *Per favore.*"

Rose kept her eyes on the meat as she ran it through the slicer. She wondered if her father had called her out here on purpose to wait on Mrs. Fazio. He wasn't as obvious about it as her mother, but Rose knew he wanted her married off just as much.

"Any word from Richie?" her father called over.

*Here it is.*

37

"Nothing since a letter a few weeks back," Mrs. Fazio said. "He complained about the weather, but I know there are worse things he's dealing with. God protect him." Tears welled in her eyes as she made the sign of the cross. "I pray to *San Giuseppe* every day." She pointed to the statue of Saint Joseph on a ledge near the front window, all that remained of the display from the feast day the prior week.

It had taken Rose and her mother weeks to assemble the altar—flowers, candles, photos of departed family members, and beautiful fig cakes shaped like fish, baskets, and wreaths. Rose found comfort in the familiar rituals, though some of the symbols were just superstitions, like the fava bean for good luck or stealing a lemon to help find a husband—always that. The war had upended so many other traditions. Even the Mardi Gras parades had been cancelled this year.

Her father brought the cleaver down with a thunk. "Your Richie and my Giovanni are probably sitting outside a bar in the Philippines right now, having a beer together and watching the girls go by."

Rose wanted to believe her father's story was true. She weighed the ham on the scale, then neatly wrapped it with twine in brown butcher paper and wrote the price on the package with a black grease pencil. She felt a small wave of guilt wash over her—complaining about such little things, like having to chat with the likes of Mrs. Fazio, when the world had much bigger problems. "Seven coupons and twenty-eight cents. Anything else today, *senora*?"

"No. *Grazie*, dear."

Mrs. Fazio counted out the ration coupons and coins, then dropped the package into her string grocery bag. "Say hello to your mother for me."

"I will," Rose said. "*Ciao*."

As Mrs. Fazio made her way out, Father Tony stood on the sidewalk, holding the door open. "Oh, Father! *Buongiorno!* Thank you." Mrs. Fazio giggled like a schoolgirl as she squeezed past him with her parcels.

Father Tony was the pastor of Immaculate Conception. Rose guessed he was about her parents' age, though he looked younger. The ladies of the parish called him Father What-a-Waste. With his dark, wavy hair and sultry brown eyes, they said he looked like Laurence Olivier. Marie had a crush on him, but he was too pretty for Rose's taste.

Rose felt for her scapular, a lump rising to her throat. These days, a visit from the priest sometimes brought a telegram with bad news from the front. "Papa, Father Tony's here."

Rose's father turned around from the meat-cutting counter, wiping his hands on his apron. The big vein in his neck pulsed. "*Buongiorno*, Father," he said. "I'd shake your hand, but. . ."

"That's OK, Frank. Hello, Rose," Father Tony said. He wiped his brow with a handkerchief pulled from the folds of his black robe. "Not even April and it's already sweltering out there. Don't worry, just a social call."

Rose let her hand drop from the scapular. Laura and Giovanni were safe.

"Frank, I hate to bother you in the store. I know you're always busy on Saturdays," Father Tony said. "I wondered if I might come by tonight to talk with you and Filomena. There's a little church business I'd like to discuss."

"What about, Father?" Rose had heard her father complain that the church was always asking for money.

"I'll tell you all about it when I come. Mind you, I'm not looking for a handout—let's say it's a special mission. We need your help too, Rose. How about I come by around seven thirty, after supper?"

"That will be fine, Father. You'll leave us in suspense until then!" Rose's father threw up his hands.

Father Tony's black robes swirled around him as he walked away. He paused on his way out the door, moving his hand to bless the blue star banner.



That night, as Rose's mother washed the supper dishes, she chattered on about neighborhood gossip—a cousin's new baby, a broken engagement, a friend's son missing in action. Rose stood next to her, drying the plates and cups, and putting them away quickly. Father Tony would be there any minute. Rose noticed her mother wore a little lipstick and a nice dress under her apron.

"Why are you looking at me like that?" her mother snapped.

"Like what? Just noticing you look nice," Rose smirked. Her mother was like all the other ladies in the parish: smitten with Father Tony.

The doorbell rang.

"Don't be silly, Rose," her mother said, removing her apron and patting her hair into place. She called out the window at the top of the back stairs. "Frank, Father Tony is here. Put out that stinky cigar and let him in at the gate. We'll be in the parlor."

Rose arranged the coffee cups on a wooden tray and added a small plate of her mother's biscotti. Her late grandmother's white china with pale pink rosebuds had survived the passage to America. Rose was terrified of breaking any part of it.

She carefully carried the tray into the front parlor. Rose couldn't remember when the family had last sat there and was embarrassed by how old fashioned the room looked. A glassy-eyed Infant of Prague statue wearing a dusty red velveteen robe stood in an arched nook in the wall. The dark wood credenza and the damask sofa covered in clear plastic seemed too large and heavy for the small room. Rose was anxious to get the visit over with. All she wanted was to shut herself in her room and reread Laura's letter.

Her mother huffed behind her. "Set it there," she directed Rose, pointing to the mahogany coffee table. "And open the window. The baking made it even hotter in here."

Rose opened the window, and a small breath of air blew into the room, ruffling the lace doilies on the end tables.

Father Tony came in with Rose's father following him.

"Father," Rose's mother said, softening her voice.

"*Buona sera,* Filomena, Rose." The priest pointed to the framed picture of Giovanni on the credenza, handsome and serious-looking in his Army uniform, the votive candle flickering as always. "Any news lately?"

"Nothing for a few weeks. Last we heard he was in the Philippines. God only knows where he is now," Rose's mother said.

Rose couldn't bear the way her mother always left Laura out. "My sister's somewhere in Italy."

Father Tony looked down at his hands and took a deep breath. "Well, hopefully no news is good news. We'll keep praying until they're both home safe and sound."

"*Siediti.* Please sit down, Father," Rose's mother said. "Have a biscotti. Fresh from the oven."

The priest settled himself on the sofa, his black cassock pooling around his legs. He wore a gold braided rope around his waist and an immaculate white Roman collar at his throat. He took a cookie from the tray. "Mmm. The best in the city," he said, dabbing the corners of his full lips with a napkin.

Rose's mother visibly blushed and sat down next to the priest on the couch. Rose cringed at the noise of the plastic squeaking. Sitting on a stiff side chair, Rose smoothed her skirt and pressed her knees together. The chair was too high for her; her toes barely reached the floor.

41

Rose's father settled himself in the big wing chair. "So, what can we do for you, *padre*?" he asked. Rose could hear a slight edge of impatience in his voice.

"Frank, I know you've had a long day, so I'll try to be quick," Father Tony said. "As I mentioned earlier, we need some help with a special project. It's about these boys they brought in over at Jackson Barracks."

"What boys?" Rose's mother asked, leaning forward.

The priest took a sip of coffee and delicately placed the cup back in its saucer. His fingernails were impeccable. Rose's own hands looked a little ragged, the skin scratched from paper cuts.

"About a year ago," the priest explained, "the Allies captured thousands of Italian soldiers in North Africa, along with Germans, of course. Mussolini left his men starving in the desert—no food, no water, no ammunition."

Rose remembered something Laura had said in one of her letters last summer about seeing Italian prisoners in their hospital when she worked in North Africa. Rose had been surprised the Army required her sister to take care of enemy fighters.

"He should rot in hell, Mussolini," Rose's father said. "That *fascista* son-of-a-bitch…Excuse my language."

"That's OK, Frank. I can't argue with you," Father Tony said. "Anyway, they brought these boys to the US as prisoners of war. I don't know all the particulars, but last week they transferred about a thousand of them to Jackson Barracks—it's been practically empty since our men shipped out."

Rose felt herself growing impatient. Why was Father Tony telling them about all this?

Rose's mother put her coffee cup down. "That's just a few miles away. Unbelievable."

"It's true," the priest said. "After Italy surrendered last fall, the Army couldn't send the prisoners back home. Not yet anyway. Geneva Convention. And they couldn't just let them go either. So, most of them signed up for Italian Service Units—volunteering to go to work at the ports and other places. Lord knows we need the manpower with our own boys overseas."

"True. Still, I hope they keep a close watch on them. They *were* on the other side," Rose's father said. "With all due respect, what does this have to do with us?"

Father Tony took another sip of coffee. "The archbishop asked for our help with organizing some volunteers to visit with these boys. I'm coming to you first because people look up to the Marinos. Filomena, I thought maybe you could get some of the parish ladies to help? Rose can come too, maybe bring Marie and some of her other friends, if you can spare her for a Saturday afternoon, Frank."

*He doesn't ask me,* Rose thought. She felt invisible, as if the priest still thought of her as a child. Not to mention that she had absolutely no interest in visiting any prisoners. She pictured the men as menacing hulks—like the dockworkers who whistled and shouted crude remarks at her when she bought fish for the store.

"Wait, you mean help the prisoners?" Rose's father asked, leaning forward in his chair. "Father, our Giovanni is out fighting the Japs who until recently were in league with these *fascisti*. I know Italy's on our side now, but they weren't when these men got captured. Why should we help *them*?"

"They're just kids, really. Some are younger than Rose here," Father Tony said. "Most of them are no more fascists than you and me, I'm told. They're just lonely Italian boys, *paesani,* a long way from home," he said. "Remember what Jesus said: 'I was in prison, and you visited me.'"

"Father, you know we always want to say yes to anything you ask," Rose's mother said. "But what can we possibly do to help these *criminali*?"

Rose sat up straighter and looked down at the coffee cup in her hands. For once, she agreed with her mother. She pressed her lips together to keep from saying anything, willing her parents to object to the priest's crazy scheme. She wanted no part of it; she and Marie had plans for next Saturday afternoon—getting ready for the dance.

Father Tony turned to face Rose's mother squarely. "I really don't think they are criminals, Filomena. A kind word spoken in Italian. Maybe a home-cooked plate of macaroni. That's all we're asking."

Rose's father wiped a hand across his stubbly cheek. "I don't know, Father," he said. "Maybe we can donate some sandwiches from the store or something. Some people still suspect we're disloyal as it is. What will they think if they see us fraternizing?"

*Yes*, Rose thought, silently cheering her father on. She thought about the rolled-up Italian flag gathering dust in the storeroom and the American flag that had taken its place.

Father Tony put his hand on his heart. "I don't think anyone here in New Orleans would question our patriotism now. Not with one of our own in the mayor's office, right?" Robert Maestri was half-Italian, at least, and had easily won the last election.

"Maybe, but I don't like the idea of my wife and daughter around prisoners."

"You have my word—no harm will come to the ladies, Frank," Father Tony said. "I would never put them in danger. The place is well guarded. We'll take the sandwiches too, but what those boys really need is a human connection. God knows what they've been through."

Father Tony turned to Rose's mother. "Imagine, Filomena— heaven forbid—if it was Giovanni held captive in a foreign land. Wouldn't you hope that some kind family there would visit with him, show him some love?"

Rose's hand went to the scapular under her blouse as she thought about Giovanni or Laura being captured. Tears welled in her mother's eyes. Rose rarely saw her mother weaken; only Father Tony could reach her like this.

"I'll be with you, Filomena," the priest said, his voice low and gentle. "And the American guards stationed at Jackson Barracks will be there the whole time."

Rose's mother looked at her father, nodded once and Rose knew it was over. Her father always had to look like he was in charge, but it was usually for show. Nine times out of ten, her mother called the shots. Meanwhile, nobody asked Rose's opinion at all. She hated them making decisions for her, as if she weren't even in the room.

Her father grabbed a biscotti off the tray. The chair squeaked as he sat back. "I don't like it, Father, but if you promise they'll be protected, I'll allow it—just this one time."

"But Papa, Marie and I . . ." Rose stammered. She felt heat rise in her cheeks. ". . . We have plans. I was going to ask for the afternoon off from the store anyway. There's a dance . . ."

"*Sta' zitta*! Quiet," her mother interrupted. She pointed to the ceiling. "This is God's work. Offer it up."

Rose slumped back in her chair, folding her arms across her chest, humiliated to be treated this way in front of Father Tony. To keep from crying, she stared at the photographs on the wall— unsmiling ancestors in old-country clothes, her parents on their wedding day, a hand-tinted picture of the three children as youngsters posed in pastel Easter outfits. Even with her Higgins job, she felt like her parents still saw her as the same little girl, standing in the shadow of her older brother and sister.

"We'll be there, Father," her mother said. "I'll make a lasagna and I'll see if I can get Inez and a couple of the ladies from the auxiliary to come too. We can keep an eye on those boys, make sure they don't get too close to our girls."

Father Tony gathered up his robes and stood, turning to Rose. "I know it's a lot to ask. We're all weary from sacrificing these days, Rose. You'll be back in time to make the dance."

Rose forced a weak smile. "I don't speak Italian very well, only a little Sicilian. I'll do my best I guess."

"That's the spirit! *Grazie,*" Father Tony said.

Rose's mother brushed a piece of lint from the priest's hat, then handed it to him. "We'll see you tomorrow at Mass, Father."

Father Tony took Rose's mother's hand. "Filomena, as always, bless you. Thanks for the coffee and the biscotti."

Rose's father was already by the door. "We'll walk you out, Father," he said.


Rose fumed as she washed the coffee cups and saucers. She tried to think about what she could say to get out of the trip to the barracks. She was a grown woman with a job and a life of her own. Wasn't it time she had control over her own decisions?

"You didn't even ask me," she said as soon as her parents came back into the kitchen.

"Don't you start, *signorina*," her mother snapped. "You talk to Marie and see if she can come. And be careful with *Nonna*'s china, for the love of God."

"Who says Marie and I want to be around those prisoners?" Rose said, placing a coffee cup on the drying rack.

Rose's father sat at the kitchen table, picking broken bits of biscotti from the baking pan. "Don't use that tone with your mother," he said. "You still live under our roof."

Rose finished washing the dishes in silence, feeling helpless and full of rage, more determined than ever to find a way out of her parents' house.

Later that night, Rose changed into her long cotton nightgown and pushed open the bedroom window overlooking the street. The soft evening breeze carried the scent of sweet olive from the tree blooming below. She breathed in deeply, trying to calm herself. She loved the French Quarter rooftops, each with its own personality: water towers, pigeon coops, chimneys. Some even held their own small vegetable gardens. And beyond? A world of possibilities within arm's reach, and yet just beyond her grasp.

She'd done the math over and over: if the war went on for another year, she'd have enough money saved from her Higgins paycheck to get started on her own. Then she felt guilty because that meant the war would have to continue. More than anything she wished she could talk to Laura like they used to. Rose kissed her fingers and touched them to Laura's nursing school graduation picture on the dresser, her sister prim and plain in her white uniform and cap. In the first few weeks after Laura left, Rose had relished the newfound privacy of having the room to herself. Now she keenly missed her sister's presence, the whispering talks they'd have long into the night. As a little girl, Rose had been afraid of the dark and Laura would reach across the narrow space between their beds to hold her hand until she fell asleep.

She heard the toilet flush down the hall and then her father's heavy footsteps heading into her parents' bedroom. Taking a deep breath, she listened one last time for any sound outside her door. Silence. The clock at Immaculate Conception chimed ten times. She crouched down, reaching under Laura's bed for the old cigar box where she kept her most precious mementos. She sat on her sister's mattress and reread Laura's letter, unsure what she was searching for. Advice? Strength?

*You never know what you can do until you have no choice.*

Maybe Marie was right, that Laura would marry her Yankee doctor and move up north. Rose pictured the big cities she'd seen only in movies—Boston, New York, Philadelphia. She had never traveled farther away than the beach in Mississippi. She loved New Orleans, with all its sweaty charm, even her neighborhood. But here she would always be "the younger Marino girl." She longed to know what it felt like out there in the great elsewhere. Now that she had real work experience, maybe she could even join Laura and start a new life for herself up north, away from this heat, the store, her parents.

A tugboat on the river sounded its mournful horn: one long blast, then two shorter ones. Rose placed the letter back, shoving the cigar box far under her sister's bed where her mother wouldn't find it. She touched the coffee can, growing fuller by the week.

She climbed under the covers and clicked off the bedside lamp. The room was dark except for the slight glow from the gas lanterns on Dauphine Street below. Nearby, a mule-drawn cart clip-clopped toward the stables for the night. Lying on her back, Rose closed her eyes and prayed that God would keep her brother and sister safe, before adding a prayer to Our Lady of Mount Carmel just for Laura. She felt she had to balance out all the extra prayers she knew her mother said for Giovanni. "*Ti amo, Lauretta,*" she whispered.

She tried to picture Laura holding hands with her handsome doctor as they looked up at the stars spilling across the Italian sky, the flash of bombs falling in the distance. As the night grew quieter, Rose thought she could hear the letter under her sister's bed beating like a heart.

CHAPTER

# FIVE

The old yellow school bus bumped along St. Claude Avenue. Outside the windows, the familiar streets of Rose's neighborhood passed in a blur—stores, schools, narrow shotgun houses, and sturdy Creole cottages. Little boys played army, using sticks for guns, and chased each other down the sidewalk. Over the noise of the engine, the ladies chatted loudly in a mix of English and Sicilian. Rose had known most of these women all her life. About a dozen of them—some with their daughters—had answered Father Tony's call for the visit to Jackson Barracks.

Marie sat by the window all dolled up in her navy-blue polka-dot dress and matching hat. Rose touched the back of her hair; she'd pinned it up and put on some lipstick. Even so, she felt a little dowdy in comparison to her friend. As usual.

"Only for you would I do this," Marie said. "You owe me."

"Just add it to the list," Rose said. An old joke—they did favors for each other all the time and kept an imaginary ledger.

"Look at that Gilda," Marie whispered, swiveling her head to look at the group crowded in the rear of the bus. Gilda Cammareri.

"The queen bee," Rose said. Gilda had been the ringleader of the group of popular girls back in high school. When most of the other girls started to develop, Rose never quite caught up, and her lack of a womanly figure was the source of endless fodder for nasty taunts. It still hurt.

Across the aisle, Rose's godmother, Aunt Inez, held a basket on her lap packed with crusty bread, fig jam, prosciutto, cheese, and olive salad. "I'm worried about the family back in the old country," she said. "The last letter talked about how hungry they were all the time." She wore an emerald-green dress with a cropped jacket and matching heels. She kept her hair dyed blond, and perfectly rolled back and lacquered in place with a lot of hair spray. Aunt Inez was always *overdressed*, according to Rose's mother, but Rose thought she looked fabulous.

Father Tony rose at the front of the bus, holding onto the seats on either side to steady himself as he faced the group. "Ladies, ladies, can I have your attention please?" he shouted over the din of conversation and the rumbling of the bus motor. "A few words." The women quieted. "When we get to Jackson Barracks, we'll pass through the gate to a big building in the back where we'll meet the prisoners. No need to worry—they're nice boys. I've met them. And there will be American soldiers standing guard."

"Father," Aunt Inez shouted, leaning forward. "What else can you tell us about these prisoners? Do you know where in Italy they come from? Do they speak any English?"

"*Aspetta*, Inez. I'm getting there. Some of them have been learning English, but you can assume they'll be more comfortable speaking Italian. They come from all over Italy, but hopefully they'll understand Sicilian!" The ladies laughed. Father Tony motioned for them to quiet down, his face suddenly serious. "Remember, they've been through a lot. Things you don't even want to know about. They've been in America for about six months now, working on farms in Texas before they were shipped here, so they're in better shape than when they arrived. You'll see they're being treated well here, but they've been away from their families for a long time. I know they'll welcome you, and the food you're bringing will be a comfort. Thank you again for making this trip. God bless you all." The ladies clapped and the chatter started back up.

"I wonder how Father Tony feels being the only man on the bus besides the driver," Marie said to Rose in a low voice. "What do you bet he likes it?"

"Marie, you're obsessed with the man. He's just doing his job." Rose looked at the priest, sitting up front next to Mrs. Panakio. She saw Mrs. Panakio's face in profile, glancing up at Father Tony with an adoring look. Even priests, Rose thought, were just men after all.

"I hope the prisoners can understand us," Marie said. "My Sicilian's not so good—my mother tries to talk mostly English in the house since my *nonno* passed. She wants us to be more American."

"I wouldn't worry. I don't think we'll be having long conversations with them anyway," Rose said.

"Yeah, and we probably shouldn't mention that we help make the boats that landed on those beaches in North Africa," Marie added. "Might have been soldiers from those units that captured these guys."

Rose hadn't thought of that. The truth was she had no idea what to expect. Would the prisoners be aggressive? Would they be behind bars? Or would they be right there next to her?

She looked past Marie out the open bus window. They crossed the bridge over the Industrial Canal and the cramped, narrow streets of the old city gave way to open fields and small farms. The warm breeze smelled of hay and the earthy aroma of manure. They had only been riding for twenty minutes, but the world outside looked like another country altogether. Rose spotted some cows grazing and thought how different it must be to live out here with the fresh air and all this space.

51

Soon there were more buildings again—a courthouse, churches, storefronts; red-white-and-blue flags everywhere, soldiers driving open-topped jeeps. The bus slowed, then took a right turn into the military base, pulling to a stop at the guard shack under a brick archway. A hand-lettered sign on the front gate read, *U.S. Army—No Visitors Allowed.* It made Rose wonder what dangers lurked beyond this gate, and why they would make an exception for them.

Father Tony stood up. "*Tutti aspettate, prego.* Wait here," he said, motioning for the women to stay seated. He exited the bus. Rose watched the priest shake hands with a young Army soldier wearing a crisp khaki uniform with a rifle slung on his back. After a brief exchange, Father Tony got back on board, and the soldier waved them through the gate, craning his neck to try and see inside the busload of women.

As the bus rolled slowly past rows of two-story white clapboard buildings, Rose stared at the small groups of American soldiers strolling down the walkways. Men. Young, fit men. Everywhere.

"Wow," said Marie, eyeing the soldiers. "I guess they're not all off fighting."

Sometimes Rose saw these same men in the Quarter. But they were generally on leave then, stumbling after a few too many beers, headed to or from the clubs and brothels. Here on the base, the soldiers looked different. Alert and attractive in their uniforms. Rose felt a sharp pain on the back of her arm.

"Ow! Ma—what was that for?" Rose rubbed the spot where her mother had pinched her.

"I see you girls." Rose's mother touched her forefinger to the skin under her right eye, pulling it down and glaring at them. "Watch yourself, or the evil eye will watch you."

Marie laughed. "Oh! Not the *malocchio*, Mrs. M! We're just looking."

"You say that now, Marie. Be careful. You don't want to end up like Cousin Paula. *Puttana.*"

*Here it is. The cousin Paula story.* Paula, who dressed like a tramp, who didn't go to Mass on Sundays, who got herself "in the family way." Paula, who had to go back to Sicily and live in a convent. Rose had been hearing the story for years; she still wasn't sure if any of it was even true.

"Filomena, leave the girls alone," said Aunt Inez. She winked at Rose. "I'll keep my eye on them, don't you worry."

"And who's going to keep an eye on *you*, Inez?" Rose's mother asked. "You're like a young girl yourself!"

Rose smiled at her godmother. Aunt Inez had lost her husband to the Spanish influenza and had never remarried, though she usually had a boyfriend or two hanging around. In some ways Rose had always felt closer to her aunt than to her own mother. Rose's mother said she pitied her sister-in-law, but Aunt Inez always seemed happy. She had her own income from her sewing and olive spread businesses, along with rental property in the Quarter. She'd always encouraged Rose and Laura to be independent too. Aunt Inez answered only to herself.

The bus pulled to a stop in front of a large steel hangar with a domed roof and a rolled-up door. Rose walked slowly behind the other women as they entered the building. Inside, it took a few minutes for her eyes to adjust to the dim light filtering in through a high row of windows. Ceiling fans spinning far overhead did little to dissipate the hot, stale air, which smelled like tobacco and sweat. Ahead were folding chairs and a blackboard with the words, *Good morning. How are you?* written on it. A few American soldiers stood at the rear, where men were milling around, smoking cigarettes and talking. They craned their necks and went silent when they saw the women.

Marie clutched Rose's arm. "There they are," she whispered into Rose's ear. "The prisoners."

The men didn't look like what Rose had expected. They wore the same sturdy boots and khaki uniforms as the American soldiers, only with green oval patches on their left sleeves that said *ITALY*. They were not shackled, as Rose had imagined. She thought they would be older, more hardened looking, but Father Tony was right; they could be any other young Italian men she knew from the neighborhood. She caught herself. They were not. They were prisoners of war and, until recently, the enemy.

"*Buongiorno*," Father Tony called out to the group of men. "Boys meet your new friends," he said in Italian. "These ladies are from the Church of the Immaculate Conception, and they've brought you some treats."

Rose stood still, holding a pan of lasagna, and carrying tablecloths from the church hall in a bag over her shoulder. Several long wooden tables and chairs had been set up along the side of the roped-off area. Father Tony motioned for the women to follow him. They walked tentatively, carrying their parcels. Their heels echoed in the huge space.

"Ladies, you can set up the food over here," he said in English, waving his hand toward the tables. "Go on, don't be afraid."

Rose and Marie unfolded the long white cloths and spread them on the rough wooden tables, then helped the other women unpack the baskets of food. Rose kept an eye on Gilda, trying to steer clear of her. Soon, the clanking of the silverware and tin plates filled the awkward silence. The prisoners watched, staring as much at the covered dishes of food as they did at the women. In short order, the women transformed the worn-out furniture into a proper dining area. Rose placed napkins at each setting, then stepped back, unsure of what to do next. She smoothed out her skirt and looked at Marie, who just shrugged.

Aunt Inez took charge. "Ladies, let's get this food out while it's still warm."

"I'll get the serving spoons," Rose said, grateful to have something to do. Meanwhile, the women took the wrappings off the dishes and placed them along the center of the tables. The men elbowed each other, murmuring more loudly as each dish was revealed—heaping bowls of macaroni, trays of lasagna cut into big squares, dishes full of mustard greens smothered in garlic and olive oil. *"Brava . . . bellissima,"* they said. Rose wondered when they last saw food like this. Like home.

The prisoners waited politely off to the side, shuffling their feet. They looked as unsure as Rose felt. A young man, at the edge of the group, caught her attention. His dark hair and eyes reminded her of Giovanni's. She felt a pang of sadness, thinking about her brother on some far-off island in the Pacific. Her eyes moved to another prisoner. He was leaning against the wall, one foot folded behind him, smoking. He stubbed his cigarette out against the concrete, slipping the butt into his front trouser pocket. Whereas some of the men's uniforms looked baggy, his fit perfectly, the khaki shirt neatly tucked into his pants, a black leather belt snug at his trim waist. His sleeves were rolled up to his elbows; even in the half-light, she could see his tanned forearms, the outline of his muscled shoulders and arms. His face was handsome, though his nose looked like it had been broken and hadn't healed right. Suddenly, he looked up at her and held her gaze, giving an almost imperceptible nod.

Rose dropped the serving spoons she was carrying, and they crashed to the floor. She felt her face flush and dropped to her knees to gather them up.

"Careful, Rose, *così goffo*," her mother yelled.

Marie was right there, helping. "Are you OK?"

"I . . . Yes, I'm fine. Just clumsy. Sorry. Thanks."

"I'll take these over to the sink to rinse them," Marie said, taking the spoons from Rose.

Rose brushed off her skirt. She kept her gaze down, embarrassed, sure that the prisoners were staring at her. She could hear Gilda and her gang mocking her.

"*Per favore, siediti*. Please, have a seat," Father Tony said to the men, mercifully taking the focus off Rose. The prisoners lowered themselves, eyeing the food but not touching it. The women stood back as Father Tony tapped his glass with a fork and rose to speak. "Gentlemen . . Grace," he began, and the men quieted. "*In nominee patris et filii et spiritus sancti*," he began, and everyone made the sign of the cross. "Jesus said, 'I was a stranger, and you welcomed me. I was in prison, and you visited me. I was hungry, and you gave me food.'"

Rose kept her hands clasped in prayer but looked around through lowered eyes. Her mother and Aunt Inez were across the room, heads bowed. Most of the men had their hands folded in their laps, looking like good Catholic boys during grace. She spotted the smoking prisoner she'd seen leaning against the wall, his head so deeply bent she could see the tendons on the nape of his neck. She felt herself blushing and looked away.

Father Tony continued. "Bless these men, and all our families back home in Italy. We pray for peace." One of the men let out a loud sob, and the priest paused.

Rose looked at the prisoner who'd cried out; he looked like a teenager. He pulled a tattered white handkerchief from his pocket and blew his nose. The man next to him patted his shoulder.

"Bless this food, Lord, and these good women who prepared it. Amen," Father Tony said. "*Mangiamo!*"

Aunt Inez and Rose's mother began spooning out food onto the men's plates. Rose and Marie poured lemonade while some of the other women passed the bread baskets. "*Grazie, grazie,*" the men repeated. "*Grazie.*"

Rose saw Father Tony walk over to the young man who'd cried during the blessing. Mrs. Panakio was there too, gently patting the boy on his back. Rose hugged herself, thinking about Giovanni.

Mrs. Panakio handed him a clean handkerchief. "*Mangi, caro,*" she said. "You'll feel better if you eat something."

"*Si, si. Mi dispiace. Grazie,*" the boy said, smiling through his tears.

Rose worked her way down the table, pouring glasses of lemonade. As she reached the end, she tried not to stare at the smoking man but couldn't help noticing the graceful way he moved—carefully, deliberately, seeming to savor every bite of the lasagna she'd made with her mother. He looked up and again, his eyes locked on hers as he chewed. She forced herself to hold his gaze, and felt a chill run up her back, despite the heat. She made her way toward him with her pitcher. He sat back as she poured. She focused on the beads of condensation on the sides of the glass, willing herself not to spill a drop.

"*Grazie, signorina,*" the young man said. His voice was low and rich.

"*Prego,*" Rose nodded.

As she withdrew, her arm brushed against his and her skin tingled. Instantly, she felt ashamed. These were prisoners of war, she had to remind herself again, not American soldiers at a dance.

The men ate quickly, asking for seconds, and some thirds. Eventually, they pushed back from the table, hands on their stomachs. Father Tony had been circulating among them, making conversation here and there. Now Rose noticed he was finally having a plate of lasagna himself. She refilled his glass with lemonade.

"Thanks, Rose," Father Tony said. "And thanks for doing this. I know you weren't thrilled about the idea, but I'm grateful."

"It's OK, Father," Rose said, now wishing she hadn't been so childish about coming. If Laura could tend to these prisoners in the field, the least she could do was serve them a meal. "I'm happy to help."

"They look just like us, don't they?" the priest asked. The men had started to get up from the tables and the women were clearing the plates, bringing them to a large kitchen area at the other end of the building.

Rose saw the smoking prisoner talking with another man. She looked away quickly, noticing three of the American soldiers chatting up Aunt Inez. The guards didn't seem too concerned about the POWs. "Yes, I suppose they do," Rose said. "But they're not really like us at all, are they?"

"We're all children of God, Rose."

"Of course, Father."

She walked back over to the tables, where Marie and some of the other women were putting out cookies and pastries. The men who had been walking around moved back to their places, while the women poured coffee from big metal thermoses. As they sipped, some prisoners grimaced and looked at each other.

"I guess they don't appreciate the chicory," Marie said. "Look out, Rose. We've got company."

Rose could hardly hear Marie over the pounding of her heart. The prisoner who'd smiled at her and the one who looked like Giovanni were both coming toward them. Rose glanced around to locate her mother, but she was busy pouring coffee, and not paying her any attention.

"*Buongiorno, signorine,*" said the one who'd reminded Rose of her brother. "I'm Vincenzo, and this is my friend Salvatore," he said in Italian, putting his arm around the other man's shoulders.

Rose struggled to understand his Italian but got the gist of the introduction. Salvatore. Now she had a name to put with the feeling. Rose smiled at them but couldn't come up with any words. Her throat had closed up and her heart was beating wildly in her chest.

58

"Thank you for delicious food. We are from Fidenza, in *Italia*. It is at the top," Vincenzo said in halting English. He pointed up.

Rose and Marie exchanged a glance. "The north of Italy, you mean?" Marie asked.

Marie spoke for them both, and Rose was grateful.

"*Si*, north," he said.

"I'm Marie. From the French Quarter. Here in New Orleans," Marie said in Sicilian. "Sorry, we don't speak much Italian."

"*Siciliani*," Vincenzo laughed, recognizing the dialect. He pressed his thumb to his fingers and shook his hand at them.

Marie smiled. "*Si*. My mother and father are from Sicily. Rose and I were both born here."

"Please to meet you, Marie. Rose." Salvatore said in English. "Thank you for bringing the food. *Come quello di mia nonna*. Like . . . grandmother." Rose was touched that the food had brought back a happy memory for him; she thought of her own grandmother, wondering what she would have made of all this.

"You have wine? Cigarettes?" Vincenzo asked.

"Um . . . no, we . . ." Rose stuttered, her mind unable to come up with the words in Sicilian.

"Is OK," Salvatore said in English. "I sorry, my English not so good. You understand Italian?"

"*Si, ma per favore parla lentamente*," Marie said, asking them to speak slowly. They all continued talking, mixing Italian and Sicilian, and the men seemed much more relaxed. Rose was surprised by how much she understood.

"How did you get here?" Marie asked.

"They captured us in the desert in Tunisia, the English," Salvatore explained. "We were so hungry and tired—we surrendered to the medics. They didn't even have guns."

Rose thought about Laura, who worked with those medics. Maybe she had been there the day Salvatore and Vincenzo gave themselves up.

"They put us on a train, all packed together like sardines," Salvatore continued. "It was . . .terrible . . ." His voice trailed off. He shook his head and looked down.

Rose could feel the pain in his voice.

"Then they put us on a big boat," Vincenzo said. "We didn't know where we were headed until we got to New York City. It was like a dream when we saw the tall buildings, the Statue of Liberty!"

"New York. Such a big city," Rose said, feeling stupid for making such an inane comment. She could understand Italian better than she could speak it. Besides, she reminded herself: they were prisoners, not sightseers. Rose noticed her mother taking in the scene from across the room. She looked at Rose, her hands on her hips, and said something to Father Tony, who was standing next to her.

"We didn't see much of New York," Vincenzo said. "They put us on a train right away and took us to Texas. From one desert to another. El Paso. We worked on some farms there. Then they brought us here, to New Orleans. So far, all we have seen is this army base."

"And now . . . you," Salvatore looked at Rose. She felt herself blush uncontrollably again.

Vincenzo touched Marie's arm lightly. "Marie, how many years have you?" he tried in English.

"*Non capisco.* How many years? Oh, you mean how old am I? Well, how many years do you think I have?" Rose couldn't believe Marie was flirting with these men. She saw Father Tony moving toward them. Had he seen Vincenzo touch Marie's arm?

"Boys, why don't you come get some of the cookies before they're all gone? Rose's mother makes the best biscotti," Father Tony said, putting his hand on the back of Vincenzo's shoulder and trying to steer the men away.

Vincenzo turned and said a polite *piacere* to Rose and Marie. He started walking with the priest, but Salvatore lingered. "Rose.

*La fattoria della mia famiglia, a Fidenza, mia madre ha molti fiori, ma la rosa è la più bella."*

Rose concentrated on the words, trying to translate them in her head. *At my mother's farm, in Fidenza, there are many flowers, but the rose is the most beautiful.* Could she have heard that right?

"When will I see you again?" Salvatore asked in Italian. He put his hand—rough, but warm, lightly on Rose's hand. Her face felt hot, and her heart was beating so fast she thought it might burst through her chest. She looked at Marie, who grinned at her like the Cheshire cat.

"I—I don't know . . . soon . . . maybe," she stuttered, pulling her hand away slowly.

"*Lo spero,*" Salvatore said, his lips pressed together in a crooked smile. "I hope," he said in English.

Rose felt dizzy as she watched him walk off after Father Tony.

"Watch out. Here comes your mother," Marie said, looking over Rose's shoulder.

Rose felt her mother's pinching grip again on the back of her upper arm.

"What's the matter with you, Rose? Flirting with those fascists. They are still the enemy. I don't care what the government says."

"Ma, we were just talking," Rose said. "Isn't that what Father Tony wanted us to do?"

"Just talk. I'm watching, and so is God," her mother said, pointing two fingers at her own eyes and back to Rose's face before turning away and rejoining the other women.

Marie grabbed Rose's arm. "Did you see that Vincenzo? Those eyes, *Madonna!*"

"What about Lou?"

"Just looking, Rose," Marie laughed. "No harm in that, right? I think he was flirting with me just a little though, don't you? I mean, it's been a while . . . And his friend Salvatore was so cute

61

too. He sure had eyes for you, Rose. We need to find you an American soldier, though, not one of these *fascistas*."

Rose nodded, looking past Marie and scanning the room for Salvatore. She glimpsed his back, his uniform shirt snug across his shoulders, his left hand in his pants pocket. She'd had crushes on movie stars before, but Salvatore was a flesh-and-blood man. Not just handsome, but seemingly smart and kind. He'd instantly made her feel special, not something she was used to.

"Ladies—I'm afraid it's time for us to head home," Father Tony shouted, clapping his hands together. The women followed him outside, carrying their empty serving bowls and pans. Marie was already ahead, chatting with Rose's mother. Rose knew Marie was trying to distract her, change the subject, downplay the exchange with the prisoners. Meanwhile, Rose lagged behind, moving as if through a dense fog. Aunt Inez came up next to her.

"Rose, I saw what happened back there," Aunt Inez said in a low voice.

"What do you mean? Nothing happened. We were just talking. Let me help you, *Zia*," Rose tried to take the tablecloths her aunt was carrying, but Aunt Inez didn't hand them over.

"These boys have been locked up for a very long time, without female company, if you know what I mean. You're not a girl anymore, Rose, you're a beautiful young woman. But you don't have a lot of experience with men. Just keep your wits about you."

Rose sighed, thinking of her mother's antics. "If I'm a young woman, how come my mother still treats me like a child?"

"She just wants what's best for you, Rose," Aunt Inez answered. "With Laura and Giovanni off halfway across the world, you're all she has. She may not tell you, but I know she loves you. She wants to keep you safe."

On the bus ride back, Marie chattered on about the dance that night, what she would wear, how she was going to fix her hair. Rose feigned interest but her mind was elsewhere as she went over

62

every detail about Salvatore: his funny nose, the slightly crooked smile, the way he looked at her like there was nobody else in the room. She'd never felt such an instant connection to someone before—not just physically, but in her soul. His words echoed in her head. *Quando ti rivedrò? When will I see you again?*

"Are you even listening to me, Rose?" Marie broke in.

"Yes, yes, the chiffon dress. Definitely." It seemed to be enough, and Marie continued her monologue. Rose felt for the rosary beads in her pocket, forcing herself to silently recite Hail Marys to calm her mind.

CHAPTER

# SIX

"I got all dressed up for this? I don't know why we bothered," Marie said, flipping her hand at the room. The gym was decorated with blue and white crepe paper streamers, and artificial flowers were tied to the basketball nets. Votive candles in small glass holders, borrowed from the church, flickered on the scattered tables. The gymnasium smelled faintly of sweaty high school boys. Big electric fans whirred in the corners, moving the hot air around. "This doesn't look anything like those USO dances we see in the newsreels," Marie said. "I thought there were supposed to be sailors here, at least. Where are they? I hate this stupid war."

"I know. Slim pickings," Rose said.

She and Marie stood by the punch bowl, surveying the scene. The nuns were scuttling around and talking in small clusters. A few of the other girls who'd made the trip out to Jackson Barracks were there too, along with some younger girls from the high school. Rose was glad to see no sign of Gilda. The dances were a chance to get out of the house, but with few men to dance with, they were like a wartime cake baked without sugar: bland and flavorless. Rose was immediately ashamed of herself. Laura and Giovanni would probably give anything to be here at this boring dance instead of wherever they were right now.

Rose couldn't even think about sailors. Her head was full of Salvatore. She wondered what he was doing at this moment. Was he thinking of her? Rose and Marie had rushed to fix their hair and get ready at Rose's house after the visit to Jackson Barracks. Rose's long black curls were caught up in a blue ribbon tied at the nape of her neck. It matched the ribbon around the waist of her modest cream-colored muslin dress. She wore a little pink lipstick and she'd rubbed some on her cheeks for rouge. Her legs felt naked with no stockings, but this dance wasn't worth risking her only intact pair.

Marie sighed. "Still, you look pretty in that dress, Rose. Not for nothing, we have to stay in practice for when the men come back, right? I wish my Louie was here. He loves to dance."

"You look great too, Marie. I love your hair that way," Rose said. Marie had teased her shoulder-length auburn hair into dramatic waves and squeezed her full figure into a black chiffon dress one size smaller than it needed to be. Her lipstick was cherry red; her mouth looked like a Christmas bow on her round face. Rose's mother said Marie dressed "cheap," but Rose knew Marie didn't care what people—especially Filomena Marino—thought of her. Rose wished she could be more like that herself. Fearless.

Sister Mary Arnold glided over to the punch bowl, her feet invisible beneath the long black robe. A white wimple covered her hair; a broad white bib framed her pale face. Beads of perspiration formed a slight mustache on her upper lip. "Good evening, ladies. Are you having a nice time?" Her blue eyes twinkled. Rose thought she must be burning up in her habit, but nuns never complained.

"Yes, sister," Rose and Marie said in unison, trying to muster some cheer. Rose had a soft spot for Sister Mary Arnold. While the other nuns told her she'd never have a use for math, Sister Mary Arnold had quietly encouraged Rose's interest and wrote her the recommendation for Soulé.

"We're grateful for the music and the nice evening," Rose said.

"So much bad news on the radio every day," Marie said. "A little fun like this takes our minds off the war. We're kind of tired tonight, though. We had a busy day with Father Tony, riding over to see those Italian prisoners at the Jackson Barracks."

"Ah, yes. I heard about that," the nun said. "What were they like?"

Rose had an instant vision of Salvatore, tucking that cigarette butt into the tight front pocket of his trousers. She felt herself blushing and looked down.

"A little strange, to tell you the truth, Sister," Marie said. "They were very polite, though. Just young men, about our age, most of them."

"I think they appreciated all the food we brought," Rose added. "We tried to talk Italian to them. I think they liked that too."

"You should be proud of yourselves," Sister Mary Arnold said. "I'm sure you had other things you could have done this afternoon. God knows there's not enough kindness in the world right now. Maybe some good will come of it."

Rose and Marie exchanged a glance. All Rose could do was smile, hoping the nun didn't notice the color rising in her face again. After Sister Mary Arnold walked away, Marie elbowed Rose lightly on the arm. "*Maybe some good will come of it, Rose!*" she joked. "I know you're thinking about that boy Salvatore. I can see it all over your face."

"Stop it, Marie," Rose said. But of course, she was. "Look, the band's coming on."

Rose pointed toward the makeshift stage at one end of the gymnasium. An upright piano, drums, stand-up bass. The clarinet player wore a threadbare tuxedo, his graying hair slicked back. He took a swig out of a Coca-Cola bottle. The drummer counted off a beat and a tall woman in a black sheath dress embraced the large silver microphone, putting her ruby-red lips right up to the RCA emblem. "Ladies and gentlemen," she purred. "Everyone out on the dance floor. Here we go with 'Night in Tunisia!'"

"Oh, I love this song!" Marie cried. "Let's go, Rose. I don't care if there are no men to dance with." The singer's silky voice followed along with the clarinet's melody as Rose and Marie took to the floor.

Rose thought of her sister's letter—Laura with her handsome doctor, gazing at the night sky. Tunisia, where Salvatore was captured. She half-closed her eyes and let Marie take the lead. Marie was a good dancer, and Rose let her push and pull her in time to the music. In her mind, it was Salvatore spinning her around the dance floor, his strong hand in hers, his arm around her waist, moving gracefully. All eyes on them, his eyes only on her.

Rose stumbled over her feet. Marie laughed and gave her a twirl. The song ended and Rose took an embroidered white handkerchief out of her purse to dab her forehead. "Let's go check out the food," she said, trying to shake off her dancing dream of Salvatore. Here she was, mooning over a man who might be a vicious killer, for all she knew, while her sister was off caring for wounded heroes on the battlefield, while so many families were losing their sons and brothers—and their sisters—every day.

At the buffet table, metal trays of miniature meatballs sat uneaten, congealing in red gravy. None of the girls wanted to risk getting tomato stains on their good dresses. Rose took a golden *pinoli* cookie from the tray. "Do you think the church will send us to see them again? The prisoners?" She asked and took a bite. No sugar, but at least the pine nuts were good.

"I don't think they're going anywhere for a long time, so I guess they might want regular visitors," Marie shouted over the music. "Ask your mother. But don't seem too eager, Rose. She'll be suspicious."

"Good point," said Rose. "Maybe I'll give it a couple of days. I would go again, though. Would you?"

"Of course! That Vincenzo was easy on the eyes—Lou, forgive me." She made the sign of the cross. "Hey, wouldn't it be great if they would let those Italian boys come to these dances?"

Rose pictured the gymnasium filled with dancing couples and Salvatore's face as he asked her to dance. "It's a nice idea," she said. "But why would the Army do that? They are still prisoners, even if they're not enemies anymore. I don't think they can leave the barracks except to work."

"Yeah, you're probably right," Marie sighed. "But maybe Father Tony could make it happen. If it came from him, people might go along."

Rose finished the cookie, flicking crumbs from her dress. She thought about Salvatore's arm brushing against hers as she poured the lemonade, and a shiver ran through her. "He *was* kind of good-looking, wasn't he? Salvatore, I mean." She couldn't help herself. If she didn't say his name out loud, she felt like she would explode.

"He sure was. *Madonna*—those muscles. He looked like he was in good shape." Marie looked around, making sure no nuns were in earshot. "Lou has muscles like that, Rose, and I'm here to tell you, it feels good when he . . . you know?"

"What?" Rose asked. Marie had much more experience with men than she did. Sometimes her stories made Rose squirm, but tonight she wanted to hear more. She felt suddenly naïve; maybe she could learn something from her friend.

"I told you about the night before he shipped out, when we snuck down to the river. Up on the levee, there's that big grassy area. You know where I mean?" Marie said, her mouth close to Rose's ear to be heard over the music. "We put a blanket down. It was a beautiful night, so romantic. Louie wanted to do more, but I wouldn't let him. Not until we're married." Marie paused, leaning in even closer to Rose. "But we did a lot of kissing, and maybe a little more."

"A little more what?"

"He might have touched me under my dress a little."

"Right out there in public?" Rose asked.

"Well, not exactly public. It was very dark. To tell you the truth I was more afraid of bugs on the grass than I was of Lou! But Lou was pretty excited."

"How could you tell?"

"Rose, are you really asking me that question?"

Rose knew what Marie meant. She thought about Salvatore. That front pocket where he tucked the cigarette butt. With all the impure thoughts she was having, she was already dreading confession next Saturday.

"Hey, maybe we could have a dance *at* Jackson Barracks," Rose said, changing the subject. She was afraid of where her mind was wandering. "That way they wouldn't have to leave."

"*Now* you're using that big brain of yours. That training hall would work just fine."

"Right. It could be an Italian culture type of thing. The Santa Rosalia feast is coming up…" Rose couldn't believe these words were coming out of her mouth. Just yesterday, she was pouting about having to go to Jackson Barracks at all. Now she was plotting her return. And all because of a man—a prisoner—she barely knew.

"Perfect. We could corner Father Tony after Mass tomorrow. Put the bug in his ear."

"As long as my mother doesn't see us," Rose said.

After a few more songs, the band leader wiped his forehead with a handkerchief. "We've got time for just one more, folks," he said into the microphone. Rose was relieved. She was anxious to get home and shut the door to her room. She needed to think. From the first moment she saw Salvatore, a part of her felt thrilled, but another part was scared. And guilty. It was all so confusing. She so wished she could talk to Laura.

"Play 'As Time Goes By,'" a girl shouted from the other side of the room.

"I guess we have some *Casablanca* fans in the house," the band leader said to scattered applause. "Boys—in C. For all the *belle ragazze* here tonight."

Rose smiled and hooked her arm in Marie's as they stood listening to the band. She pictured Ingrid Bergman in the film, her face glowing and wet with tears, sobbing in Humphrey Bogart's arms. Rose had cried through most of the movie; her heart aching for the lovers—the sacrifices they both had to make, the love they'd never find again.

The piano player was singing now, the clarinet winding out the mournful melody as a few couples slow-danced across the gym floor. Rose thought about Laura and her doctor facing danger every day and every night. The war had thrown people together who would never otherwise cross paths. Rose wondered if Laura's love would survive the war, or if it would become a sweet memory, like Paris had for Rick and Ilsa in the movie. It had been up to them to act, right or wrong, rather than let the moment pass by. Maybe this was her moment too, her Paris, with Salvatore.

# SEVEN

Rose sat back on the bench to relieve the pain from the wooden kneeler. The church was stifling hot and smelled of sweaty Sunday clothes mingled with incense. She saw beads of moisture on the back of Father Tony's neck as he recited the Latin prayers. She hoped he was as uncomfortable as she was, so he would speed up the service.

Her mother elbowed her. "Jesus suffered six hours on the cross, the least you can do is kneel for a few minutes," she whispered.

Rose rolled her eyes as she leaned forward to kneel again.

"A reading from the book of Matthew," Father Tony began. "Jesus said, 'For I was hungry, and you gave me to eat, I was thirsty, and you gave me to drink, I was a stranger, and you invited me in, I was in prison, and you came to visit me.'" It was the same passage he had quoted to convince Rose's mother to visit Jackson Barracks.

Rose looked around at her neighbors in the pews. She could feel the grief all around her as people offered up special intentions for their loved ones. She said a prayer for Giovanni and Laura, trying to keep her mind off the image of Salvatore. Rose wondered if her act of good will in visiting the POWs would be cancelled out by her thinking about Salvatore obsessively since meeting him, of her plotting the dance so she could be near him again.

After the sermon and the consecration, Rose and her parents kneeled at the altar rail for communion. Father Tony, in his dark green and gold chasuble, was flanked by two altar boys dressed in white robes. They moved down the row of kneeling parishioners, dispensing the hosts. "*Hoc est Corporis Christi, Filomena,*" he said to Rose's mother.

"Amen," she replied.

Rose watched out of the corner of her eye as the priest gently placed the host on her mother's outstretched tongue. Her mother kept her eyes closed, swallowed the host, then blessed herself. Rose accepted the host in her own mouth, and followed her mother back to the pew, her father walking behind her. In her head, Rose was rehearsing the conversation with Father Tony she would have; Mass was nearly over.

"*In nomine patris et filii et spiritus sancti,* amen," Father Tony blessed the congregation as the service ended. Everyone started for the exits.

"I'm going to run ahead and get the coffee set up in the hall," Rose's mother said. "I'll see you over there." She turned on her heel, adjusting her navy-blue dress and matching hat as she headed for the side door.

Rose breathed a sigh of relief. Her mother's absence would give her and Marie an opening to talk to Father Tony alone. "Papa, I'm going to say hello to Marie and Mrs. Leonardi. I'll meet you at the hall, OK?"

"OK, baby. I'm going to light a couple of candles up front. For Giovanni and Laura. I'll meet you over there."

Before the war, her father used to joke about the offerings being just another way for the church to take his money. Now Rose watched his back as he slowly made his way toward the rows of flickering candles. Other parishioners were already there, sliding coins into a small metal box, making promises to God in exchange for healing a sick parent, a soldier's safe return.

Rose met Marie at the rear of the church. Father Tony was standing outside greeting the parishioners, silhouetted by the bright sunshine. Rose gave him a shy wave from behind Mr. Lupo, who owned the Central Grocery, one of her family's competitors. Mr. Lupo shook the priest's hand and walked away. Marie's mother was on the sidewalk, chatting with some of the neighborhood women. It was now or never.

Father Tony turned to Rose and Marie. "Oh, *buongiorno*, girls. I was just telling Mr. Lupo about our outing to the Jackson Barracks yesterday. Thanks again for coming."

"Good morning, Father," Marie said. "Well, it's the least we can do. Those poor boys, so far from home. I can only hope people would do the same for my Louie if he were captured in Europe somewhere, God forbid."

"Your sermon today made me think about it some more," Rose said. "When you said that Jesus would want us to help our enemies, and people who weren't like us."

"Well, it's nice to know someone was paying attention!" the priest said.

"I thought about my sister and brother, fighting to liberate people we don't even know."

"May God protect them," Father Tony muttered, making the sign of the cross.

"But then I thought about those prisoners—something we could do here at home, for the war effort." Even as the words left her mouth, Rose felt like a fraud.

"Speaking of that, I was just asking Mr. Lupo if he and the Italian Club might be willing to sponsor some more activities over there at Jackson Barracks," Father Tony said.

"Really? What were you thinking, Father?" Marie asked.

"I'm not sure yet—maybe a Saturday evening Mass? Maybe a luncheon like before?"

"That sounds good," Rose said, starting to panic. A Mass was not what she had in mind. "Another thought. Marie and I were at the church dance last night. You know, dancing with each other because there were no men. It's probably a crazy idea, but what if we could hold a dance at Jackson Barracks?" Rose smiled and blushed a little as she looked into Father Tony's dark brown eyes. She felt as if she were outside herself, watching as this strange, bolder person took take action. It felt more like something Laura would do: asking for what she wanted, making her own decisions, not waiting for permission.

"A *dance*? Well, I'm not sure about *that* . . ." Father Tony frowned, stroking his chin.

Marie interrupted him. "You know, the Saint Rosalia feast is coming up. That might be a fun way to celebrate. We'd need our parents' permission, of course. And chaperones."

Marie was laying it on a little thick. Rose watched the priest's face to see if he would catch on to their ploy. "Maybe we could have it on the Saturday night of the feast week," she said.

"Well, I'd have to think about it," Father Tony said. "I told your parents I would watch out for you girls. Those men haven't been with women in a long time. Your parents might be a little wary."

If he suspected anything, Rose thought, he wasn't letting on. "You're right, Father. We would be careful, of course. Just some music and maybe a little dancing. If you can get my mother to agree, Marie and I could help round up some of the other girls to come."

"It's the dancing part. I don't know. I'd have to talk to the commanding officer over there. I don't know if there are rules against that sort of thing," Father Tony said. "They're supposed to be prisoners, but I know they're trying to keep them happy, so they don't cause any trouble."

"Whatever you decide, just let us know," Marie said. "The feast is three weeks away, so we have plenty of time to figure it out once we get through Easter."

"*Va bene*," Father Tony said. "Rose, your mother's over in the hall. I'll speak to her and maybe she can get the ladies' auxiliary to help with food, and chaperones too, of course."

"We'll see you back there in a few minutes, Father. We'll give you a head start," Rose said. "And probably better not to mention the idea came from us."

"*Capisco.* I understand." Father Tony winked at her.

They watched the priest's black robe swirling around his feet as he walked into the church. "I think he took the bait, Rose," Marie said.

"I'm not so sure about that. I think he knew it had nothing to do with Jesus," Rose said. "I hope my mother goes along."

"You know she can't turn *him* down," Marie said. "And I'm proud of you—you weren't afraid."

Rose was afraid, though. Would she feel the same when she saw Salvatore again? Would he? Three weeks. It felt like an eternity.

"Oh, my aching back," Marie said. Two weeks had passed since they'd spoken to Father Tony about the dance, and now she and Rose sat by the bayou on their lunch break. Clusters of workers on their break sat in every available shady spot; a slight breeze off the water cut through the stifling heat. "They've got us working double time on the line now. I'm glad for the extra money, but I'm exhausted. All I can hear when I close my eyes at night is the roar of those machines."

"I saw the production reports this morning," Rose said. "I hope all these new boats will help speed things up over there. This war is wearing us all out."

The newsreels brought home frightening footage—the Allies were even bombing the Vatican to drive out the Germans. Everyone in the neighborhood worried about family in Sicily, trying to send food and clothing to relatives, unsure if the shipments were getting through. The radio reports were full of news about the Germans sinking American ships in the Atlantic. It had been almost two months since she'd received the letter from Laura. Rose knew the fighting was fierce in Italy. And still no word from Giovanni.

"Are you getting excited about Saturday night?" Marie asked, unpacking her sandwich.

"Yes, and also a little nervous," Rose said.

"What are you nervous about?" Marie asked. "It's just another dance. It'll be fun to have some real men there for a change. Father Tony says there's going to be a live band. I hope the Italian guys like jazz. I know my cousins in Cefalú are crazy for it."

"This dance feels different to me," Rose said. "I don't know. Maybe I'm just making a fool of myself even thinking about Salvatore. What if he's not even there still?" Rose said.

"And where would he go?"

"I don't know. But what if it's all in my head?"

"I saw the way that boy looked at you," Marie said. "It's not in your head. But hey, even if he's not there, I'm sure you won't lack for dance partners."

But Rose wasn't interested in just any partner, only Salvatore. It didn't make any sense—she didn't even know him. She knew she was a little obsessed, fretting about her imaginary romance while overseas the war raged on.

"What time are you finished at the store tomorrow?" Marie asked through a mouth full of sandwich.

"I should be done by four," Rose replied.

"Bring your dress over to my house so we can get ready together. And then we can walk to the bus. That way your mother won't be hovering all over us, all due respect."

"Good idea," Rose said. "I'm so glad my mother isn't chaperoning. Did you figure out which dress you're going to wear?" Rose was relieved when her parents said they had plans at the Italian Hall the night of the Jackson Barracks dance.

"Well, I'm going with the tried-and-true red crepe de Chine. None of them have seen it, so it's new to them, right?" Marie said. "What about you?"

The whistle blew, and they started packing up their things. "You'll see," Rose said. She'd rummaged through Laura's closet and found a pretty dress with a sweetheart neckline. It was a little too big, but Aunt Inez was altering it. "All I can tell you is it's not what you'd expect from me."

# EIGHT

The morning of the dance, Aunt Inez arrived early. "Knock knock," she sang as she walked through the kitchen door, carrying a cloth garment bag. "Only for my goddaughter would I get up this early on a Saturday!"

Rose gave her aunt a kiss on both cheeks. Even at this hour, Aunt Inez managed to look glamourous. She wore a stylish canary yellow wrap dress and leopard print pumps. She pulled a cigarette and gold lighter from her purse and lit up.

"*Buongiorno,* Inez," Rose's mother said. She looked worn out in a faded floral chintz dress and frayed apron. Rose had to remind herself her mother and her aunt were nearly the same age. "Where are you going, dolled up like that?" Rose's mother looked Aunt Inez up and down.

"It's called life. You should try it sometime. I hope you have some coffee ready—I had a late night over at the Dew Drop."

"I don't even want to know!" Rose's mother held up one hand as she poured Aunt Inez a cup from the big silver pot. Rose knew her aunt spent time in the jazz clubs, probably with people her parents wouldn't approve of. Inez' world sounded mysterious and exciting to Rose, though her aunt didn't share many details.

Aunt Inez shook her head, a small smile at the corner of her mouth. "Enough of that. Today it's about our Rose and this dress."

The radio was on. There was a news report about German U-boats being spotted in the Gulf of Mexico, just a hundred miles or so from New Orleans. "Scary news," Rose said. "I feel a little selfish, worrying about dresses and dances."

"Nonsense," Aunt Inez said, sipping her coffee and stubbing out her cigarette in the oystershell ashtray on the table. "You Higgins girls work hard. You deserve to have a little fun. Let's go finish with the dress before my brother starts looking for you downstairs."

"I'm off to the market," Rose's mother said, untying her apron. "See you later, Inez. Thanks for helping Rose."

"Don't you want to see the dress?" Inez asked.

"I saw it before, when her sister wore it to her prom," she said with a wave of her hand. "I'm sure it'll be fine. It's just a dance, for heaven's sake. I need to get going. I have things to do. I have a life too, you know."

She couldn't even say Laura's name, Rose thought, biting her lip. For once, her mother wasn't meddling; still, Rose was hurt. Her mother was so uninterested in the dress, the dance—anything about her life. Even her work at the factory.

"Your daughter's going to be the belle of the ball," Aunt Inez said.


In her bedroom, Rose stood in her slip and bare feet as Aunt Inez pulled the dress from its bag and held it up. It was a deep indigo blue, almost floor-length, with ruffled straps over the shoulders. "It looks like a whole new dress!" Rose said.

"I added some embroidered netting over the taffeta to snazz it up a little," Aunt Inez said.

"I hope Laura doesn't mind," Rose said.

"I think she'd be happy. Your sister's very practical. Reusing an old dress—she'd like that. Besides, she's one of the most unselfish people I ever met. Now, let's try it on one last time. I want to make sure I got the length right. Watch for the pins." Rose pulled the dress over her head, letting the silky fabric shimmy over her hips. Her aunt zipped it up in the back and spun her around. "My, my," Aunt Inez said, stepping back and nodding her head. "*Che bella. You look like a grown-up woman, Rose.*"

Rose turned to look at her reflection in the vanity mirror and felt a lump in her throat. Her face looked the same, but from the neck down she didn't recognize herself. Her aunt had taken the dress in to fit her waist, and tulle the skirt made her slim hips appear fuller. The neckline dipped, making her neck look longer, more elegant. "Oh, *Zia.* I love it," she said, giving her aunt a hug.

"I do wish I could give you some of my bust, though!" Aunt Inez laughed.

Rose saw her aunt smiling in the mirror. "I wish you could too!" She twirled around to see the back of the dress, then pulled her hair up on top of her head. She was a little embarrassed to be caught acting so vain but liked the way she looked. She hadn't felt this way in a long time. Maybe never.

"*Si, si.* You make me wish I was young again." Aunt Inez dabbed a handkerchief to her eyes. "But knowing what I know now, *capiscimi?*"

"Knock knock! What's going on in there?" Rose's father shouted through the door. "We've got a store to open, or have you forgotten?"

"You'd better come in, Frankie," Aunt Inez yelled back. "But watch out. You may not recognize your own daughter."

Rose's father opened the bedroom door slowly and peered around it into the room. "Rose?" He stood in the doorway, his mouth open, staring at Rose in her dress. He let out a low whistle. "*Che bella* You're not kidding, Inez. Who is this lovely woman?"

Rose blushed. She looked down and ran her hands over the skirt. "You like it, Papa? For the dance tonight. Aunt Inez made it from one of Laura's old dresses, so it didn't cost anything."

"Even if it had, it would be worth it. Look at you, my baby girl, all grown up," he said, clearing his throat. "When did this happen, Inez? You and I remain the same age, but *cara*? Suddenly a young woman."

"She looks a bit like Fil when she was young, doesn't she?" Aunt Inez asked.

Rose looked at herself in the mirror again, looking for signs that it was true. She couldn't see it.

"Yes…well, yes, she does." He wiped his eyes with the back of his hand. "I remember…You look beautiful, Rosita. *A pretty girl is like a melody . . .*" he sang—the theme song from the *Ziegfeld Follies* program on the radio. "Now I'm a little nervous about you being around those boys. Your mother won't be there to keep an eye out this time."

Rose couldn't tell him how grateful she was for that. "Don't worry, Papa. I'll be fine. Father Tony will be there, plus Mr. Lupo from the Central Grocery. You'll have plenty of spies."

"*Va bene.* When you're finished here, I *could* use your help downstairs," her father said, heading back out the door.

"Go on, Rose," Aunt Inez said, pulling out a needle and thread from her sewing box. "I'll finish up and leave the dress hanging here for you."

Rose changed out of the gown into her plain Saturday work skirt and blouse. She glanced at herself in the mirror again. "*Zia,* do you really think I look like Mama when she was my age?"

Aunt Inez snipped a piece of thread and looked at Rose. "You're as beautiful as she was at your age, Rose. But you're very different from her in a lot of ways."

"How so?"

"You have to remember how we grew up. Your father and I—we came over here with nothing. Your mother's family too. It made us a little hard, I think." She pushed the needle through the delicate fabric with her thimbled finger. "Happiness was a luxury."

Rose considered her aunt's words. It seemed like happiness was a luxury now too, because of this war. "She never talks about those days," Rose said. She had a fleeting image from an old photo she'd seen of her mother as a young, single girl. Rose thought how little she knew of her own parents' youth. Her mother was only ten years old when she got on a boat with her family and came to a strange country to start a new life, speaking no English. She never thought of her mother as brave, but she must have been, once upon a time.

"And she could never have imagined her daughter dancing with prisoners of war, I'm sure of that!"

"Me neither," said Rose. She pictured Salvatore, hoping he'd like the dress.

"You should take happiness where you find it, *cara.* You never know what life will throw at you." Tears welled in Rose's eyes; she knew her aunt was thinking about her dead husband. "Oh, I almost forgot," Aunt Inez said. "I brought these for you." She pulled a small satin bag from her purse and shook drop pearl earrings into her palm. "They're from Sicily. I wore them as a girl. Maybe they'll bring you some luck tonight." She winked and handed them to Rose.

Time crawled while Rose worked in the grocery store. Rose's father cut cheese for a customer, using a piano wire to slice through the thick wheel of fontina.

"Papa, I wonder if it might be quicker to cut up the cheese ahead of time, put it into packages—a pound, half-pound—so when the customers come in you can just hand it to them?" Rose asked when the customer had gone. "Seems like that would make it easier and faster."

Her father didn't look up, just shook his head. "If it ain't broke, don't fix it, Rose. First rule of business. Besides, they like to gossip and visit while they're waiting for their cold cuts. They might see something else they want to buy. Why would we want to rush them?"

*Why do I bother?* Rose asked herself. He never took her suggestions seriously—so different from Mr. Sullivan at the shipyard.

Between customers, Rose restocked the shelves with her cousin Carmine. He'd been needling her all day, digging for details about the POWs. His constant interruptions annoyed her; she needed to mentally rehearse for the dance tonight. She couldn't wait to get out of the store.

"You and Marie are all excited for your big dance with those *fascistas* tonight, I'm guessing." It was the third time he'd mentioned it.

"Why do you care, Carmine?" Rose asked. "It's just a silly dance, something to do. It's not like I've ever seen you at one of our dances. We could use some more men, you know."

"All I'm saying is these guys were the enemy." Carmine blinked at her through his thick glasses. "Who knows how many of our boys they may have killed? They were fighting right alongside the Krauts just a few months ago. Don't take my word for it—your boss Mr. Higgins agrees with me."

Rose caught her breath. "What are you talking about?"

"Don't you know?" Carmine sneered. "He was on the radio the other day, testifying in Washington about those guys being coddled. You'd better watch yourself."

"You're making that up," Rose said. "He was probably talking about the Germans." She hoped she was right but made a mental note to be careful what she said around her boss. She climbed up on the step stool and made room on a higher shelf for the pickled pepperoncini they were unloading. "Besides, it's none of your business who I dance with. I'm a grown woman."

"Oh, listen to you now. A few dollars in your pocketbook from your factory job and now you're Eleanor Roosevelt?" Carmine handed a jar up to her. "Pretty soon Rocco will be back, and you'll be here with your father and me every day, just waiting for Prince Charming to come along."

"I'm not even going to respond to that," Rose fumed.

"Not to mention what people will think of us. It's hard enough convincing people we're loyal, without giving them excuses like fraternizing with the enemy."

"Italy's on our side now, remember?" Rose said. "Just because the Army didn't want you, don't be dragging me into it." Rose knew he was sensitive about his rejection from the service, but she didn't care anymore if she hurt his feelings. "I do my part every day. Nobody's questioning my patriotism." She turned toward him too quickly and dropped a jar. It shattered spilling glass and pepperoncini all over the floor.

"Jesus, Rose!" Carmine jumped away.

Rose's father yelled, "What happening over there? You OK?"

"It's fine, Papa. I just dropped a jar." Rose climbed down from the stool and stepped around the slimy puddle. "Just get out of my way, Carmine. I'll clean this up."

"Fine with me," he said, mumbling curses in Sicilian. "Your mess."

Rose was mopping up the last of the glass with a cloth when her father stood over her. "Your head is in the clouds today, Rose. You're lucky you didn't cut yourself. Why don't you go on upstairs and get yourself ready for the dance? Carmine and I can finish up here."

"Really, Uncle Frank?" Carmine protested. "You're letting her off early to go to a dance with those *fascistas*? With Giovanni fighting those Jap bastards."

"*Basta*, Carmine," Rose's father said. "Enough. They're different. These are Italian boys. *Paesani*. Like us. It's not their fault Mussolini dragged them into the war."

Carmine shook his head. "A lot of people don't see it that way, is all I'm saying."

"Since when do I care about a lot of people? I care about my own."

Rose knew that wasn't entirely true. The Italian flag was still in the drawer. Still, she loved her father for backing her up.

"Thank you, Papa," Rose said, giving him a hug and slinging her apron onto a hook by the back door. "I'll make it up to you, I promise."

"You can make it up to me by having a good time tonight. But not *too* good a time, *capiscimi?*" He touched his thumb to his fingers and shook them at her. "*Piano-piano!*" he called. "Go easy-easy."

Rose carried her dress and shoes in a cloth bag and headed down Decatur Street toward Marie's house, on the end of the French Quarter near the market, where the houses were a little run-down. The smell of the river mixed with rotten vegetables.

Mrs. Leonardi opened the door wearing her white waitress uniform. "*Buona sera,* Rose. Go on back. Marie's in her room getting ready." Her hair was caught up in a hairnet, which pushed a V into her forehead.

"*Grazie*, Mrs. Leonardi." Rose said. Marie was just seven when her father died in an accident on the docks. Her mother took a job at the diner after that and never remarried. Since Marie's grandfather passed, it was just the two of them living on one side of a rented double shotgun-style cottage. All the rooms led into each other without a hallway, with the kitchen at the very back of the house. Rose walked from the cluttered front parlor, passing through Mrs. Leonardi's room, to Marie's tiny bedroom, where her friend sat in her slip, putting on makeup. She looked at Rose in the reflection of her makeshift vanity, a small mirror propped on a table.

"Rose! Just in time. Help me?" Marie wriggled into her dress, a low-cut shirtwaist, deep red to match her lipstick and shoes.

"Breathe in," Rose said as she tugged the zipper up Marie's back.

"Try not to rip anything!"

"There you go," Rose said, fastening the hook-and-eye at the top. "I've always liked this dress on you. You look gorgeous."

Marie smiled. "I hope the boys like it. I do think it highlights my . . . assets." Marie pushed her breasts into place, her cleavage on the verge of risqué. "And I'm ready to do some real dancing!" She shimmied her hips. "Now, let's get some makeup on you."

"You know I don't like a lot," Rose said. "I don't want anyone to think—"

"I know, I know," Marie interrupted. "And you almost don't need it, with your beautiful skin. Just a little to bring out your eyes. Trust me, you're going to look your usual pretty self. Only better."

"All right," Rose said. She sat on the little stool, her back to the mirror and her face tilted as her friend applied mascara, eyeliner, and eye shadow. Marie had been wearing makeup since she was a young teenager and knew her way around cosmetics. Rose was quietly grateful but also a little embarrassed at her own lack of knowledge in these areas.

"And a little rouge, a little lipstick—it's important to get the curve just right—and . . . *eccola!*" Marie stood back.

Rose turned around. For the second time that day, she almost didn't recognize the woman looking back at her in the mirror. She sat up a little straighter, turned her head to one side, then the other. In a matter of minutes, Marie had transformed her. Maybe her father and Aunt Inez were right. She did look older, maybe like the kind of woman who'd catch the eye of a handsome man.

"Can you help with my hair too? Just put it up for me and pin it?"

"Now you're talking!" Marie said. "You're going to look like a movie star. Put the dress on first."

Rose unwrapped her dress from the bag and held it up for Marie to see. "What do you think?"

"Oh Rose, it's beautiful!" Marie ran her fingers over the embroidered netting. "How did you pull this off?"

"I found it at the back of Laura's armoire, and Aunt Inez fixed it up. We had to take it in at the waist and the bust, of course. She took the sleeves off and shortened it a little. It came out all right, yes?"

"All right? Are you crazy? It's drop-dead gorgeous. Your aunt sure knows her stuff—I can't see any of the alterations. Put it on." Rose took off her blouse and skirt, then stepped into the dress. She turned around for Marie to zip it up in the back, then stepped into black sling-back pumps with a peep-toe opening.

"Wow . . ." Marie said, her red mouth an O to match the ring she formed with her thumb and index finger. "Va-va-voom! I can't wait to see Salvatore's face when he gets a load of you."

Marie's mother knocked lightly on the doorframe. "*Madonna mia!*" Marie's mother said, clapping her hands together. "You both look beautiful! Rose, that dress!"

Rose smiled. "*Grazie*, Mrs. L," she said. "It was my sister's. *Is* my sister's," Rose felt her throat tighten a bit, thinking about Laura. How she wished she were here.

"God bless her," Marie's mother said, making the sign of the cross. "It's lovely, dear. You girls have a nice time tonight. But be careful with those men. I'm still not sure whether they are *paesani* or enemies."

"We'll be careful, Ma. You know Father Tony organized this whole thing," Marie said with a wave of her hand. Marie caught Rose's eye and winked. Her mother was not immune to Father Tony's magic.

Mrs. Leonardi patted Marie's arm lightly. "I know you'll be good, *Marieooch,*" she said.

"I'll tell you all about it when I get home."

Rose envied the way Marie and Mrs. Leonardi got along—so different from her own relationship with her mother. Mrs. Leonardi was a widow, like Aunt Inez, but they had such different lives, Rose thought. Neither of them had a man to support them, but Aunt Inez had her own money, and that made all the difference.

Rose and Marie stepped out onto the sidewalk, walking arm-in-arm, holding their dresses off the ground. A man on a bicycle wolf-whistled as he rode by. Rose blushed; normally she'd turn away, but she held her head up.

"What'd I say? Gorgeous," Marie laughed, waving to the man.

# NINE

Rose looked out the window as the bus pulled into Jackson Barracks. The drab buildings on the base seemed to glow in the setting sunlight. She thought about how different she felt compared to the last time she'd been there. Then she'd dreaded the visit. Now she was excited, even if she had a knot in her stomach.

Some of the girls checked their lipstick and hair in compact mirrors one last time. Gilda wore a tight-fitting silver dress with sequins; her friends were fluttering around her.

"She looks like a tramp, that Gilda. *Bruta*, inside and out," Marie whispered.

Rose couldn't disagree, but shushed Marie. Her mind was on Salvatore; she didn't want any trouble.

Father Tony climbed down from the bus with the nuns and a few of the other chaperones before the girls filed out. They tottered on high heels and held up their long skirts away from the dusty ground, then went silent as they entered the cavernous hall. Dim light from candles made the room look almost romantic. The musicians were setting up their instruments on a riser at the far end—a full swing band with fancy shells in front of the players, like in a real show. The horns gleamed. Chairs and tables were scattered around, and a wooden dance floor had been laid in front of the stage. Rose's heart pounded as she scanned the hall, looking for Salvatore. But except for the musicians and Father Tony, there were no men in sight.

"Is it warm in here or is it me?" Rose asked. She dabbed at her forehead with a white linen handkerchief. Suddenly, she understood the old expression "hot and bothered."

"Oh, it's warm in here. But it still might be you," Marie smiled. "Don't worry. He's gonna be here. Deep breaths."

"My dancing is a little rusty. I hope I don't trip over his feet."

"When's the last time you think these guys were dancing? You'll be fine. Try to relax, play it cool," Marie said.

Rose envied her friend's confidence. So self-assured. The girls had fanned out, some sitting at the tables, some over by the food. Slowly, the rear door opened, and the men filed in. Rose looked at each face, her heart in her throat. A handful of American MPs came in first, smiling when they saw all the women. Then the Italians, in groups of two and three, tentatively followed.

"Told you," Marie said. "There he is."

Rose saw Salvatore, but he was talking to his friends, his head turned, and he didn't see her. It occurred to her that she might have been building something up over nothing—a look? A few pretty words? For all she knew, he used those lines on girls all the time.

"And there's that Vincenzo . . . Oooh, just as handsome as I remember," Marie said. Marie waved and Vincenzo gave her a little salute back. Rose wondered if Lou would even cross Marie's mind tonight. "Let's get some punch."

They walked over to the refreshments table, pouring punch into Dixie cups, and taking in the scene. The prisoners stood in a tight knot on the far side of the room as the band started tuning up. Rose spotted Salvatore, talking with some of the other POWs. He paused from his conversation to smile at her and take a drag from his cigarette, exhaling slowly as he held her gaze. Rose blushed. Suddenly unsure of what to do with her gloved hands, she fumbled with her purse. She said a silent prayer of thanks for Laura's dress, and an extra prayer for herself: for courage to be the woman she'd seen in Marie's mirror.

The band leader leaned into the microphone. "Welcome, *signorine*. You all look beautiful tonight," he said. "Here's one of my favorites to get us started, from our own hometown hero, the great Louis Prima. It's called 'Old Black Magic.' Hit it, boys!"

Rose had heard the song a hundred times before, but now the words—all about kissing and flames of desire—raised goosebumps on her bare arms, despite the heat. A couple of girls headed to the dance floor with each other as they usually did, but the men quickly cut in to dance with them.

Father Tony came over to them. "Well, girls, what do you think?" Father Tony asked. "We did it."

"*You* did it, Father," Marie said. "You and Central Grocery. We're just happy to be here."

"The prisoners are excited about the music. Turns out they love American jazz over there, just like we do. I'm sure you girls will be popular—there are fifty of you and a couple hundred of them, so the odds are pretty good." He turned to pour a cup of punch for one of the chaperones.

Rose looked over at the bandstand, and her heart skipped a beat. Salvatore was there alone, listening to the music and tapping his foot. She saw Gilda moving toward him with her gang and felt sick to her stomach.

"*Buona sera, miei amici!*" Rose and Marie turned in unison to find Vincenzo, his face clean-shaven, black hair slicked back. Rose thought she smelled a whiff of Old Spice and wondered where POWs were getting aftershave.

Father Tony nodded to Vincenzo. "*Buona sera,* son."

"*Ciao, Vincenzo,*" Marie said, batting her eyelashes.

Vincenzo was not bashful about checking out Marie's assets. "You can dance, *si?*" he asked Marie in broken English.

"*Si!*" Marie said. "*Andiamo!*"

They left Rose standing with the priest and the chaperones. The band was in full swing now, and the floor was crowded with Lindy Hopping couples. The dancers tried to outdo each other with spins, dips, and jumps. Rose was grateful for the hot band and the loud music, which helped drown out her thumping heart. She ached for Salvatore to walk away from Gilda, who was now talking into his ear, her hand on his shoulder.

Rose turned her back to the bandstand so she wouldn't have to watch. "My mother always talks about when she first came over from Sicily and heard the music here," she told Father Tony. "Hearing live jazz for the first time must've been so exciting."

"I remember too," the priest said. "I was still in the seminary: Saturday nights they would let us out and we would head to the clubs in the Quarter. For the music, of course."

"With your collars on?" Rose joked.

"Well, we might have left our collars at home . . . I don't really recall." He smiled. "You know tonight, in this dress, look a lot like your mother did then."

"So I've heard," Rose said.

"But that was a long time ago. Before the Depression, before this war . . ." He looked at the dancers.

One of the other POWs approached and asked Rose to dance in broken English. She nodded to Father Tony and took the man's sweaty hand. He was slightly built, just a little taller than Rose, and he smelled faintly of body odor. Rose was grateful it was a fast song—Cab Calloway's "Jumpin' Jive" from the movie *Stormy Weather*—so she wouldn't have to get too close. She tried to smile and pay attention to the young man, but also kept an eye out for Salvatore. She didn't see him anywhere at first in the dim light, then she felt a chill run up her spine as she spotted him dancing—with Gilda.

She watched as he twirled Gilda around the dance floor, tight and graceful, a lock of sandy brown hair on his forehead, his uniform shirt pulled taut across his chest and shoulders. Gilda had her hand on his arm, his waist. Of all the girls in the room, it had to be Gilda. Rose caught his eye and he smiled over Gilda's shoulder. She looked away.

Another boy tapped Rose's partner on the shoulder and cut in before whisking Rose off to the other side of the room as the band began the next number. She tried to enjoy herself, but her eyes kept returning to Salvatore, watching him as he cut in to dance with several other girls. She felt nauseated. How could she have been so foolish?

Meanwhile, Vincenzo had refused to let anyone else dance with Marie. When the band took a break, Rose saw Vincenzo kiss Marie's hand. She made a comical curtsy, bowing down in a gesture Rose knew was designed to give him a good look at her cleavage. It had worked before. Poor Louie. Vincenzo openly stared at Marie's ample backside as she walked back toward Rose.

"*Madonna!* What a dancer! The man has some moves." Marie took a handkerchief out of her purse and dabbed at her face and throat. "Did you see how Vincenzo kept all the other boys away? I think he likes me."

Rose was distraught but didn't want to detract from Marie's moment. "Of *course,* he likes you! What's not to like?"

"I saw you were pretty popular out there yourself. Have you talked to Salvatore?"

"Didn't you see him? Dancing with Gilda?" Rose asked.

"No, I guess I was a little distracted. Let's find the ladies' room, I need to powder my nose." The latrine had a makeshift sign saying *Ragazze* on the door. Inside, a gaggle of women crowded around a small mirror, applying lipstick, fixing their hair, talking all at once. There was Gilda, of course, at the center of it. She sneered as her eyes met Rose's in the mirror.

"Nice *dress*, Rose."

"Thanks," said Rose, pretending it was a compliment. It was steamy in the restroom—now she was worried about all that eye makeup running. "It was my sister's. She's off at the front." As the words left her mouth, Rose regretted them. Gilda didn't deserve to know anything about Laura.

"Not bad for a hand-me-down. I had to talk my father into buying me a whole new dress." Gilda's friends giggled.

Such a show-off, Rose thought, steaming. She felt like she was back in high school.

Gilda pointed at Rose's chest. "Guess you have to work with what you've got, right?"

"You done?" Marie pushed past Gilda. "Some of us need the mirror too."

"I'll say." Gilda flipped her hair. "Some more than others. Let's go, girls."

When Gilda's flock was gone, Rose whispered. "God forgive me, but I want to slap her."

"Let it go, Rose. She's not worth your *agita*."

Rose took a quick look in the mirror. In the harsh fluorescent light of the latrine, she felt garishly made-up, like someone else entirely. She touched her bare chest where her scapular usually sat, conjuring her sister's presence. She so wished Laura were here.

When they emerged from the restroom, Marie nodded at the edge of the dance floor. "There's your fella," she said. Rose held her breath. Salvatore was walking toward them.

"*Buona sera, signorine,*" Salvatore said, and gave a little bow.

"*Buona sera,*" Marie said.

Salvatore smiled at her but turned to Rose. "You came back." He said her name and she felt herself blush. "Your dress is beautiful. As elegant as you."

"Oh! *Si.* Yes. *Grazie.* I—we did come back. *Buona sera,* Salvatore." The words were getting all twisted. Instead, Rose extended her gloved hand and Salvatore bent down to kiss it lightly. The gentle pressure of his lips through the soft white leather of her glove, his hand firmly holding hers—she felt as if she might faint. The band members took the stage again.

"Who's seen *Cabin in the Sky*?" the band leader asked to a smattering of applause. "All right, well here's a little number from that movie, which featured New Orleans' own Louis Armstrong on trumpet. It's called 'Taking a Chance on Love.'"

"May I have this dance?" Salvatore asked. Rose nodded, transfixed, and Marie gave her a little shove. Salvatore took Rose's hand and led her onto the dance floor. She looked around for Father Tony, who caught her eye and gave her a gentle smile.

Rose and Salvatore started dancing, just a simple box step at first, then picking up speed. He gently held her left hand in his, his right hand sitting lightly on her waist. He smelled of soap and tobacco. He was a little taller than she remembered, but not too tall; she reached up to place her left hand on his shoulder. She could feel muscles through his shirt, and it sent an electric thrill through her body.

Rose was glad Salvatore's English wasn't very good; the words of the song were making her blush. She was sure she was red as a beet.

*"Piano-piano,"* he said. Just like her father always said to her. He seemed to sense her nervousness, and she tried to relax into the beat.

Salvatore moved her around the dance floor, smoothly steering her and protecting her from the kicks and whirls of the other dancers. She noticed Vincenzo and Marie swinging over their way. Marie's head was tilted back, and her red mouth was open in a hearty laugh, which made Rose smile. It felt like years since she'd seen Marie so happy.

When the band took another break, Salvatore led her by the hand over to the refreshment table. "Where did you learn to dance so well?" Rose asked as she tried to gather her wits.

He poured them both a cup of punch. "My boxing coach. He made me take dancing lessons to help me move lightly in the ring."

"Were you a boxer before the war?" Rose asked. It explained the crooked nose.

"Not professional, only on the side for fun. Mostly I helped Papa on the farm."

She'd been to a few farms outside New Orleans with her father, and tried to picture Salvatore working with a pitchfork, plowing a field, tending to the animals. He was so close to her she could feel the heat coming off him.

"Well, I'm grateful for your coach, then," she said. "My father loves boxing. I'm sure you two would have a lot to talk about." She immediately regretted bringing up her father. She hoped it wouldn't scare Salvatore, or make him think she had designs on him, even though she did. She was just no good at this.

"What does your father do for work?" he asked.

"He owns a grocery store," she said, trying to maintain her composure. "Tell me about your family. Do you have brothers and sisters?"

He nodded. "Sergio, Anna, and Nunzio," he said. "I am the oldest. Sergio, he had a bad fever when he was a baby, so he can't see too well. I help him with his schoolwork. My mother says, 'Sal is Sergio's eyes.'"

"Your mother calls you Sal?"

"Everyone calls me Sal."

She stood up a little straighter and took a sip of punch. "Well, I'm going to call you Sal from now on then. Tell me more. What do you grow on your family's farm?"

"Not that kind of farm. We have cows. A dairy farm. Milk, cheese. My mother makes the best ricotta." The band started playing Duke Ellington's "Somebody Loves Me" and the floor erupted in a swirl of dancers. Sal raised an eyebrow at Rose, and she threw her paper cup into the trash. She nodded at him, and they joined the crowd. Sal danced them close to the stage. "I love this music!" he shouted into her ear, spinning her around.

As the song wound down, Sal twirled her one more time, then caught her gently, pulling her close. She felt his breath on her neck, his long eyelashes tickling her ear. "You are the most beautiful girl in the room," he whispered. "I could dance with you all night."

Her heart began beating even faster. Nobody outside her family had ever called her beautiful, let alone a man like Sal. She was out of breath now and grateful for her sleeveless dress, as she was sure she was sweating.

"We've got time for just one more," the band leader said. The couples on the dance floor groaned. "I know, I know. How about we make it a nice slow, romantic number so you can all cool off a bit."

Sal gently took Rose by her elbow, waving off another man who was approaching her to cut in. "*Un altro?*" he asked.

"*Si,*" said Rose, nodding as the band leader called out the next song.

"From our *paesano* Mr. Frank Sinatra—this one's called 'There Are Such Things.'" Sal waltzed her around slowly, holding her firmly but gently, his chin resting on the top of her head. Meanwhile, the rest of the room faded away—no Father Tony, no Gilda, not even Marie—as if she and Sal were the only couple on the dance floor—like she was in a movie—excited, beautiful, free.

As the song ended, the room came back into focus. Sal kept holding her hands and leaned down as if to whisper something in her ear. Instead, he kissed her, brushing his lips against her cheek. It was brief, but Rose felt her toes curl. She found her own lips near his ear, and kissed him back, at the top of his neck. He gripped her tighter. Then he leaned back, and she saw Father Tony, looking right at them. Rose pulled away.

"*Mi dispiace,*" Sal stammered, dropping her hands.

"*Va bene.*" Rose smiled up at him. She didn't dare look at Father Tony again but could feel the priest's stare. Maybe he would report her to her mother after all. She worried she'd confused Sal. He looked at her without speaking, and she could see gold flecks in his hazel eyes. Never had she seen eyes that color before.

"Thank you for the dance." It was all she could think to say.

The band members were beginning to pack up their instruments and someone turned on the bright fluorescent lights overhead. Other couples were also stranded on the dance floor making awkward small talk. The American soldiers on guard duty started rounding up the prisoners, tapping shoulders and waving them toward the rear exit door. Rose hadn't thought through how the night might end. She didn't want it to. She missed Sal already.

"This has been wonderful," Sal said. "But it went by too fast."

Rose nodded, glancing at Father Tony who still stood watching them. She didn't care. She might be in trouble, but it was worth it. A guard tapped Sal on the shoulder.

"*Buona sera, mi bella Rosa. Arrivederci.*" Sal gave her a little nod.

Rose stood alone, watching him follow the rest of the men, her head spinning. She wondered if this was what it felt like to be a woman, not a girl. To be in love.

Her parents were in bed when she crept back into the house, although she knew they were listening for her. Fortunately, they didn't come out of their room. Rose couldn't bear to have a conversation with them right now. She didn't want to break the spell. Marie had gabbed on about Vincenzo on the bus; but Rose was silent. The only person she wished she could talk to was her sister.

She sat at her dressing table in her nightgown and tried to remove Marie's makeup with a washcloth and Pond's cold cream. Laura's dress, now her dress, was draped across her sister's bed next to Rose's old Raggedy Ann. The doll seemed out of place now, childish. She shut off the light and opened the big window onto her balcony. The spring air outside was just a little cooler than inside. She smelled the mustiness of the river, mixed with the perfume of the gardenia bushes in the courtyard. The Quarter was mostly dark, still under blackout rules; a few stars winked dimly above the steeple of Immaculate Conception church.

She lay down in her bed, but her mind was reeling, replaying the feeling of Sal's body against hers, his soft lips brushing her cheek. She switched on the bedside lamp and took a pen and a sheet of thin blue airmail paper from the drawer of her nightstand.

*Dear Laura, I hope you are well and safe. I need to thank you. You didn't know it, but you lent me your dress tonight. I hope you don't mind. I had a special reason for 'borrowing' it. I don't know where to start.*

Rose paused. Usually, the news she shared with Laura was so mundane. She wasn't sure what to say.

*A dance, your dress, the music, a kiss . . .*

*May 1944*

*Dear Rose,*

*It's "three o'clock in the morning," like the song says. I'm on duty, but all the patients are asleep and I'm borrowing a little of Uncle Sam's time to write letters. We finally got some pictures developed so you can see my doctor friend. Thanks for sending the struffoli— a big hit with the girls. I was so excited when they yelled my name out at mail call and there was a package from you!*

*We just moved our whole operation into a real hospital in a city. The Germans must have left in a hurry, because it's still in pretty good shape—a big improvement from our field operation. Nurse McCarthy somehow got us sheets and blankets. The roof leaks and it smells old and musty, but it feels luxurious compared to our tents in the mud. We've been very welcomed here. People are so happy to be rid of the Jerrys, they poured out of their homes as we passed through villages a few weeks ago. Children ran alongside the trucks and flashed the V for victory sign. They all look like cousins and kids we grew up with in the Quarter. They giggled when I spoke to them in Sicilian—my accent must've sounded funny to them.*

*We're working most of the time, but we manage to have a little fun in between long shifts. Last Sunday Frances and I went on an outing to the countryside with Nicholas and one of his buddies. On the way back, we had a scare: a plane flew overhead with that horrible swastika painted underneath. Luckily, Nicholas had put down the glass windscreen on the Jeep so the Krauts couldn't spot us from the reflection, and they kept going. It's getting so I can tell our planes from theirs just by the sound of the engine. I don't think I'll ever hear a plane overhead without looking up and making the sign of the cross.*

*I know they'll need more doctors as the front moves on, and I'm worried Nicholas and I will be separated. We're spending as much time together as we can. The other night, he told me he loved me, that I'm what keeps him going through the rough days, that he feels safe with me. Rose, I feel the same way. When I'm with him, it feels like I'm home. We talk about the future sometimes but try not to get too far ahead of ourselves. You never know what's going to happen. I've lost so many friends already.*

*I'm glad Aunt Inez was able to remake my old dress. I bet you looked like a stunner for your dance. I had no idea they were bringing Italian prisoners to Jackson Barracks. Sounds like our Army is taking much better care of them than Mussolini did. A few months ago, they were over here shooting at us—now they're dancing with you and Marie? Promise me you'll look out for yourself. I've learned the hard way: you must be careful who you trust. Especially with your heart.*

*I'll stop now—one of the patients is moaning and I need to tend to him. Thanks for all the news from home. I'm worried nobody has heard from Giovanni. I try not to think about those Japanese kamikazes sinking ships in the Pacific. I'm glad to hear things are good at the shipyard. I tell all my friends here my kid sister is helping to make the Higgins boats so we can win the war. I'm so proud of you, Rose.*

*Buona notte,*
*Your loving sister, Laura*

CHAPTER

# TEN

Rose sat on the stool in the corner of the mail room. She felt tears welling in her eyes as she finished reading the letter. Laura was proud of *her*? All she did was enter numbers in a ledger. No blood. No moaning patients or German planes. She felt guilty again for fretting over her petty little life: dances and boys, dresses and makeup. She reread Laura's warning about Sal, worried her sister might disapprove of him. *They were over here shooting at us—now they're dancing with you and Marie?* Letting Sal sweep her off her feet like that, like a silly girl in a movie. She barely knew him.

Irma was humming softly to herself, absorbed in her task of sorting the mail. Rose tucked the letter back in the thin blue envelope, then lifted the photograph to the light, studying it for clues about Laura's life. At home, her sister had always been so put-together, never a hair out of place. Now she looked so different in her rumpled fatigues and work boots, her bobbed hair flying in the wind. In the background, Rose could just make out tents and jeeps. Holding the photo closer, Rose saw lines on Laura's forehead that hadn't been there before, crinkles at the edges of her eyes. Nicholas was handsome in his uniform: tall and square-jawed. His arm was around Laura, hugging her close as she leaned into him.

A machine whirred somewhere out on the factory floor. Rose looked at her watch with a start. Her break had ended ten minutes ago; Mr. Sullivan would be looking for her upstairs. She wiped her eyes with a handkerchief and carefully put the photo back into the envelope with the letter.

"Bad news?" Irma asked, looking up from the bin of mail.

"Not really," Rose said. "But things sound pretty tough over there."

"Any idea where she is?"

"Italy, I'm pretty sure," Rose said. "She can never say. The censors, you know."

"Sure. Such a brave girl," Irma said. "You must miss her a lot.

"I do," said Rose. "And Giovanni." Fresh tears welled up in her eyes just saying Giovanni's name. It had been months since his last postcard. Laura was worried about him too, which made Rose even more concerned.

"I write my boy Alfred every week, even if I have nothing to say," Irma said, her soft brown eyes glistening as well. "Then so much time goes by before I hear back. It's hard."

"Sometimes it feels like too much. I know my parents worry about it all the time. How do you handle it?"

"I pray a lot," Irma said. "And work is a blessing. Sometimes my back hurts from hauling the mail bags around, but I tell myself the harder I work, the sooner my boy comes home."

"That'll be a happy day." An image of Giovanni and Laura coming through the kitchen door flashed in Rose's mind, and she smiled.

When Rose got back upstairs to her office, Mr. Sullivan was scurrying around, emptying ashtrays and litter into the trash bins. She'd never seen him clean before. "Ah, Rose. Thank goodness you're back. I just got a call from Mr. Higgins himself. He's coming for a visit."

Rose stowed her purse in her desk drawer. "Here? When? What for?" she asked.

"Today. I have no idea. Some sort of announcement."

"And you think he'll be coming up here?" Rose looked around the cluttered office. Paper everywhere. Dusty venetian blinds hung crookedly on the windows.

"Who knows?" Mr. Sullivan said. He sounded flustered.

"Let me help," Rose said. She started gathering up piles of paper, straightening them into neat stacks. She had never met Mr. Higgins, only seen photographs, and read about him in *Eureka* magazine. She'd heard him on the radio news a few times—he was quite outspoken about the war and all sorts of issues of the day, always urging people to buy bonds or give blood.

"I wish I had known. I would have worn something nicer," she said.

"You look fine, Rosie, just fine," Mr. Sullivan said. "Mr. Higgins will address everyone outside, right after the lunch break." He looked out the window by his desk. "Looks like they're setting up a stage now. And there are the lads from the Higgins Band too."

Rose pictured a group like they had at the dances, but when she looked out the window, there were dozens of musicians milling around and setting up sheet music on stands. "They look like the marching bands they have in the Mardi Gras parades."

"Over a hundred members strong, from all five plants," Mr. Sullivan said. "They only come out for big occasions. Speaking of, I should go down to the boss' office and see what's going on."

Rose found a rag and started wiping the venetian blinds. "You do what you need to do. I'll make sure everything here is shipshape."

"Shipshape," Mr. Sullivan said, wiggling his finger. "Good one, Rose."

When she was satisfied the office looked tidy enough, she ate her sandwich at her desk. She hadn't even finished when the speaker on the wall crackled to life.

*Attention, attention. All hands are requested to proceed to the yard on the bayou side of the plant for a special ceremony.*

Rose checked her face in a compact mirror for crumbs before adding a little lipstick. Mr. Sullivan had not returned, so she assumed he was already out there. She made her way downstairs and joined the growing crowd abuzz with questions and speculation. Outside, she spotted Marie and waved her over.

"What's this all about?" Marie asked. "You office people always know more than we do."

"Mr. Higgins himself is coming," she whispered.

"Good, because I have a few suggestions for improvements," Marie said. "The ladies' room, for one . . ."

"Don't make trouble, Marie. We should be grateful we have jobs at all. Where else could we make this kind of money?"

"Yeah, yeah. OK. Teacher's pet, just like in school. Hey, let's watch from that staging so we can get a good look."

They climbed up on a scaffold that surrounded a huge ship's hull, just to the right of the stage. Rose ran her hand over the smooth wood. She didn't usually get so close to the boats. She'd seen them in action on the newsreels, rolling onto the beaches in the massive invasion of Normandy just a few weeks before. The Higgins boats were helping win the war, and it made her proud.

"See this?" Marie said, pointing to a large metal piece, fastened to a plate screwed into the boat. "That's my hinge. I welded that. Or one like it. When the ramps came down on Omaha Beach and our boys rolled off, I was right there with them. How do you like that?"

"Who'd have ever thought you'd be so good with a blowtorch?" Rose asked, touching the metal.

A group of men was gathering on the platform. A large American flag stood behind a podium and red-white-and-blue bunting skirted the stage. The Higgins Band was tuning up and the brass of dozens of trumpets, trombones, and tubas gleamed in the hot sun. A slight breeze came off the bayou, and Rose had to hold her skirt to keep it from flying up.

"This is a great view," Marie said, looking down at the platform.

A few of the men below whistled. "Sure is," one called up.

"Hey, I think I see Mr. Higgins. Isn't that him in the white hat?" Rose said. A stocky man was shaking hands with workers in the crowd. He wore a double-breasted suit with a dark shirt, a red tie, and matching pocket square.

"I think so," Marie said, craning her neck. "Are those radio microphones on the podium? This must be a big deal if they're broadcasting it."

"I wish I could let my parents know—hopefully Papa has on NBC in the store."

Mr. Haddock, the plant manager, walked up and tapped the microphone, then blew into it. His office was on the other end of the hall from Rose's, though she doubted he knew her name. Once she'd heard Mr. Sullivan call Haddock a *hard-arse.*

"Is this thing on? Can you hear me?" he shouted. The crowd grew quiet. "We won't keep you long—we know you have work to do." The workers chuckled. "We wanted you to be the first to hear about a high honor we're being given today. We're joined by some special guests from Washington." He introduced a couple of the other men on stage—some in uniform with lots of medals and stripes. "Now it's my honor to introduce Admiral Henry A. Wiley, head of the U.S. Maritime Commission."

The workers clapped as Admiral Wiley approached the podium. In front of the stage, two men unfurled a giant red and black flag with four white stars on it. *ARMY* was printed on the left, *NAVY* on the right. In the center was a large E surrounded by a gold wreath. A murmur went through the crowd. "What is that?" Marie asked.

Rose craned her neck to get a better look. "Beats me."

Admiral Wiley shouted into the microphone, "Thank you for that warm welcome. It's my honor to be with you today. Because of your magnificent boats, our boys can land directly on the beaches, deep in enemy territory, avoiding the ports where the Japs and Krauts are waiting for them. Because of the Higgins boats, we took North Africa and then we took Sicily!" The workers roared, and Marie let out a loud whistle. "Now we're working on France!"

Wiley made no mention of the Pacific, where Giovanni was. Rose knew the boats were there too—she'd seen the magazine pictures of landings on jungle island beaches. But the latest news was grim: heavy Allied casualties. Meanwhile, the Japanese just kept on fighting.

"Therefore, on behalf of a grateful nation, I have the honor of presenting you with the Army-Navy E for Excellence, the highest award that the armed forces can bestow upon a company. It shows our appreciation for a job well done. Keep it flying!" The crowd erupted in wild cheers. Wiley held up his hands for quiet. "And none of this would be possible without the man himself, your own Mr. Andrew Jackson Higgins!"

The band struck up a lively tune as Mr. Higgins walked up to the podium. He wiped his brow with a white handkerchief then returned it to his trouser pocket. "How 'bout our wonderful band?" he boomed. Once again, loud whoops and clapping. "I love that song, the 'Higgins Victory March,'" he said. "The words say, 'Let's all work hard and fight for liberty.' That's what we do every day. We've gone from seventy-five people to 20,000 strong in just a few years." He gripped the sides of the podium and looked out over the cheering workers, then broke out into a broad grin.

"President Roosevelt himself called me yesterday," Mr. Higgins paused, letting the crowd quiet. "Our commander in chief told me personally, that we are the NUMBER ONE BOAT BUILDER IN THE NATION. As of today, we've produced more landing craft than all the other shipyards in the country combined!"

Rose and Marie clapped along with everyone. "Number one," Marie said. "Can't wait to tell my Ma. Makes you kind of proud, doesn't it?" Even her small job was helping, and Rose felt like she was part of something important—helping the good guys win the war.

On the podium, a photographer with a large camera took photos of Mr. Higgins and the E banner, then turned his lens on workers, many of whom were flashing the V for Victory sign. Mr. Higgins motioned with his hands for quiet again. "Now, I know you're proud and so am I. But let us take a moment and think of the men who are doing the fighting and the dying." The crowd was silent; many bowed their heads.

Rose closed her eyes, thinking of Giovanni and Laura.

Mr. Higgins leaned into the microphone. "We sacrifice every day, and I know you're working harder than you ever have before. We're on the radio, so I'll watch my language." Scattered chuckles. "But I want to leave you with this: from the Industrial Canal to Guadalcanal, from City Park to the distant shores of Africa, Anzio, and Normandy—these boats deliver our boys by the thousands, so we can kick Jap and Kraut . . . behind. Don't let up. They're depending on you. Now, get back to work!"

Rose was glad he didn't mention the Italians along with the Japanese and Germans. Sal's face flashed in her mind, and she remembered Carmine's claim that Higgins objected to the POWs being "coddled." She and Marie climbed down from the scaffold as the band struck up "America the Beautiful." Everyone sang along as Mr. Higgins waded into the mass of cheering workers. Rose wiped away a few tears; the words to the song always made her a little emotional. She wasn't the only one. Maybe the Allies would win, and the war would be over soon.

Marie gave Rose a hug and headed to the welding shop. As Rose walked back to her building, she spotted Mr. Sullivan standing just inside the doorway with Mr. Higgins. An entourage of suited men surrounded them. Before she could change direction, Mr. Sullivan motioned to her. "Rose, come meet Mr. Higgins," he shouted through cupped hands.

Rose felt herself blush. She stood up as straight as she could but still only came up to Mr. Higgins' chest. He reached down, his meaty paw crushing her small hand. She tried not to wince. "Pleased to meet you, sir. Congratulations on the E—we're all very excited," Rose said, holding his gaze and trying to contain her trembling. His bright blue eyes glowed in his ruddy face, and he smelled faintly of cigars and whiskey.

"My Irish brother Mr. Sullivan here tells me you're his right-hand gal."

"I was telling Mr. Higgins about your idea for a better inventory system," Mr. Sullivan said. "No downtime waiting for parts."

"That E is as much yours as anyone's, Miss Rose," Mr. Higgins said.

"Thank you, sir. I'm proud just to play a small part," Rose said. "My brother and sister are both serving, so I really appreciate what you said."

Mr. Higgins smiled down at her. "Good to know someone was listening. Your sister too, you say?"

"Yes, sir. She's an Army nurse. In Europe."

"Well, I guess I should have said 'sons *and daughters*' in my remarks. God keep them both."

The photographer asked them all to turn, and his flash bulb went off. Rose wondered if her picture with Mr. Higgins would be in the newspaper.

"I'm sure you'd rather be keeping the home fires burning, Rose. Don't worry, we'll get you back there soon enough," Mr. Higgins said. "In the meantime, we're grateful for all your hard work here. We can't miss a beat—there's too much at stake, right?"

"Yes, sir," Rose said. She tried to smile, but his words hit her like a punch to the gut.

Mr. Higgins shook Mr. Sullivan's hand. "Give my best to Matilda and the kids." Mr. Higgins tipped his hat to Rose, then walked off with his men following in his wake.

"How about *that*?" Mr. Sullivan said to her. "You know that photographer is with *Life* magazine? They're doing a big spread on Mr. Higgins. Maybe you'll have your picture in there with him—wouldn't that be something?"

"It sure would," Rose said. "I'll see you upstairs." She stopped in the ladies' room on the way back to the office. She patted at her sweaty face with a handkerchief, looking at her reflection in the mirror. The E award and President Roosevelt's words made her feel important, like she was really contributing, not just slicing deli meat and making sandwiches at the store. Even her mother would have to be impressed if she got her picture in *Life* magazine. But Mr. Higgins' words rang in her head too. *In the meantime.* A reminder that all this was temporary. She had no home fires, only her family's grocery. She just wanted to keep working. Hadn't Mr. Higgins and Mr. Sullivan just told her how important her job was? Who would ever want to stop?

At the end of the day, Rose saw Irma at the streetcar stop. "Wasn't that exciting about the award?" Rose said.

"It makes me feel proud," Irma said. A man standing next to her cleared his throat and jutted his chin at Irma. She looked down and moved to the *colored* section of the waiting area. Rose moved away from the man. She was unsure whether she felt more embarrassed for Irma or for herself. It made no sense that she and Irma could have a friendly conversation in the mailroom, but not out here. And the factory would never have received the E flag without the efforts of everyone who worked there.

Rose climbed aboard the streetcar and found a seat. Irma smiled as she walked by toward the rear. For a fleeting instant, Rose felt like she wanted to see what would happen if she just asked Irma to sit next to her. But she quickly checked herself—she wouldn't be the one to get in trouble.

The streetcar rolled forward. She started thinking through the conversation with Mr. Higgins again. *Keeping the home fires burning* kept repeating in her head. She wasn't keen on spending her days in the kitchen and resented him assuming she'd rather be at home than working at the shipyard. She liked having her own money in her pocketbook and the growing nest egg in her coffee can. She didn't want to go back to relying on her parents, biding her time in the grocery store until she got married only to then depend on some man.

The streetcar crossed Broad, clanging its bell as it rattled downtown. Of course, the war couldn't end soon enough. She worried about Laura getting hurt by one of those German planes, about her unit being moved closer to the front. She felt for her scapular under her blouse. Rose wanted her sister and brother back home safe. But then what? Rose took Laura's photograph out of the envelope in her purse, tilting it toward the grimy window, and saw what she hadn't seen in the mailroom: a fierceness in her sister's eyes. Laura had one hand around Nicholas' waist, the other pressed to the front of his shoulder. Rose imagined herself standing close to Sal the same way. Laura and Nicholas were both officers, working together, leaning into each other, loving each other. Rose wondered if she would ever have that herself.

116

# ELEVEN

Rose brushed her hair, looking in the mirror and trying to stay focused on the monthly report she had to finish for Mr. Sullivan that morning. But her mind kept wandering to Sal. Since the dance a few weeks ago, she and Marie had made a few Sunday trips to Jackson Barracks with the other girls. Rose was looking forward to another visit this weekend. The more she got to know Sal, the more she liked him. He was gentle but strong. And the way he talked about his family with such tenderness touched her. Most of all, Sal listened to her—really listened—when she spoke. She tried to contain her excitement, especially around her parents. They didn't know all her Sunday outings were to the barracks. Pretty soon she'd have to come clean with them about her growing attachment to Sal. For now, she wasn't ready to face all their questions.

Rose pinned her hair up, then went to close the small side window. She looked down into the courtyard, where her mother was hanging laundry out to dry. Rose watched her clip one of her father's large white T-shirts to the line, a clothespin in the corner of her mouth. Rose wondered if one day she'd be hanging Sal's clothes on a line. She noticed the gray in her mother's hair, the loose skin at the back of her arms jiggling as she reached up. Her mother was just forty-six and yet she seemed so old.

Rose heard the vegetable man go by outside, the clip-clop of mule hooves punctuating his chant: "I got merlitons, I got ripe strawberries and cantaloupe, watermelon red to the rind. I got spinach, I got onions." Rose smiled, remembering when she was little, how Giovanni would make up silly songs to the peddler's melody. Her brother would even juggle vegetables while he sang in a bad fake Italian accent, always trying to make her laugh. *I got Rose-a with the pretty curls-a!* She walked to the window overlooking Dauphine Street, the bright summer sun making her squint. The vegetable peddler had moved on, but her eyes landed on a black taxicab with a white top pulling up to the curb across the way. All around, people on the sidewalk stopped in their tracks. Everyone knew about the extra job taxi drivers had to do now: delivering telegrams with bad news from the front. Rose felt sick to her stomach as she watched the driver slowly get out of the car, a pale-yellow envelope in his hand. He squinted at the front of Rose's building, then stepped into the street to cross. Rose wheeled around and scrambled through the kitchen and down the outside stairs to the alley, determined to get to him before he could ring the bell. *Please not Laura. Not Laura.*

"*Cosa fai?*" Her mother yelled after her from the courtyard. "What's all that racket? You're going to slip on those stairs!"

Rose flung open the gate. The man stood there, his arm reaching for the bell. He stopped at the sight of her and stepped back, removing his cap.

"Good morning miss. Is Mr. Marino at home?" He stumbled over his words.

"He's at the market," Rose said. "I'm his daughter." *One of his daughters*, she thought. The driver reached out with the envelope. She kept her hands behind her back, gripping the gate; refusing to take the telegram. It felt like everything was happening under water, as in a dream. Out of the corner of her eye Rose could see

118

Mrs. Fabucci on her stoop across the street. Mrs. Fabucci made the sign of the cross then held her hand over her heart.

"I'm sorry, miss. There's no good way to deliver this news." The taxi driver was hardly more than a boy, his narrow face pale and pockmarked, his neck long and skinny. Rose stared up at his Adam's apple, working up and down. He bowed his head, holding out the envelope with one hand, his cap in the other. "My condolences to you and your family."

She shook her head. "No." She wanted him to go away, to say it was the wrong address, the wrong name. Laura's face flashed in her head. She felt through her blouse for the scapular.

"Please miss, you have to."

He stood there quietly, and she took the telegram from him, her hand trembling. The envelope was addressed to her father; she tore it open anyway. *"The Secretary of the Army regrets to inform you . . ."* She scanned the words until she came to his name. *"Giovanni Marino."* She leaned against the building. *"Killed in action . . . disposition of remains . . ."* Not Laura. A wave of nausea and guilt washed over her for having made the trade-off in her mind. Giovanni's life for Laura's.

The driver was already back in his cab, starting the engine. Meanwhile, Rose stood frozen on the sidewalk with the telegram in her hand, not caring who saw. Her mind was spinning. Her brother was dead. Had been dead for days, maybe weeks. At this moment, nobody else in the family knew, just her. She should have just handed the envelope off to her mother—now she'd have to deliver the news herself. She closed her eyes and held onto the gate to steady herself, then heard footsteps.

"Rose!" Father Tony called out. He wore a priest's collar, but no cassock, just a black shirt with the sleeves rolled up to his elbows. His face was red; she'd never seen him run. "The Army chaplain called the rectory," he said, trying to catch his breath. There were beads of sweat on his forehead. He touched Rose's shoulder. "I came as soon as I heard. I'm so sorry. Your mother, is she . . ."

"She doesn't know. This just came," she held up the telegram. "My father's at the market and I . . . Oh, Father," Rose stammered, and the priest drew her into a hug. She melted into him, closing her eyes. She wanted time to stop. "I don't know what to do."

"I'll go with you," Father Tony said. "I'll tell her."

Rose nodded and led the priest through the gate to the back steps. Her mother was standing at the bottom of the stairway to the second floor. "Father Tony, how nice . . ." she stopped, her eyes on the yellow telegram in Rose's hand, then back to Father Tony.

"Filomena, I'm so sorry," the priest said, moving toward her.

Her mother's face paled and her eyes went wide. "NO, noooo, noooo," she cried, shaking her head and holding her palm out. Her other hand still held the bag of clothespins. "Don't come any closer." She turned and ran up into the apartment.

Rose looked at Father Tony, utterly helpless.

"Go ahead," he said. "I'll be right behind you." He followed Rose up the stairs.

In the kitchen, Rose held the telegram out again, just as the taxi driver had. "Mama, I . . ." She couldn't get any words out.

Her mother shook her head, slapping at Rose's hand. The telegram fluttered to the kitchen floor. "*State zite!* I said NO! Not Giovanni! NO!"

Rose's hand stung; she was paralyzed with fear and confusion. How did her mother know it was Giovanni and not Laura?

"Filomena let's all sit down," Father Tony said, his voice trembling. He reached out his hand to Rose's mother, but she crumpled to the floor, the clothespins scattering.

"I think she's fainted." He sat down and pulled Rose's mother's head into his lap, patting her gently on the cheek. "Filomena. Wake up. Are you OK?" He looked at Rose. "Do you have any ammonia?"

120

"Yes, yes, Father." Rose nodded. Beyond words.

"Get it, then. And a rag. Quickly," he said.

Rose grabbed the jug and a clean *mapine* from under the kitchen sink and handed them to the priest. Father Tony quickly spilled some ammonia onto the dishcloth, waving it under Filomena's nose. Her mother's eyes fluttered open, and she coughed, clutching his arm. Her tears stained the front of his shirt.

"Not Giovanni. Not my boy. Tell me it's not true, Antonio," her mother cried.

Father Tony took a white handkerchief from his pocket; her mother clutched at it. "*Questa maledetta guerra.* This damned war."

"It should be me lying dead, not him."

"Don't talk like that, Filomena," he said.

Rose backed up against the sink. Father Tony was brushing a damp lock of hair from her mother's forehead. She'd never heard her mother call the priest by his first name. She couldn't take it all in. Her mother's words, the priest on the floor, his cursing. And Giovanni, gone. Rose was shaking and felt nauseated, yet no tears came to her eyes.

She stepped forward, reaching for her mother's shoulder. "Mama . . ." she tried, but her mother twisted away, sobbing into Father Tony's arms. He was talking quietly in Sicilian, trying to soothe her. Rose wanted them to get up, to move apart.

"Antonio, Antonio . . . They took my boy," her mother wailed through her tears, ". . . *il nostro ragazzo* . . ."

Rose couldn't stand to watch for another moment. She had to leave, to get her father. "I'll go find Papa." Father Tony just nodded; tears ran down his own face. Her mother said nothing.

She ran downstairs; even outside she could hear her mother crying Giovanni's name over and over. A few neighbors had joined Mrs. Fabucci on the sidewalk. "Rose. . ." Mrs. Fabucci called out. Rose ignored her, turning away, and headed toward the riverfront. She ran as fast as she could over the cobbled streets, dodging pushcarts and cars. By the time she got to the market, her blouse clung to her, and her hair had fallen out of its bun. People yelled at her in Italian and English as she pushed her way through the crowd, searching for her father. She felt faint. The heat. The ripe smell of the produce. Flies buzzed about. She spotted her father and called out to him. She leaned backed on a column; the market was spinning. She closed her eyes. Suddenly her father was there—his rough hands holding her up, his familiar smell of cigars and sweat. Somehow, he would make it all right, wake her from this nightmare.

"Rose, what is it?" She saw the panic in his face. "*Che è successo? What's happened?*"

She couldn't bear to say it. "A telegram came." Her eyes met his. "Giovanni. Gone."

"Oh, no. *Gesù, Maria, e Giuseppe.*" He grabbed Rose by the shoulders and kissed her on the forehead. "Giovanni. *Povero ragazzo.*"

"Father Tony is at the house. Mama is hysterical," Rose said. An image flashed in her head: Father Tony and her mother on the kitchen floor. "You have to come."

Her father had tears in his eyes now. "*Andiamo. Let's go.*"

He gripped her hand all the way home, just like when she was little. The crowd of people in the market parted to let them through, murmuring and blessing themselves. She did her best to keep up with him, his long legs outpacing her. At the gate to their house, he stopped and took a deep breath at the same spot where Rose had read the telegram. It seemed like hours had passed since then, since her brother was alive.

Upstairs, Father Tony sat alone at the kitchen table, smoking a cigarette; he stood when they came in. He looked pale, his thick hair a mess, dark circles under his eyes, as if he'd aged a decade in the short time she'd been out. "Frank, I'm so sorry."

"Where's my wife?" her father asked. Rose flinched at his sharp tone.

"She's lying down. Such a shock." The two men just looked at each other for a moment, then Father Tony looked down and stubbed out his cigarette in the oystershell ashtray. Her father didn't respond. The yellow telegram waited on the table; Father Tony must have picked it up.

"Rose, call your Aunt Inez," her father said. "Tell her to come."

"Yes, Papa," she said. Their only telephone was downstairs in the store.

"And leave the shades down. The store is closed today." Her father walked down the hall and Rose heard the bedroom door close softly behind him.

"I should go, now that your father is here," Father Tony said. "But I'll check in with you later. I'm so sorry, Rose, I…" he sighed heavily. Laying a hand on Rose's shoulder, he looked at her directly, his eyes red-rimmed. "Listen to me. This is going to be hard, especially on your mother. She'll need you, even if she won't admit it. Do you hear me, Rose? You and Laura are her world now. And your father, of course. You must be strong. Pray for her."

"I will, Father," Rose said. A part of her didn't want him to go, to leave her alone with her parents.

"Good girl," he said. He wiped his brow with the same damp handkerchief her mother had used. "I'll light a candle for Giovanni. He was a good boy, Rose. God must have needed another angel. He loved you girls so much."

Downstairs, Rose walked to the front of the store, feeling numb. It was cooler here, in the dim light with the shades drawn. She pulled the blinds aside and looked out as people walked by, going about their business like it was any other morning. Other than Christmas and Thanksgiving, she couldn't remember when they'd ever closed the store on a weekday. She touched the service flag hanging on the front door. Two blue stars. Now one would have to be gold.

She made her way to the stool behind the front counter, trying to gather herself. She felt exhausted and edgy at once. She so wished Laura were here. Rose would have to get word to her somehow. She envied Laura not knowing, oblivious to the loss of their brother. Out of reach of their parents' grief.

She lifted the heavy black receiver and dialed Aunt Inez' number. Her aunt picked up on the third ring. "*Zia,* it's me."

"What's wrong?" her aunt asked.

"Giovanni . . ." She couldn't continue; her voice shook.

"*Madonna . . .*"

"There was a telegram. Father Tony was here, and Mama fainted."

"*Basta.* I'll be right over." Aunt Inez hung up.

Rose glanced up at the Coca-Cola clock and suddenly remembered Mr. Sullivan would be wondering where she was by now. She dialed the Higgins switchboard and asked the receptionist to let him know there'd been a death in the family. She hung up the phone, lingering behind the counter and dreading going back upstairs. She breathed in the comforting smells of the store. Coffee, cheese, citrus, smoked meats. But it didn't help. She felt so alone. Incomplete. Brotherless. From now on, there would only be before and after this day. Her parents would need her, Father Tony had said. For what, she wasn't sure. She had so little experience with real grief. She'd been just six when her grandmother died. She pictured her *nonna,* hunched over and dressed in black, her stockings rolled down around her ankles like little donuts, stirring a pot of red gravy on the stove. Rose could almost smell her sweet scent—flour and garlic, a whiff of anisette. People were sad but said her *nonna* was old, had lived a good life. This felt different. A true loss. Like there was a hole in the universe, in her family, in her heart, that would never be filled.

Jake padded out from the storeroom, panting, and wagging his tail. She sucked in her breath at the sight of the dog. He put his chin on her thigh, and Rose scratched him behind his ears. "Poor Jake. Your buddy's gone," she said. "I know you'll miss him as much as I will, won't you boy?"

The dog licked her hand, and the tears finally fell. Rose sobbed as images flashed through her mind: Giovanni as a little boy horsing around at the beach, singing carols with their father on Christmas eve, standing up for her at the playground when kids were teasing her. She regretted every time she'd been annoyed at him when they were teenagers. She'd give anything to have him back. It was so unfair. She bent down and rubbed her damp cheek on Jake's soft fur. He whimpered softly, getting as close to Rose as he could. "Don't worry, boy. We'll take care of each other now."

# TWELVE

Rose braced herself for the onslaught of people who would come by the apartment to pay their respects after Mass. Walking past Giovanni's bedroom, she heard her mother crying behind the closed door; she'd slept in Giovanni's room for the last week, ever since the day the telegram arrived. She'd refused to come to Mass with Rose, her father, and Aunt Inez. Carmine had come with them too—kind to Rose for a change. Giovanni had been like a little brother to him. Without a body, there could be no real funeral; instead, they'd had to settle for a memorial mention along with four other Immaculate Conception Parish boys killed in action that month. Rose hadn't seen Father Tony since the day they'd gotten the news. She'd expected him to be on the altar that morning, but it was old Monsignor Carroll who read out Giovanni's name.

Now back in her own room, Rose took off her gloves and hat. She picked up Laura's telegram from the top of her dresser and read it for the hundredth time.

*DEAR FAMILY. HEART=BROKEN. R.I.P. GIOVANNI.*

*ALL MY LOVE, LAURA*

Rose touched the scapular under her black dress, offering up a silent prayer to the Virgin to keep Laura safe. She had hoped they would let her sister come home, but the Army needed her where she was.

People would be coming any moment to pay their respects. Rose didn't feel up for this but knew she didn't really have a choice. If only Laura were here. Then she could take over, and Rose could gladly just take orders. Instead, with their mother hiding in the bedroom, Rose would have to play hostess.

In the kitchen, she tied an apron over her dress and looked out the window. Her father was down in the courtyard with cousin Carmine, a bottle of whiskey and two half-full glasses on the little black wrought iron table next to them. Jake dozed with his muzzle resting on her father's foot. A wave of sadness hit her. As crushed as she was to lose her brother, she knew her father was devastated to lose his only son. She didn't know which was more unbearable: her own loss or the thought of his.

In the kitchen, Aunt Inez was making sandwiches with a lit cigarette in the corner of her mouth. Rose waved away the smoke and gave her aunt a hug from the back. Marie and her mother came in the door carrying glass casserole dishes wrapped in dishtowels, and the kitchen felt a little less sad. "Stuffed artichokes. Where should we put them?"

"On top of the stove is fine," Rose said. "*Grazie,* Mrs. Leonardi. This is a big help. My mother is . . ." Rose hesitated. "She's not feeling well."

Mrs. Leonardi gave Rose a hug. "No trouble at all, Rose. We're so glad we could do something. We know what it's like to lose someone you love. You just tend to the guests and let us take care of the food."

The doorbell rang. Rose went downstairs and through the alley. She was already tired just thinking about how she would get through the next few hours. Irma and her husband Melvin stood on the other side of the gate. "Rose, we wanted to come pay our respects," Irma said, holding out a basket of bright orange fruit."

"We brought some satsumas from our backyard." She wore a blue dress and a white lace doily pinned to her hair while Melvin wore a pressed brown suit, yellow tie, and matching pocket square. They must have come from their own church, Rose thought. They stayed on the sidewalk and Rose realized they were hesitant to come in. They'd never been inside the house before, only the store.

"Please, please come on in," Rose said, taking the fruit. "Thank you so much, they're beautiful. My mother is resting but my father will be happy to see you, I'm sure." They followed her down the alley and up the stairs. At the landing, Rose leaned over the railing and called to her father in the courtyard. "Papa, Miss Irma and Mr. Melvin are here." Her father looked up and raised his eyebrows at her. He swallowed the last of his drink and stood up. Carmine stayed seated, smoking a cigarette.

Rose brought Irma and Melvin into the kitchen and looked at Marie with pleading eyes, since Marie knew Irma from the shipyard. "Hello, Irma," Marie said, introducing them to her mother while Aunt Inez took the basket of satsumas.

Rose's father came in, looking awful. His white Sunday shirt was wrinkled and open at the neck. "Sorry for your loss, Mr. Frank," Melvin said. The men shook hands.

"I remember Giovanni as a little boy, that puppy following him everywhere," Irma said. "I lit a candle for him at St. Augustine this morning."

Rose was touched by Irma's words. She remembered Irma and Melvin's son was still fighting in the Pacific. "That means a lot to us, Irma," Rose said. "I'll say a special prayer for Alfred tonight. I hope he's home safe soon."

People came and went for another couple of hours. Rose tried to stay busy, serving food and chatting with cousins, neighbors, and customers of the store. Her father sat in the parlor, doing his best. She didn't have much time to dwell on it, but every now and then there was a lull in a conversation, and Rose would remember why the people were here: Giovanni was gone. Killed in action. She couldn't bring herself to think of that part yet. The sadness would almost overwhelm her, but then someone would ask her a question and she would snap out of it. Surrounded by people all day, and still she'd never felt so alone in all her life.

After the guests were gone, she sat with Aunt Inez at the kitchen table, reviewing who had showed up and who had not. The kitchen was spotless, and all the dishes done, thanks to Marie and her mother. Rose's father had disappeared to the Italian Hall with Carmine. Aunt Inez had just kicked off her high heels and lit a cigarette when Rose's mother appeared in the kitchen doorway. Her hair was disheveled, her eyes swollen and red. Rose felt pity and anger at the same time.

"Are they all gone?" she croaked, a gray housedress hanging from her thin frame. Rose hadn't seen her eat much beyond a piece of toast and coffee for the last week. She wondered when her mother had last taken a bath.

Aunt Inez turned in her chair. "Yes, Fil. We had a nice crowd here. Everyone sends you their love," she said. "You should eat something. There's plenty left. You don't look so good."

"Give me a cigarette," Rose's mother said.

Aunt Inez sat back. "You don't smoke anymore."

"I do now." Her mother sat down with a grunt. She took a cigarette from Aunt Inez' pack and snapped the lighter.

Rose had never seen her mother with a cigarette. "Ma, Mrs. Leonardi made nice artichokes. There's some left. Let me fix you a plate." Rose tried to keep the alarm out of her voice.

"I'm not hungry."

Rose fought back tears. It had been a long, emotional day and she was just about at her wits' end. She tried not to feel sorry for herself, but Giovanni's death had propelled them all into a different world. Her parents had dumped the responsibility of the makeshift wake on her. It was as if her mother was hoarding all the grief, as if nobody else had a right to feel pain.

"She's just trying to help, Fil," Aunt Inez said. "Rose did well, you know, handling all the company. Are you sure I can't warm up some food for you?"

Rose's mother took a drag from the cigarette and held in the smoke. "I told you I'm not hungry." She exhaled. "You wouldn't understand."

"Understand what?"

"I killed my son."

Aunt Inez gave Rose a concerned look. "You've got to stop that nonsense. The Japs killed Giovanni," Aunt Inez said. "I'm worried about you, Fil. You haven't eaten a proper meal in days."

"Worry about yourself, Inez. This is God's doing. My punishment." She started coughing and Rose brought her a glass of water.

"That's crazy talk, Fil," Aunt Inez said. "Look, try to get some rest. Have some warm milk or something. I'm exhausted. I'll talk to you tomorrow."

"Thanks for everything, *Zia*." Rose stood and gave her aunt a hug. Aunt Inez patted her back and Rose held onto her godmother for a long minute, wishing she could just leave with her.

Then Rose was alone with her mother, and there was nothing left to do but sit with the wall of silence. She desperately wanted to comfort her mother, to remind her she still had two daughters, a husband, a family who loved her. "Mama, I don't understand—"

"You *can't* understand. You're just a girl, young and ignorant, same as I was. You think life is going to be one big dance, flirting with the boys, going to your little job, and pretending you're so important. Just like your sister."

Her mother's words hit like a slap in the face. "Laura is doing God's work over there, Mama. Saving lives. She's a hero, just like Giovanni is—was . . ." Rose felt the tears coming and wanted to

131

run from the room. She gripped the table edge, forcing herself to stay. "You shouldn't talk about her like that."

Her mother held up her palm. "Don't you tell me what I should and shouldn't do, Rose. I'm still your mother. I know more than you ever will."

Rose felt like she was talking with a stranger. Her mother had always been difficult, but rage had transformed her. Rose hugged herself, folding her arms over her chest, her fingernails biting into her palms. "I'm sick over it too, Ma. I miss Giovanni every minute of every day, but we have to—"

"What? We have to what, Rose. 'Get on with our lives?' That's what your father said. I have no life to get on with. God has taken my boy from me." Tears were running down her mother's cheeks; she made no effort to dry them.

Rose wiped her own eyes with the hem of her apron. She felt hollow and shaky. "You still have us, Mama. Laura, Papa, and me."

Her mother wouldn't even look at her. "I have no son," she said, brushing invisible crumbs from the table. "Nothing anyone says can bring him back."

Rose was out of words. She ran to her bedroom and threw herself on Laura's bed, sobbing. It was as if her mother wished Laura had been killed instead of Giovanni. And where was her father? He should be dealing with this, not her. All her life she'd been suffocating under their control; just when she needed them most, they'd abandoned her. Her head pounded. Her mother's anger was contagious. She was furious at the war, at her parents, at God, even at her brother for getting himself killed, for leaving them. For leaving her.

# THIRTEEN

Rose woke up the next morning, hot and sticky after a restless night. She hadn't bothered to wash her face or change out of her slip before collapsing on her bed the night before. Now she dragged herself through her morning routine, groggy and sullen. She was nervous about leaving her mother alone in the apartment, but relieved to be returning to the shipyard. She'd been out for a week and knew Mr. Sullivan would be anxious for her to get back to work. Plenty of other people at Higgins had lost someone; most of them didn't get the kind of time off Mr. Sullivan had given her, but she'd go crazy if she had to spend one more day locked up with her mother's bitterness.

Her father was already downstairs in the store. Carmine and Aunt Inez had kept things running as best they could for a few days, but the business needed her father's attention. Rose found him arranging a shipment of cold cuts in the deli display. She stood on her toes to give him a kiss on the cheek. "I hate to leave you all by yourself," she said. The front door stood open; already Aunt Inez had sewn a gold star over one of the blue ones to honor Giovanni.

"It's OK. Carmine will be here soon," her father said. "And I have Jake for company." The dog was dozing in the corner and raised his head when he heard his name. Her father had been keeping the dog close. The radio was playing Glen Miller's "American Patrol." Rose thought it was a good sign her father had the music on. Even so, he looked weary.

"I don't know how I'm going to get through the day," Rose said.

"Just do your best, baby. Like you always do." A glimpse of the old Papa warmed Rose's heart. His quiet sadness over Giovanni shook her even more than her mother's unpredictable outbursts. "You're helping make those boats, and that's an important job."

It was the first time she'd heard such words from him.

"Giovanni sacrificed his life. We have to honor that, *cara,* stay strong, and beat those sons of bitches."

Rose nodded. "I'm so worried about Mama."

"One day at a time. It's all we can do," her father answered. "I'll see you tonight. *Vai piano-piano.*"

As she headed out the front door, she touched the gold star and said a silent prayer that Laura's star would stay blue.

Sweaty bodies crowded together on the streetcar as Rose made her way to work. A soldier stood to give her his seat and she was grateful, though the sight of a young man in an Army uniform almost made her start to cry. On the ride in, she thought about Sal. It had been so long since she last saw him; he seemed like someone she'd dreamt up. Maybe her mother was right, that she was a silly girl, not taking life seriously enough. He'd fought for the other side, the side that killed Giovanni. Before, she'd been able to push that aside. Not now. Only guilt remained. She missed Sal, but it didn't feel right. Whatever it was they were getting into, it was time to back out.

Mr. Sullivan was at his desk, a mess of green ledger sheets in front of him. "Ah, Rose. So good to see your face," he said and stood. "I'm so sorry I couldn't come by the house yesterday. We had a family event across the lake and didn't get home until late. How are your folks holding up?" He walked over to her and touched her shoulder lightly.

"They're doing the best they can. It's been rough, but I know we're not alone," Rose said, trying not to cry. "My mother's taking it especially hard. I really appreciate your letting me take time off to help out at home."

"A mother's love for her son is a special thing," Mr. Sullivan said. "She's lucky she has you. And your sister, of course." Mr. Sullivan's lilting brogue made her feel comforted, and he always remembered to mention Laura.

"I'm anxious to get back to work," Rose said.

"Glad to hear it. The Navy put in another huge order while you were out, and Mr. Higgins is on our behinds. He wants us to move even faster, though I don't know how that's possible. Maybe you can help us figure out a way to tighten up the schedules."

"Whatever it takes. I can work overtime," Rose said. It would be better than spending time at home. Here, she could finally breathe, apply herself. She dove into the reports on her desk and felt the gears of her mind start up again. She looked for patterns in the numbers, seeking out ways to meet the production challenge. Gradually, thoughts of Giovanni retreated to the back of her mind, replaced by the order pipeline, forecasts, and inventory projections.

When the lunch whistle blew, Rose walked outside to meet Marie. She looked forward to getting back to their routine, to spending time with her best friend. Marie could always make her laugh, no matter how grim things were.

Marie gave Rose a long hug. "Good to have you back."

"Let's go sit near the bayou," Rose said. They made their way down to the water's edge and spread the brown woolen blanket on the grass. Clouds of small insects swarmed just above the surface of the murky brown water. There wasn't a breath of a breeze, but it was slightly less stifling than inside.

"Thanks for being there yesterday. And thank your mom again too. The artichokes were a godsend."

"Happy to help. How are you holding up?"

"Sometimes I feel a little better, but then out of the blue I'll start crying again," Rose said unpacking her lunch—a leftover olive salad and salami sandwich from the day before. She offered half to Marie. "You want this? I can't eat the whole thing."

"If it'll help you out," Marie smiled and took the half sandwich. "I know it's a lot better than my bologna."

"My mother is a mess," Rose said. She hadn't wanted to say anything about it, but she had to get it off her chest. "She's still sleeping in Giovanni's bed and won't talk to us unless she's ranting and raving. After everyone left last night, she said some awful things."

"Like what?"

"Like her life is 'over.' I really don't know what to do about it."

"What about your father?"

"He's doing his best, trying to keep the store going, putting one foot in front of the other. It's hard." She took a bite of her sandwich, wiped olive juice off her chin with a cloth napkin.

"Poor guy," Marie said. "Losing a child. It goes against the natural order of things. I was so young when my Papa died, but I remember how sad my mother was. I didn't understand and kept asking when he was coming home. I must've broken her heart all over again."

"Yeah. I feel like there's a huge hole that won't ever heal. But what can we do? We have to go on with our lives, right? Giovanni would hate to know we were all moping around," Rose said, hearing the words but not feeling them.

"Well, I have something that might cheer you up," Marie said. She pulled an envelope from the pocket of her coveralls and waved it in front of Rose. "Wipe your hands."

Rose put down her sandwich and cleaned her fingers on the napkin. Marie presented the envelope to her with a flourish. "What's this? You already gave us a Mass card."

"It's not from me," Marie smirked.

Rose saw her name scrawled on the front of the envelope and a pencil sketch of a rose, thorns and all. Her heart skipped a beat. She held the envelope with both hands and studied the drawing. It was meticulously detailed. "Sal?" she asked.

Marie nodded. "Turns out he's quite an artist, in addition to being dreamy-looking. And one heck of a dancer."

"When did you . . . where did you . . ." Rose was hesitant to open the envelope, afraid of what he might have written.

"For the love of Saint Christopher, just open it, Rose," Marie said. "He gave it to me last week when I went to visit Vinny. I didn't want to hand it to you yesterday, obviously. I've been waiting over a week to know what's inside!"

Rose opened the envelope carefully, trying not to damage the drawing. She unfolded the single sheet of paper. He had written in Italian, and she could hear his voice as she read.

*Dear Rose,*

*I was so sad to hear from Marie about the death of your big brother. I can't even imagine how I would feel if something happened to one of my own. I lit a candle for him in our chapel here and said a prayer to San Giovanni. I know you must be with your family now, but I am counting the minutes until I can see you again. In the meantime, you are in my heart.*

*Yours, Sal*

Tears welled up in Rose's eyes, and Marie touched her friend's hand. "What is it, Rose? Why are you crying? I thought it would make you happy to hear from him."

"It's OK," Rose sniffled. She wasn't sure why she was crying. She was tired of all the tears but couldn't stop them. "Really, it's very nice. He was thoughtful to send it. Here, you can read it. It's in Italian." She handed Marie the note. She didn't know what to say. She'd been so sure of her plan this morning to quietly let him go. Now Sal's beautiful words had her more confused than ever.

Marie finished reading and held the letter up to her heart. "So sweet," she said, then handed it back to Rose. "He's a good man."

"I don't think I can do it," Rose said. "They may be nice, but those boys were technically the enemy. On the same side as the Japs who killed my brother, and the Germans your Louie is fighting. How can we just date them like it's no big deal? Look where we work. The war is real, Marie."

"They're not the enemy anymore, though. Plus, Vincenzo told me they were drafted—forced to be in the army," Marie said, looking down at her sandwich and shaking her head. "Besides, I think it's too late for me anyway. I've got it bad, Rose. Vinny's making me forget all about Louie."

"Really?" Rose had been so caught up in her own troubles, she hadn't even thought about how Marie was doing.

"I haven't heard from Lou in two months anyway. He's probably hitting on all the pretty mademoiselles over there in France."

Rose couldn't argue with that. Though Marie and Louie were practically engaged, Rose knew the war probably hadn't changed his ways. If anything, he was probably using it as an excuse to misbehave.

"I made up my mind to write Louie a letter and break it off—I was going to ask you to help me. You're so much better with words than I am, and—"

"Whoa, wait a minute," Rose said, looking up from Sal's drawing. "I mean, I'll help you if you want, but think about it. You don't really know this Vincenzo. You really want to break it off with Lou? Just like that?" She wasn't sure if the question was for Marie or for herself.

"I've never been surer of anything. I think God sent him to me or something," Marie said. "I was there last week when you were dealing with your family. We spent hours just talking. He's as crazy about me as I am about him. I know it's quick but it's like the war has sped things up."

Rose had never heard Marie talk like this. "That's . . . great, I guess. Have you told him about your job?"

"Well, yes, but I tried to downplay it. And I didn't tell him you worked here too. I knew he'd tell Sal. They think you just work for your father at the store. Let's go visit this Sunday and you can tell him yourself."

"I really don't think so, Marie. My mother's still not well and I have to help out at home."

"Come on, Rose. They can spare you for a few hours. It's the least you can do after that beautiful note. Can't hurt to see him one more time, right?"

"I don't know. I can't push away the thought of Sal in North Africa, shooting at soldiers like my brother."

Marie pressed her. "That's your mother talking. Sal had nothing to do with Giovanni's death. Nothing. You *know* that."

"Maybe." Rose slipped Sal's letter into her pocket. "I'll think about it. I need to get back to work."

CHAPTER

# FOURTEEN

The following Sunday, Rose met Marie at the bus stop. Some of the other girls from the neighborhood were there—Dorothy and Mary Messina, along with the four Battaglia sisters—dressed up and carrying baskets of food. Rose knew they were all angling for husbands; the oldest Battaglia girl was almost 30. Rose was relieved not to see Gilda among them.

"I'm so glad you decided to come," Marie said, hooking her arm in Rose's. "I brought some cookies—they can be from both of us."

"Thanks," Rose said. She wore an old off-white, sleeveless dress of Laura's, belted at the waist because it was too big on top. Her hair was pinned up and she wore a small hat she'd had for ages, its edges slightly frayed. She'd tried to make an effort, but looking at the other girls now, she felt underdressed.

The city bus pulled up and they boarded. All the windows were open, but it was still stifling hot, and Marie pulled a fan out of her handbag as they got settled. Rose dabbed at her forehead with a lace handkerchief, glad not to be wearing much makeup in this heat. She could see the foundation melting a little on Marie's face. "I love that dress, Marie. Vinny won't be able to take his eyes off

141

you." Marie had lost a little weight, Rose noticed. Her dress showed off her figure, and her round face was beaming.

"Aw, thanks doll. That's the idea. By the way, I mailed the letter to Louie at work yesterday. Thanks for your help."

"Well, I guess that's the right thing to do," Rose said. *Poor Lou*, she thought. She agreed with Marie's decision but felt a little bad for the guy—even if he was a lout. She pictured him reading Marie's Dear John letter while stuck in some filthy foxhole in France.

Rose gripped the seat in front of her as the bus lurched forward. "How do you know . . . that Vincenzo's the one for you?"

Marie shrugged. "It's like they say: you just know. Love. I can feel it in my bones."

Rose wondered what love would feel like for her. Laura was in love; Marie was in love. Aunt Inez had been in love with her dead husband. She assumed her parents had once loved each other, but did they still? She thought about Sal's kiss, the drawing with the sweet note—was that love? She rested her head against the window frame as they crossed the Industrial Canal, the view more familiar to her now. She wished she could just suspend time, turn back the clock. Things had been so much simpler just a couple of months ago, when her biggest problem was what to wear to a boring dance with the nuns. Before the POWs came, before her brother was killed. Before her mother lost her mind. Before Sal.

The bus stopped at the entrance to Jackson Barracks to let the women out, and the guard waved to them as they walked through the gate. Tini Battaglia reached into her basket and handed him a cookie—he didn't ask what was in the packages or bother checking their handbags. "We could be smuggling anything in here," Marie whispered. "Lucky for them we're all good girls." From what Rose could see, what little security the Army had started off with at Jackson Barracks was pretty much gone. The prisoners left base in the morning to work at the Port of Embarkation and came back at night. None of them had ever tried to escape; in return the Army had given them even more freedom.

The August sun was relentless—not a cloud in the sky. Heat shimmered off the asphalt path. "*Madonna,* let's get out of this oven," Marie said, fanning herself. They passed a group of shirtless, sweaty men playing soccer. They chased a ball around the muddy yard, wearing clumsy boots.

Rose scanned the field. "I don't see them," she said, feeling a slight panic rising in her throat. *What if he isn't here?* She knew the POWs had been transferred a few times before they reached New Orleans. Maybe the Army would just keep moving them around. Maybe it would be better. Then she wouldn't have to decide after all.

"You're right, I don't see our boys. Too bad," Marie said. "I wouldn't mind seeing my Vin with his shirt off."

Rose blushed and shot her a pretend scowl, though she had the same thought about Sal. "You'd better watch it, Marie. You'll have to talk about that in confession next week."

"Some things I keep between myself and the Virgin Mary," Marie said. "Those priests don't need to hear *every*thing."

They entered the cavernous building. Rose spotted Sal before he saw her, sitting in a corner the Army had set up for games and movies. He was playing cards, his shoulders square in a clean, pressed shirt tucked into uniform pants. His hair had been cut short on the sides, leaving a mop of light brown curls on top of his head, and making his ears stick out a little, like orecchiette pasta. For some reason, the imperfection touched her. He looked up and locked eyes with her, then placed his cards face down on the table. Her heart raced as he walked toward her.

"*Cara mia,* I'm so happy to see you again," Sal said in rapid fire Italian, gripping her lightly by both elbows. "I'm so sorry about your brother."

Rose had told herself she wouldn't cry in front of him, but the tears welled up. "Thank you for your beautiful note . . . and the drawing," she said. Her knees gave way, and Sal caught her in his strong arms. He smelled of shaving cream and tobacco. She closed her eyes and rested her head against his chest as he pulled her tight.

One of the guards yelled out, "Hey, Dilisio. No touching." Sal took a step back. It was the first time Rose had heard his last name.

Marie cleared her throat. Rose had forgotten she was still standing there.

"*Buongiorno,* Marie. Vincenzo is in the kitchen," Sal said. "He'll be happy to see you."

"You OK, Rose?" Marie asked.

Rose nodded, embarrassed, and wiped her cheeks with a handkerchief Sal produced from his pocket. A couple of the other girls were staring at her. "Yes. Thanks. Go ahead," she said, and Marie headed off to the kitchen. Meanwhile, the guard had returned his attention to his magazine.

Sal sat Rose down on a threadbare brown sofa. "*Acqua, per favore,*" he said to one of his friends. "I no like to see you cry," he said in broken English.

His accent made her smile.

"I say something wrong? Sorry, my English . . ." he looked down.

"No, no. Your English is getting much better," Rose said. "You just surprised me. Pretty soon your English will be better than my Italian."

"We are studying, Vincenzo and me. So I can talk to you better in your language."

Rose was touched that he was so eager to learn English for her. One of the other POWs brought over a glass of water. "*Grazie,*" she nodded to him. She took a sip, then put the glass down on the battered green army chest that was serving as a coffee table. Sal took her hands in his and squeezed them gently. Rose looked at his hands, so much larger than hers, tanned and strong.

"I was so upset when Marie told me about your brother," he said, switching back to Italian.

"It seems impossible that he's not coming back, that I'll never see him again," Rose said.

"How are your parents?"

"Not too good. I think it's hardest on my mother," Rose said. "She doesn't talk—some days she doesn't even get out of bed. She's very angry." She stopped there. How could she make him understand her mother's condition when she didn't fully understand herself?

Sal kept his eyes on hers, waiting for her to finish before asking more questions, so patient. At home she had to walk on eggshells all the time. Her mother and father were locked up in their private grief. The silent dinners were excruciating. With Sal, she felt safe, comfortable, like he was on her side, nothing like an enemy.

"And your father?"

"My father is quiet. He just keeps working. Because my mother doesn't leave the apartment, my father is left to run the store alone with my cousin." Rose caught herself. Sal didn't know she had someplace else to be during the week.

"It's good he has you there to help him," he said.

"Let's talk about something happier," Rose said, dabbing at her eyes. She looked around but didn't see Marie. The other girls were deep in their own conversations with men; a few played cards at the table where Sal had been.

He dropped her hand and pulled a pack of cigarettes and matches out of his shirt pocket. "It's OK?" he asked in English.

"Please, go ahead," she said. "Tell me about the picture. The rose was so beautiful. Where did you learn to draw?" Rose asked.

"From my mother. I used to trace over her drawings when I was a boy. She finally got me my own set of colored pencils and I would sketch all the farm animals." He pulled a small, battered, leather-bound notebook out of his shirt pocket and held it out to her.

"You've kept this the whole time?"

"Yes."

She turned the pages, some of which were torn and stained: life in the Army camp in El Paso and here, the ocean waves—she assumed it was what he saw during his passage to America. Further back, desert scenes. "Where is this?" she asked, pointing to a drawing of camels and strange figures wrapped in sheets leading them. There were hills on the horizon, shadows and light. It looked exotic, the land wide open. So different from New Orleans.

"Tunisia," he answered. "Where we were captured. We had a lot of time waiting for them to decide what to do with us, so I drew. The local people there, the Arabs, were kind. They brought us water, fruit from their gardens. Some of them even spoke a little Italian—they told us there were Italian settlements in the area. The English soldiers made fun of them and made them work, but they never complained."

"My sister was there," Rose said, looking more closely now at the sketch. She wondered if this was how Laura's world had looked and felt a sudden pang in her heart. Where was her sister now? Was she safe?

"The nurse," he said. "I remember. I hope someday I will meet her. You miss her very much, no?"

Again, Rose felt her throat tighten. "*Sì*. Very much." She handed the notebook back to him. "These are really beautiful, Sal. We have many artists in New Orleans. Some of them sell their paintings and drawings in the alley near my house. Maybe you could do that . . ." She caught herself. She was getting too far ahead.

"Here, keep this one." He carefully ripped out a drawing of camellias and handed it to her. "I'll give you a new one every time you come to visit."

"Camellias," she said. "Beautiful. We have these in our courtyard."

He tucked the notebook back in his shirt pocket. "We have them at home in Italy too," he said.

*Home,* she thought. Of course, he'll be going back there, to his family. She felt foolish imagining a future with him here in New Orleans. She decided this was her moment to tell him about her job. She had rehearsed the conversation in her head, but now she struggled for the right words. "Sal, you said something earlier about my father having my help at the store," she began.

"*Sì.*" He took a drag on his cigarette and turned his head to blow the smoke away from her. A momentary silence fell between them. Sal took her hand again. He was rubbing his thumb slowly on the inside of her palm; for a moment she lost her focus. They both started speaking at the same time and laughed.

"Go ahead," she said.

"No, you first," he said. He looked at her with those hazel eyes, his eyelashes long, like a girl's. She could lose herself in those eyes.

"It's just . . . so nice to see you again." It was so much less than what she was feeling—she wanted to throw herself into his arms. She hesitated. "About the store. There's something I should tell you about that. Papa has my help on Saturdays, but during the week, I work at a shipyard. We make boats for the war, the kind that land on the beaches." Her words came out in a rush.

"Wait," Sal said, coughing out some smoke. "You are making warships? With these tiny fingers?" he held up one of her hands.

She laughed. "I'm a bookkeeper. But Marie does. She's a welder."

"Now that, I can believe," he laughed. "Yes, I know. Vincenzo told me about Marie's job."

"I was afraid to tell you. It's possible it was one of our boats that captured you and—"

"I'm glad they captured me, *cara*. We were starving in the desert—no food, no water, no ammunition. Heaven sent the English and American soldiers to us. Without them, we would have died. Then I came to America, to you. God bless your boats."

Rose felt a wave of relief. "I took my cousin's place when he joined the Army. I'm hoping I can keep working, even after the men come back." She stopped. It was the first time she'd said it out loud to anyone but Marie.

Sal's face was expressionless.

"Sorry, that was probably more than you wanted to know," she said.

"No, please. I want to know everything about you."

It was a nice thing to say but Rose was hesitant to share much more. She changed the subject. "But what about you? What do you think *you'll* do? Afterward?" she asked.

"I don't know. We hear they will send us back, but I don't know what things will be like at home. The farm, my parents, my sister, and brothers. I'm sure it's been hard on them without my help. I worry about them all the time, especially with all the bombing."

Rose felt her stomach sink. Of course, that would be his answer. His loyalty to his family made her like him even more. It also made her sad to think about him returning—forgetting about her once he was back among his people. Would she just become a fond memory of his time in America? A nice distraction from his captivity? Or maybe this was just a story she'd invented to keep from caring more deeply for him, to protect her heart like Laura had told her.

Marie startled Rose, plopping down on the sofa next to her. "Hope we aren't interrupting anything," she said.

Vincenzo sat down next to Marie, his arm slung around her shoulders. "*Buongiorno*, Rose," he said. "So sorry about your brother."

"*Grazie*, Vincenzo," Rose answered, though Vincenzo had already turned his attention back to staring at Marie, discreetly holding her hand.

"Time flies, and we're going to have to catch the bus back to town," Marie said.

"What? So soon?" Sal asked.

"I'm afraid so. But we can come again next Sunday, right Rose?" Marie asked, raising an eyebrow at her.

"Yes," Rose nodded. On the bus ride over, she hadn't been sure she even wanted to see Sal. Now she was sorry to be leaving.

"*Molto brava!*" Sal said. "But that sounds like such a long time. I don't know if I can wait."

"Maybe we can break out of here before then," Vincenzo laughed. "Come on, Sal. Let's walk the ladies out."

Rose gathered her purse and stood. Sal took her hand as they headed for the door. "I want to kiss you," he whispered in her ear as they walked. "But I don't want to get us in trouble."

She saw the guard at the exit, looking right at them. She squeezed his hand, and he pulled her closer. She felt his heat on her bare arm. "*Presto*. Soon," she whispered back.

Back on the bus, the other women chatted away, swapping stories about their new boyfriends. Rose tuned them out, reviewing every detail of her conversation with Sal in her head. She thought about the little sketchbook; it had opened a window into his life. Every time they met, she found there were deeper layers to him: his devotion to family, his observations about the war, his art. The drawings made her want to know even more about him, to be alone with him and crawl inside his head and his heart. She liked the feeling of his hands on her and wanted much more, though she knew it was a sin even thinking about it. But it wasn't just physical, this attraction. She felt her mind meeting his too. It was thrilling.

Marie elbowed her in the side. "Ow, what's that for?" Rose asked, feigning pain.

"You're a million miles away," Marie said. "Let me guess: in Sal land. By the way, I told Vin about Louie."

"Was he mad?"

"For about a minute. He said I should have told him earlier that I was engaged. But then I asked him what difference that would have made, and he said, 'None—I would have fought for you anyway,'" Marie put up her fists like a boxer. "Can you see it now Rose? The two of them fighting over me?"

"I'm glad you told him," Rose said. She thought about how different she was from her friend; she would be so uncomfortable with two men fighting over her.

Marie rearranged her purse on her lap and was quiet for a minute. "You two looked pretty cozy over there. I think you might be a goner yourself."

Rose smiled and looked out the window. As they came up over the Industrial Canal bridge, the late summer sun was a huge orange fireball in a purple and red sky. The Mississippi River glistened in the distance, snaking its way around the city. Her feelings for Sal were so different from the crushes she had as a schoolgirl. For a few minutes, Sal had kept her mind from Giovanni and her almost all-consuming grief. Maybe Marie was right, maybe she was a goner. She felt so good when she was with him and wondered what it would be like to feel his touch each night and each morning.

*September 1944*
*Italy*

*Dear Rose,*
*Sorry I haven't been able to write sooner. We've been working pretty much round-the-clock for a couple of months now. It's been a quiet night, but I know it won't stay that way. Any time I'm not working, I try to catch some sleep. I've been so sad about Giovanni. He was my first friend, such a good big brother. My heart hurts every time a memory of us as kids flashes in my mind. Everything else I've wanted to write about has seemed beside the point—until now.*
*I hope you're doing well. I appreciate your letter so much. I never heard anything back from Mama after my telegram, and I guess I won't. I did get a package from Aunt Inez—a new lipstick and some stockings. Hopefully sometime soon I'll have a use for them. Papa . . . well, I know he's thinking of me, but he's never been much of a writer. My heart aches for him, losing his only son. Give him an extra hug for me.*
*Please write soon and tell me more about your fella. I wonder if they'll still be at Jackson Barracks when I get home? Now that the POWs work for the Army, maybe people will be a little more open-minded. The Italians I talk to over here hated Mussolini and never wanted to side with the Germans in the first place.*
*Conditions here are a little better now, though when we play the game of "what do you miss the most?" I must admit my soft bed in our little room is high on my list, along with Mama's cooking, and Papa's hugs. Luckily, we're not as close to the front as we were when we first arrived, so things are a little more orderly now. I was put in charge of our ward, and it's good having more say over things. Nurse McCarthy said she put me in for a promotion to First Lieutenant, which would make a big difference. The Army may not like all us women running things, but they have to respect the rank.*

*OK, I've saved the best for last. I have some good news to share. Are you sitting down? I'm engaged. Well, not quite. But almost! We had a rare break in the action, and Nicholas and I took a walk along the sea wall. He got down on one knee and asked me to marry him! It was so romantic. No ring, but he made a little placeholder out of twine. So sweet. I told him yes, of course, but I said he had to ask Papa's permission, so it's not really official. Here's the hard part: PLEASE don't say anything to ANYONE, even Aunt Inez or Marie. We'll wait until the right time—I didn't want to get Mama and Papa involved, so soon after Giovanni, but I HAD to tell you! Nicholas makes me so happy, Rose. I can't wait for you to meet him. I know you'll love him too.*

*I don't know what will happen next or what life will be like when this war is over. I've dreamed of getting my RN, maybe working in a hospital trauma ward since I have all this experience now. I think Nicholas would be OK with that, at least until we start a family (yikes!). And we haven't figured out where we'll settle down either, although I can't imagine living anywhere but New Orleans. What I wouldn't give to be sitting with you and Marie on the levee, eating a sno-ball and watching the tugboats on the river. Hopefully I can convince Nicholas we should set up shop there, instead of in the cold and snow up where he's from.*

*I can feel you starting to fret that I'll move away from the family. Please don't worry. We're a long way from that decision. But you <u>can</u> start thinking about your maid-of-honor dress (smile). I'd better get some shut eye. Write back soon. Vai piano-piano.*

*Love, Laura*

# FIFTEEN

On the bus ride to Jackson Barracks, Marie chatted with Dorothy Messina across the aisle, leaving Rose alone with her thoughts. The letter she'd received from her sister two days before drifted through her mind. *Laura engaged.* Rose wondered how her parents would react, even if she needed to keep the news to herself for now. It had been two weeks since Paris was liberated—for a few days people were so joyful, saying things like, "There's a light at the end of the tunnel." In her own house, though, Rose continued to feel smothered by the heavy curtain of grief hanging between her parents.

They found Sal and Vincenzo playing on the bocce court the prisoners had made. They waved Rose and Marie over. The weather had cooled off a little, so now it was bearable to sit outside. They sat in folding chairs in the shade of a big magnolia tree next to a small table with a pitcher of lemonade and glasses on it. The barracks didn't feel much like a prison camp anymore, though the men still couldn't leave without permission.

"*Buongiorno!* We'll be right there—almost done," Sal called to them. He was wearing a sleeveless white T-shirt. Rose had never seen him without his uniform. She stared at his arms—so muscled and tan as he tossed the bocce ball.

"That looks like fun. Maybe we can try it?" Marie shouted.

"It's a man's game, Marie," Vincenzo said. "We wouldn't want you to get your pretty dress dirty. I'll be over as soon as we finish beating these guys."

Sal gave his ball to another prisoner. "That's enough for me. I don't want to be that far from my Rose," he said. He sat down next to her and kissed her hand. "We made lemonade from the lemon trees here—just like on my farm back home." Sal poured glasses for them. Rose thought about that first time she had poured lemonade for him, how his arm had brushed against hers. She could not have imagined this day. She looked at him and blushed.

"What are you grinning at?" Sal asked.

"Nothing," Rose said.

"*Mysterioso*," he laughed. "Let's take a walk. Do you mind, Marie?"

"No, I'm fine here watching Vinny play. You go ahead." Marie winked at Rose.

Sal took Rose's hand and they walked down a small path in front of rows of white-washed cabins. Laundry flapped on improvised clotheslines hooked to the small stoops. Rose was excited, but a little nervous—it was her first time alone with Sal. She felt his strong arm around her shoulders. He asked about her family, how things were going at work. He always seemed genuinely interested, not just making conversation. She prattled on a bit but didn't dare talk about details. *Loose lips sink ships* rang in her head when she talked about her work to anyone, let alone Sal.

"Are you OK listening to all this?" she asked. "I know you were on the other side."

Sal shook his head. "Italy was on the wrong side. Now that I'm here and learning more about America, I feel foolish that we ever thought we could win this war. Mussolini was crazy. An idiot."

Rose was relieved. "You sound like my father."

They were quiet for a few minutes as they walked along the dirt path; the grassy slope of the river levee rose in front of them. "I got a letter from home," Sal said to her. "Yesterday."

*Home*, she thought. *Italy*. She braced herself for whatever news he had to share. "Is everything all right?"

"My mother pretends they're fine, but I know she's worried. She says it's hard. There's fighting nearby. The younger children are scared all the time."

In her letters, Laura had mentioned the noise from the bombs. "That must be terrifying. I'll pray they stay safe." It was all she could think of to say. She tried to picture the Italian children, crying and scared, explosions all around them. On the newsreels, she'd seen the terrible damage in London, buildings reduced to rubble, people fleeing their homes. The threat was never far from her mind, even here in New Orleans. There were still German U-boats sinking ships in the Gulf of Mexico, not that far away.

They reached the end of the dirt path and Sal steered her toward the levee. "Let's rest for a minute," he said. They sat down on the soft grass. "I love seeing you on Sundays, but in between it gets lonesome here. We try to stay busy, but there's not much to do when we're not working. I have too much time to think. I worry about my family a lot."

Rose rearranged her skirt around her bare legs. In her mind's eye, she imagined his family farm like the ones she saw on the bus to Jackson Barracks. Maybe some pretty village girl was waiting for him there. "I'm sorry. I hope you'll get to go home and see them as soon as the war is over." The words were out of her mouth before she could think—did she really hope that?

Sal took her hand. "But then I would be apart from you. It's making me crazy, thinking I will have to go and leave you behind. I can't explain it, I don't have the right words, but I think about you all the time. Maybe you could come with me—I could show you our farm. My mother would love you."

Rose was a little alarmed. Did he mean to take her home to Italy, make her a farm wife? "Oh, I don't know about that, Sal. We're a long way from the end of things. Who knows what the Army will do with you guys between now and then?"

He looked down and pulled up a few tufts of grass. "I know. It's a dream," he said. "Maybe after the war I can send for my family instead. Things were hard in Italy, even before. Maybe they could have a little farm here in Louisiana. Everybody needs milk, right?"

"Of course. But that would take a lot of money." She didn't want to discourage him, but she couldn't imagine how all that would happen.

"There is always a way," Sal said. "I thought I would be dead many times in North Africa, but here I am, in America. I survived. I am strong, I can find work, save money. Maybe your family would help. When can I meet them? Some of the other girls bring their mothers to visit now."

Rose's heart was racing. She looked out at the river, not sure how to answer him. She wasn't ready for all this. Her parents didn't even know of Sal's existence. Even if they hadn't been so grief-stricken, she wasn't entirely sure she would have mentioned him to them. Not yet. "Let's just enjoy our time together today. I don't want to think that far ahead."

"Of course, *cara*," Sal said, brushing her knuckles with his lips. "I'm sorry. I just get so excited about the future when I'm with you." He turned her shoulders toward him.

She looked up into his eyes, the crooked smile. She felt a little overwhelmed; she knew he would try to kiss her, and it scared her, though she didn't know why. "We'd better get back to the group before the guards start thinking I've kidnapped you."

"You have kidnapped my heart," Sal said. He tipped her chin up with his forefinger and kissed her gently on the lips.

She kissed him back and he hugged her close, his arms wrapped all the way around her small body. She pressed herself against him as tightly as she could. "That was nice," she said into his shoulder. She squeezed her eyes tight; wanting to remember this moment. Her first real kiss. It wasn't as scary as she had imagined; it was sweet. He smiled and they were quiet as they slowly walked arm-in-arm, back to the others.

Inside the hall, the girls were watching a movie across the room with a group of men. Rose could hear John Wayne's voice— *Giovanni Weena*, Vincenzo and Sal called him. The Italians were fascinated with American westerns, even though they were all in English. She and Sal sat holding hands on the sofa next to the card table where Marie and Vincenzo were playing a game. Marie looked up at her, arching one eyebrow. Rose wondered if the kiss showed on her face.

That week, Rose threw herself into her work, looking for any possible means she could find to speed up inventory to meet the crazy production schedule Mr. Higgins had demanded. She broke down the whole timeline, from ordering through delivery and warehousing, tracking essential components. She found some unnecessary steps in the process and made recommendations for streamlining. She also found a new vendor in Mississippi for some critical parts, including the propeller shafts. The old vendor was in Indiana; having a new supplier closer by, and initiating some competition between the two companies, would help speed up production *and* cut costs. Every time she figured out another piece of the puzzle, she felt energized. She wanted to help as much as she could, telling herself it was for Laura. But she also wanted to make herself indispensable.

Mr. Sullivan came in, his brow furrowed. "Sorry to interrupt, Rose. I need to talk to you for a moment." He shifted from one foot to another. "Look, I know you don't like to be singled out."

She was instantly concerned, had someone found out about her and Sal? "Have I done something wrong?"

He smiled. "Oh, no, dear. I didn't mean to scare you. It's just that you'll be getting an award at the next all-hands meeting, and I couldn't keep it a secret any longer."

Relief washed over her. "An award for what?"

"For figuring out how to speed up the parts supply to meet our production targets, for saving us money to boot. Your suggestions were brilliant. Mr. Higgins himself will be here for the ceremony. You can invite your family if you want. I know it's hard for them to get away from the store, but they're welcome to come."

Rose felt proud but also a little uncomfortable with the thought of so much attention. "Well, I really don't think I deserve any awards. I'm just doing my job." She looked through the interior office window near her desk to the shop floor below. She thought of Marie in her coveralls and tool belt. "The workers down there, they do the hard work."

"Don't say that again, Rose. You've earned it. All the extra hours. And here's another good thing: the award comes with a little cash bonus too. Treat yourself to something nice."

Rose saw the books and knew they'd given a $25 bonus to a guy from the warehouse last quarter. Maybe she could finally spring for that new dress—and add a little more money to the coffee can.


Lying in her bed that night, Rose closed her eyes and listened to the sounds of the city. The breeze coming through her open window smelled like the river, damp and earthy, and carried a slight whiff of diesel from the ships in the port. She conjured up Sal's face, the feeling of his strong arms around her, that kiss. She knew she should be happy: she was falling in love, proud of her work, enjoying life like Marie did, despite the war. Instead, she had a knot in her stomach all the time. She worried about all the things she couldn't control—whether Sal would be shipped back to Italy soon, her mother's bottomless grief, her sister so far away and in constant danger. And how soon she would have to tell her parents about Sal.

Over the weekend, she had started writing to Laura for advice but couldn't find the right words and ended up tossing the letter. How could she ask Laura for anything when her sister was going through God knows what over there? But Rose couldn't pretend nothing was happening either. Laura had defied their parents and followed her calling. Now Rose wondered what *her* calling was. She'd been the obedient Catholic girl who'd won awards in grade school for her good conduct. As a little girl, she'd listened hard for angels, praying they would visit her like they did her favorite saints, and call her to some great purpose. But they never did. She'd have to figure it out on her own.

CHAPTER

# SIXTEEN

At the all-hands meeting on Friday morning, Rose waited nervously in the front row, where Mr. Sullivan had reserved seats for her family. Her father sat next to her, beaming with pride in his clean white shirt and dark trousers. Aunt Inez sat on her other side. Her mother volunteered to stay behind and look after the store with Carmine. Rose was hurt, but also a little relieved. Her mother was so unpredictable these days; she didn't want any trouble.

Mr. Higgins greeted the workers with a rousing speech about the Allied victories in the Philippines. Photographs were propped up on easels beside the stage: jeeps and tanks rolling off a Higgins boat onto a beach in the Pacific. *Too late for Giovanni.* Rose tried to push the thought away. A small group of musicians from the Higgins Band chimed in with drumrolls and trumpet flourishes. It was all so festive, and Rose tried to relax and take in the moment. She wanted to memorize the details to write to Laura about it later.

"And now we'd like to call up one of your own for a special award," Mr. Higgins said. "Rose Marino—come on up here, little lady." Rose heard him as he turned to a man behind him. "Get Miss Marino a box or something to stand on—they won't be able to see her!"

Rose was mortified, but climbed up on a crate they brought, and looked out over the crowd. She relaxed a little when she spotted Marie smiling up at her.

"Miss Marino here has been an unsung heroine of our recent success," Mr. Higgins said into the microphone.

Rose felt herself flush, the eyes of hundreds of workers on her. She was just an office girl, not a real worker like them. Even so, she did allow herself to feel a little proud.

"Miss Marino has helped us come up with a new inventory system and worked with our suppliers, so we'll always have what we need to meet our ambitious production schedule," Mr. Higgins read from a sheet of paper. "No gaps, no waiting means more boats and quicker delivery."

She looked at Mr. Sullivan and he winked. He must have prepared the remarks for him, she thought. *He was so busy. When did he find time to do that? For me?*

Mr. Higgins looked up from the script and surveyed the crowd. "This is the kind of go-get-'em spirit we need to get these boats to our boys, am I right?" he shouted.

The workers responded, "Yes!" and "Damn right!"

"On behalf of all of us here at Higgins Industries, and I daresay on behalf of our brothers in arms, thank you, Miss Marino. You are this month's Higgins Hero! How 'bout a big round of applause for our girl?" The band played and the audience applauded as Mr. Higgins handed Rose a small wooden plaque. "ROSE MARINO— HIGGINS HERO," it said, with the date and an engraving of a Higgins boat.

Rose saw her father wipe away a tear; it was hard not to choke up too. If not for all the people looking on, she would have. She hadn't been up in front of a clapping assembly since she won the spelling bee in eighth grade. This was different, though—like she'd made a difference in the war. She stood up a little straighter.

"And here's a little something for you, a token of our appreciation," Mr. Higgins said, handing Rose an envelope. "Buy yourself some perfume or maybe a new pair of shoes—if you have the right ration coupons." The crowd laughed.

Rose took the envelope and shook Mr. Higgins' hand. "Thank you, sir," she said. "I was just doing my job, but I'm grateful."

He leaned down. "I know you lost your brother recently, Miss Marino. My condolences, but you honor his sacrifice with your work."

Rose was touched that he knew about Giovanni. "Thank you, sir. That means a lot."

She returned to her seat. Her father leaned over and kissed the top of her head. "I'm proud of you, *cara*. Giovanni would be too," he whispered. Rose pulled her handkerchief out of her pocket and dabbed at her eyes.

"What's in the envelope?" her father asked.

Rose tried to open it discreetly. Inside was a ten-dollar bill.

"Nice!" her father said. "Nobody ever gave me a bonus at the store."

But Rose was disappointed. "The last guy got $25."

"Well, he probably had a family to support. Ten dollars is still a lot of money. And it's the recognition that counts."

Rose nodded. She supposed he was right. Still, it didn't seem fair.

On the way home from work that night, Rose held her plaque on her lap and watched out the window: young boys on bicycles tried to race the streetcar, trucks laden with scrap metal were headed for the salvage yard, an old woman with a cane gingerly made her way along the sidewalk. She replayed the day's excitement, wishing Sal could have been there, as impossible as she knew that was. But for this war, Sal would be home with his family, sketching and practicing his boxing, working on the farm, helping his brother study. Giovanni would be closing up the store with their father right about now, trying to harmonize with the radio with Jake howling in the background. She might be tallying up grocery receipts for the day, making plans to see a movie with Laura and Marie. It was hard sometimes to know how to feel. Not all the changes the war brought were bad. She felt sad for all the dead brothers, the children hiding from bombs over in Europe, the refugees she'd seen in the newsreels, the ruined lives. But she also felt like her life was finally arriving.

Early the following Saturday morning, Rose was stocking a display of eggplant, getting ready to open. She liked this time of day— working in the dim light before the store filled with people—and breathed in the familiar smells: coffee, spices, cheese, and vegetables. Carmine was nearby, unloading crates into the icebox while her father arranged the cold cuts in the glass case and hummed along to the radio. In another half hour, the store would open. Aunt Inez came through the door pulling a pallet of olive salad jars on a red Radio Flyer wagon. She wore a blue-and-white checked blouse, and a royal blue skirt with low-heeled black Mary Janes—about as dressed-down as her aunt ever got.

"*Buongiorno a tutti!*" her aunt called. She gave Rose's father a kiss on the cheek. "Give me a hand with these, would you Rose?"

Rose began unloading the jars. "I'm glad you came today. We were running low."

Her aunt leaned over to whisper in Rose's ear. "I want you to have dinner at Turci's with me tonight. Just the two of us."

"Sure, but what for?" Rose asked.

"Because you're my goddaughter. Do I need any other reason?"

Rose laughed. "No, that would be nice. I can't remember the last time I ate in a restaurant."

"And to celebrate your award. Half past six. Meet me there."

"What are you two yakking about?" Carmine asked, coming up behind them suddenly.

"Well, if it was any of your business, I'd tell you Aunt Inez invited me to have dinner with her tonight. Is that OK with you?" Rose said. She noticed Carmine was getting a little paunch. His white T-shirt stretched tight across his belly.

Her father shot her a look. "Carmine, do me a favor and bring more of the big olive oil cans out from the storeroom."

"Why do you have to talk to him that way?" Rose's father asked when he was gone. "The poor kid." Her father had always had a soft spot for Carmine, alone in America without his parents. And now Carmine's brother Rocco was at war as well. With Giovanni gone, her father had been spending more time with Carmine, smoking cigars in the courtyard almost every night after work. Her cousin was perpetually unhappy, but Rose was fed up with his attitude. She felt like he held a grudge against her for her ambition, the Higgins job. The fact that people liked her.

"Poor kid? Please, Frank," Aunt Inez said. "He lives the life."

"He's always on my back," Rose said. "He treats me like we're still little kids."

"He's just jealous of you," her aunt whispered to Rose.

"He does the best he can," her father said.

Carmine came out carrying two large cans of olive oil, his arms straining and his face red. "Move, Rose," he said. "By the way, what's this I hear you about you and your girlfriends still visiting those *fascisti* over at Jackson Barracks." He was speaking loudly. Rose understood. He wanted to make sure Rose's father heard him.

Rose glared, felt her face turn red. In that moment she could have slapped Carmine. Aunt Inez placed the last jar of olive salad on the pyramid and stepped closer to Carmine. "I've met them," she said. "You're out of line, Carmine. They're nice boys."

"Is that right? Well, I hear Marie is sweet on one of the prisoners," Carmine said. "Real sweet. And that Rose might be too. A boxer or something?"

Rose glanced at her father. He'd stopped moving the cold cuts and was looking at her. "Shut up, Carmine. You don't know what you're talking about."

Carmine feigned offense, raising his hands and making an innocent face. "I'm just repeating what I heard from Doris. You know Doris."

She did know Doris. One of Gilda's gang. She felt the conversation unravelling fast.

"Is it true, what Carmine said?" her father asked. "Have you been seeing one of these Italian prisoners?" He moved closer, hands on his hips.

"We're all just friends," Rose lied. She'd wanted to tell her parents about Sal in her own way, not have Carmine force it out like this. "You know we went back a few times over the summer— Marie, the Battaglia girls, a bunch of others. There was that dance with the church group. There's no secret." She looked at Carmine and he pointed to his eyes, then at Rose.

"Let it go, Carmine." Aunt Inez to the rescue. "Frank, I can vouch for what's going on over there. Not to worry."


After the store closed, Rose changed into a pale pink dress and beige pumps with a low heel. She ran a brush through her hair, put on lipstick, and rummaged in Laura's closet until she found a small hat with a pink ribbon that would work with the outfit. Her father was out at the Italian Hall with Carmine again, and her mother was sitting at the kitchen table alone. Her mother looked tired, her eyes puffy. It had been nearly three months since Giovanni died, and her mother continued to sleep in his room at night. For a moment, Rose pitied her.

"I'm going to meet Aunt Inez for supper."

Her mother gave her a withering look and lit up a cigarette; the smoking habit had stuck. In the past, she would have interrogated Rose, but now she said nothing. Rose wondered if her mother cared what happened to her at all. "I won't be late," she said, as if her mother had asked.

Rose walked the six blocks to Turci's on Bourbon Street. It was a mild evening; the air felt soft, and it was good to be out. Mr. DiGregorio was sweeping the sidewalk in front of his cobbler's shop. He tipped his cap and smiled. A gold star hung in his shop window. The sadness in her heart over Giovanni felt permanent now, but it was oddly comforting to know she wasn't alone.

Rose could smell the garlic a half block before she reached Turci's. She walked into the restaurant through an archway of artificial grapes. Heavy tapestry drapes covered the windows, and it took her eyes a few minutes to adjust to the dim light. On the wall to the left was a huge painted mural with scenes of various Italian landmarks—the Leaning Tower of Pisa, the Coliseum. Photographs of the Turci family with local politicians and celebrities hung behind the hostess stand. Rose spotted Mayor Maestri and the bandleader Benny Goodman in one of the pictures. Italian opera played softly, and Rose heard someone singing along in the kitchen.

The maître d' led her through the restaurant, passing a few couples, a serviceman and his date, their heads almost touching over heaping plates of spaghetti. Aunt Inez sat in one of the banquettes against the back wall, a glass of wine in front of her next to a flickering candle and an ashtray.

"Here she is now," Aunt Inez said to the tuxedo-clad waiter as he lit her cigarette. Her aunt wore a light blue sleeveless dress, a rhinestone broach at the V-neck. Her hair was pinned up and topped by a matching, blue-feathered fascinator. Rose wondered if she'd ever have the confidence to dress so boldly.

Rose leaned in to kiss both her aunt's cheeks. "You look like Bette Davis, *Zia*. I love that dress."

"And you look a little thin, *cara mia*. We need to get some food into you, maybe a little wine too. Mario, bring another glass for my beautiful niece, *per favore*," she told the waiter. "And for dinner just bring us whatever Chef Joe's cooking back there tonight, will you?"

"*Si, signora*," he said and retreated to the kitchen.

"This will be a treat. Papa and I have been doing the cooking," Rose said, settling into her chair. She reached for the basket of bread, next to a dish of olive oil on the white tablecloth. "I don't have the knack for it that Mama does, or you. Maybe you need to give me some lessons."

The waiter poured Rose a glass of wine and left the green bottle on the table. Her aunt touched glasses with her. "To you, *cara*. Congratulations on your award. Well deserved. You make us proud."

Rose took a sip of the wine. She wasn't much of a drinker, but the Chianti tasted rich and smooth. "Thanks, *Zia*."

"How is she, your mother?"

"Still pretty impossible. One minute she's curled up in Giovanni's bed crying, the next throwing things around the kitchen."

"Go easy on her, Rose," Aunt Inez said, tapping her ash. "You can't know what she's feeling. It takes time. You have your work at Higgins to keep your mind occupied. Your mother just has her home; even the store is really your father's, not hers."

"My mother acts like I'm invisible most of the time. She's so bitter and negative when she talks at all."

"She's like that about everything these days. I've tried to get her to snap out of it. But it's like talking to a wall," Aunt Inez said, taking a sip of wine.

"She's mean to Papa too, so I know it's not just me," Rose said, but the thought wasn't a comfort. "I miss Giovanni too. We all do. It's unbearable sometimes. I keep thinking I'm going to wake up and it'll all be a bad dream." The waiter brought a plate of antipasto—brown and green olives, salami and cheese, pepperoncini, and cherry tomatoes. Rose wanted more wine but told herself to slow down. She was already feeling lightheaded.

"Your brother will always be with you, Rose," Aunt Inez said. "I sent a message to my Roberto, to look out for him up there," she pointed to heaven, then blessed herself with the sign of the cross, murmuring, "*L'uomo buono.*" Aunt Inez often called on her dead husband for special favors. "Roberto loved your brother too. Used to put him on his lap and let him pretend to drive the streetcar."

"I wish I had known *Zio* Roberto," Rose said. She wasn't yet born when her uncle died from the flu. "It must have been such a scary time."

"It was. A different kind of fear from what we have now with this war, but very bad. So much death, and you didn't know who was going to catch it next," Aunt Inez said. "And it hit just when we were getting over the first war. Plus, we had that idiot Wilson as president, which made it worse—at least we have Mr. Roosevelt now." She exhaled. "Just thinking about it still riles me up."

Rose dipped a piece of bread into the dish of olive oil. "Do you ever wonder what your life would be like if Uncle Roberto had lived? Or if you had remarried?" Rose realized that sounded bad. "Well, I guess it's not too late for that."

"Never too late. I've had offers over the years," her aunt said. She extinguished her cigarette.

"So why didn't you?" Rose asked.

"I don't have to marry another man to enjoy their company. Nobody ever really measured up. Besides, I'm content just as I am. I have my property to manage, the olive salad business, and

Roberto's little pension from NOPSI. I do what I want when I want to. I don't need permission from anyone, *capiscimi*?"

Rose nodded. It's what she'd longed for—to be her own person. But now there was Sal. The waiter returned and refilled their water glasses. Rose waited until he left to speak. "But don't you want to fall in love again?" She knew she was pushing it, but she really wanted to know. "Don't you get lonely sometimes?"

"Ah, to be young again. Love." Aunt Inez lit a fresh cigarette. She waved her hand. A trail of smoke followed the cigarette between her fingers. "Me? No. I have my cat, I have my friends, and I have you, my precious goddaughter," she smiled, taking a long drag, slowly blowing out the smoke. "And Laura, of course. But what about you? That boy at Jackson Barracks? I saw you blush when Carmine was teasing you this morning. You might be able to fool your father, but not me. What's his name?"

Rose made a little sandwich with a small piece of bread, pepperoni, and cheese. She couldn't help smiling. "Sal. I've seen him a few times. Mama and Papa don't really know about him—yet—so thanks for rescuing me this morning."

"You know your secrets are always safe with me, *cara*. That's what godmothers are for. But why keep it from them? Don't you think they'd approve?"

"I don't know. Every time I think about telling my mother, I feel sick to my stomach."

"You might want to start with your father," Inez said. "Not for nothing—I love your mother, but she's no role model for happiness."

"Plus, I don't know if it's a good idea, what we're doing," Rose said. She wondered what she and Sal were doing. She still wasn't sure. "They were the enemy, right? I feel guilty sometimes. And what if they find out about it at work? I heard Mr. Higgins wasn't too keen on the POWs. What do I say if my boss finds out and asks about Sal?"

Her aunt shook her head. "Admit nothing. It's none of anyone's business what you do on your own personal time."

"I wouldn't want to get in trouble. I really like my job. I want to stay for the duration, and maybe even after that. Mr. Sullivan's been so good to me. He put me in for that award."

"You earned that award," Aunt Inez said. "You do the job, they pay you. Then you go home and live your life. That's how it works. You think they spend one minute thinking about you after they punch out? They don't. It's business." She took a sip of wine. "Plus, they need you. Remember that. Who's going to do that job if they fire you? After the war, it'll be a different story, but it won't have anything to do with Sal. Then it'll be about your cousin Rocco coming home. The men taking over everything again."

Rose took a deep breath. She hated thinking about that, even though she prayed every day for the war to end, for everyone to come home safe. For Laura. Even so, that day wasn't now. Her aunt had a way of seeing things clearly. She wasn't afraid. "You're so smart, *Zia*."

"I'm no smarter than you. Just older and a little wiser," Aunt Inez pinned Rose's hand to the white linen tablecloth. Her voice was gentle, but her eyes held a steely look. "Listen to me. Don't borrow trouble, Rose. See what happens with Sal. Maybe you stick with him, and he sticks with you. Maybe not."

"Thanks for letting me talk about it, *Zia*. Except for Marie— who's not exactly unbiased—I can't really talk to anyone else about this.

Rose's head was spinning a little, whether from the wine or her aunt's words she wasn't sure. The waiter brought two plates of veal ravioli, swimming in a buttery cheese sauce and topped with sprigs of parsley. Such a luxury compared to the dinners she and her father had cobbled together these last few months.

"*Eccola, signorini,*" he presented the plates with a flourish, and refilled their wine glasses.

"*Grazie,*" Rose said, suddenly famished. She took a bite of the ravioli and her mouth watered.

"It's good, right?"

"So good."

"Tell me this: does he make you laugh? Sal?"

"He does," Rose said, looking down and feeling her face flush.

"Be happy. Follow this," Inez said, touching her heart. "And don't worry what other people think. You're a woman now. Nobody else is in charge of your life. Not your parents, not me, not Andrew Higgins, not the nuns—just you."

Rose leaned back, heard people talking softly at the other tables, the clatter of silverware, music drifting from a speaker in the corner.

Aunt Inez pointed her long red fingernail at Rose. "Your life is yours to make." Her aunt raised her glass. "*Saluti.* To Giovanni." They clinked their rims together.

"And to Laura," Rose said.

"To love," her aunt added. "And to the end of this goddamned war."

CHAPTER

# SEVENTEEN

Rose came into the store late Saturday afternoon after running a payment to the bakery. Carmine had the afternoon off; Rose didn't miss him, even though it meant she had to do his share of the work.

"Rose, you're just in time to hear the good news in person," her father said.

Mrs. Fazio was at the counter. "Mrs. Fazio. Nice to see you." Rose put her purse down behind the counter and took her apron from a hook. "What's the news?"

Mrs. Fazio was beaming. "I know you'll be excited too, Rose. We've had a telegram from Richie."

"Oh?" Rose took a clipboard and pencil out from under the cash register.

"He's coming home! Thank God and Saint Michael the Archangel." She blessed herself and kissed her fingertips. "He was wounded, but just enough to send him home for good. I'm not sure of the details. We're just so happy he's on his way back to us."

Rose looked at her father and saw a hint of sadness in his eyes. Giovanni wouldn't be coming back. Rose tried to muster some enthusiasm. "That's great news, Mrs. Fazio." She was genuinely glad for the woman but knew what was coming next.

"And once he's healed up, we'll make sure we get the two of you together, right Frank?" Mrs. Fazio winked at Rose's father.

"I'm sure she'll have all kinds of suitors, but Richie's a good boy," her father said.

Rose shuddered, imagining Mrs. Fazio as her mother-in-law.

"I'd better be going. *Grazie*, Frank." Mrs. Fazio hoisted her shopping bag over her shoulder. "See you *soon*, Rose," she sang on her way out.

"*Ciao*," Rose said, locking the door behind her. She flipped the "open" sign to "closed" and watched through the window until Mrs. Fazio was safely away, then turned toward her father and shook her head.

"You could do worse," he said. He began unpacking hams, roast beef, and turkey breasts from a crate.

"I'd rather join the convent."

Her father raised his eyebrows. "Don't be so quick to judge. The family has money. Undertakers always have business. He'd be a good provider. You'd have a fine home, nice clothes. A comfortable life is important, Rose. Trust me, I didn't have one growing up. You kids take a lot for granted."

Rose bit her tongue. She took the feather duster from the hook and began tidying the shelves. She knew her parents had it hard when they first emigrated to America, staying in overcrowded apartments with other families, sometimes going to bed hungry. Maybe her father was right that she was spoiled. But that didn't mean she had to marry Richie Fazio. Aunt Inez's words came back to her.

"Is that what you were to Mama? A good provider? I always thought you married for love."

"*Si, amore*," her father said, looking down at the hams. "Watch out for that. It'll get you in trouble."

"Good trouble, though, right?" Rose smiled at him. "You really want me to marry Richie Fazio?" Rose asked, her hand on her hip.

He returned to arranging the meat. "All I'm saying is, think a little. Reflect, before you act. The things you decide now can change the rest of your life."

Rose thought about Sal, whether he'd change the rest of her life. Her gut told her he would. She hung up the feather duster and started straightening out the cans on the shelves, facing them forward in even rows. "Papa, when did you know Mama was *the one*?" Rose asked.

He didn't hesitate. "The minute I laid eyes on her. She was in Inez' class, a grade behind me. She was the most beautiful girl I'd ever seen. I just felt it, here." He pointed to his heart.

Rose wondered if he still felt that way. She'd never thought much about her parents' love, how it was when they were young.

Her father cleared his throat. "I proposed three times before she said yes." He looked off toward the front of the store, though nobody was there. "It's not easy to make a marriage work over the long haul. Your mother knew that better than I did, even back then."

Rose began unpacking boxes of macaroni, tallying them up on her clipboard. She thought about what her father was saying. Sal would start off with nothing. Would it be too hard to make a life with him? Suddenly her future seemed like all the figures she entered into the books at the factory: a calculation.

"So Carmine was right?" her father said, as if reading her thoughts.

"Right about what?"

Her father tipped his head to the side the way the dog sometimes did. "This boy at Jackson Barracks. The Italian prisoner."

The question surprised her. Still, she was glad her father had waited until they were alone, without her mother, to have this conversation. Now there was no turning back. "Well, sort of . . ."

"I could tell there was something going on. What's his name?"

Rose blushed. "Salvatore." Somehow saying his name to her father made him more real. "He's a good man. Very kind. From Parma, in the north near Milano."

"Oh, the *north*," her father said, his brows knitted. "I hope he doesn't look down on us like they do."

She moved the empty macaroni carton aside and started helping him with the cold cuts. "No, he's not like that. His family has a small dairy farm there. They sound like simple, hard-working people. Like us."

"And he fought for Mussolini."

"Well, yes. But he was drafted. He fought but his heart wasn't in it—he's not a fascist or anything, Papa."

"But you don't really know anything about him, his family, *cara*. Just whatever he's told you."

Rose felt herself getting angry. Did he really think she was that naïve? "I know how to judge people, Papa."

He held up a hand, his face softening. "You're right, *cara*. My Higgins hero. Just know you'll always be my baby girl, no matter how old you are. I'm used to the boys around here, boys I know. This man who's stolen your heart, he's a stranger. Go ahead, tell me more about him."

Rose handed him a round of pastrami. "He did a little boxing back home, so you and he would have fun talking about that. He's a great dancer and loves music. He's kind and smart. And he's an artist too, does beautiful drawings."

He slid the pastrami into the case, crouching down to push it towards the front. "Well, there's one thing your mother would like. Her sister in Sicily, your aunt Katarina, is an artist."

"I didn't know," Rose said, surprised at another part of her mother's history she'd never heard. "I don't know if Mama would like anyone I picked out for myself."

"I know your mother's tough on you, *cara*, but she loves you in her own way. She just wants what's best for you, to see you settled, once things get back to normal. We both do. Especially now. This war . . ."

Rose took a deep breath. There would be no "normal," ever again. She knew that.

"How can I be settled if she's always trying to keep me in the house? I'm a grown woman. Mama already had Giovanni when she was my age."

"*È vero*," her father said. He stood up. "We were so young."

"You were happy though, right?"

"We were too tired to be happy," he said. He put his hands on his hips, flexing his back with a groan. "And now, Giovanni's gone, and Laura—who knows?" He wiped a rag over the top of the deli case. "Just be sure, Rose. That's all I'm saying. Real life isn't like the movies. Happiness may be as simple as looking across the kitchen table at that person you love, drinking a cup of coffee together without speaking. Just knowing."

Rose was afraid she had made him even sadder, bringing up Giovanni. There was no making up for what they'd lost, but she and Laura marrying and raising families here would make her parents happy.

"I'm going to take a walk down to the market before it closes. I need to pick up a few things."

Rose knew he didn't really need to pick anything up, and that the market was open for another hour. He'd walk down and clear his head, see a few friends, and smoke a cigar. She noticed the dark circles under his eyes. Her mother's gloom was taking a toll on him too.

"Sure, Papa. I'll finish closing up here."

He hung his apron on the hook. He suddenly laughed. "I can't believe it. My baby girl's in love! Seriously though, I want to meet this Salvatore. Set him straight on a few things. Soon, *capisci*?"

"*Capito*," Rose said. "I suppose I should say something to Mama."

He held up a hand. "Let me take care of telling her. Maybe we can invite your Sal and this one Marie's dating to dinner. It would do your mother good to see young men eating her food again."

He left the store, and Rose locked the door behind him. She saw him pause on the sidewalk and light a cigar in the failing light. She wished she could make him happier. She tried to picture Sal in her house, fitting into her world—helping in the store, joking around with her father, maybe even making friends with Carmine over boxing and cars. She knew they would all love him. And he might save her from the likes of Richie Fazio, or worse.

Jake came padding out of the back room and nuzzled against her leg. She reached into the deli case and found a rind of salami. The dog took it from her fingers and wagged his tail. His muzzle had some gray in it now. He was getting older; Giovanni never would. In a couple of years, she would be older than he'd ever be.

CHAPTER

# EIGHTEEN

"The *cucuzza*'s ready," Rose said. She took the black cast-iron skillet off the flame and covered it with the metal lid. "Where's Papa?"

"I wish I knew. He left to get the bread an hour ago," her mother said. "Hurry up and change. They'll be here any minute, and I'm not dealing with them by myself."

Rose was glad to see her mother cooking again. Under her apron, her mother wore a dark green linen dress. She'd finally started making an effort with her appearance too. Rose caught a faint whiff of White Shoulders perfume cutting through the kitchen aromas of lasagna and roasted bell peppers. Rose had wanted a little more modern menu, but her mother insisted on the old family recipes.

In her room, Rose threw her apron over the chair. After weeks of planning this dinner, she'd had a restless night, working through all the possible ways the dinner could go wrong. Her mother was finally out of her funk most of the time, but Rose was still afraid something might set her off. Or maybe there would be some embarrassing talk about Rose's childhood, or her parents wouldn't warm up to Sal. She put on a gray dress with a crimson pinstripe, tight at the waist—it was old but flattering. Aunt Inez had raised the hem and added lace at the collar and cuffs. She had worn her sensible Mary Janes to Mass that morning, but now slipped into her higher heels. She took out her hairpins, letting her black curls fall over her shoulders. She put on a little makeup— enough to look pretty for Sal but not so much that her mother would call her a *puttana*.

That morning before Mass, her father had pushed the parlor furniture to the edges of the room to clear space and brought card tables and folding chairs up from the storeroom. With Sal and Vin, there would be ten for dinner: Marie and her mother, Aunt Inez, Father Tony, plus the guard the men were required to bring. Carmine was not invited. She'd discussed it with her father; he'd conceded. Rose didn't want her cousin's negative attitude adding to her anxiety.

"Ma, I'm going to set these tables for five and five," Rose yelled into the kitchen.

"No. Get *Nonna*'s big tablecloth, Rose. In the bottom drawer," her mother yelled. "Push the tables together to make one. And put the good candlesticks out—make sure they're polished." Rose sighed and dug around in the sideboard for the white tablecloth from the old country, its edges embroidered with tiny flowers. She combined the tables and spread the cloth, placing the candlesticks strategically to hide a couple of red gravy stains. She glanced around the room, wondering how her house would look to Sal. She drew back the heavy drapes and let in the thin winter sun; the wrought iron on the balcony outside cast shadowed stripes on the rug. Everything looked a little shabby, but there was no time to worry about it now.

She'd just finished setting out the silverware, dishes, and glasses when Aunt Inez came in the parlor door with Father Tony. Rose took a deep breath. "*Buona sera*, Father."

"*Buona sera*, Rose," Father Tony said. "Inez let me in downstairs." He shook Rose's hand and looked her in the eyes. He looked sad, his shoulders a little slumped—a far cry from his usual upbeat demeanor. He had changed out of the robes he wore at Mass that morning into his uniform of black pants and shirt, white clerical collar. They had seen him at Sunday Masses, but the priest hadn't been to the house since the day the telegram came about Giovanni.

Aunt Inez held a white box from Brocato's bakery tied with green string. "*Buona sera*," she said.

Rose kissed her aunt on the cheek. "Cannoli?" she asked.

"Of course. Your favorite."

"Ma—Father Tony's here," Rose shouted into the kitchen. *Where was Papa?*

"I'll be there in a minute," her mother called, her voice high and pleasant, almost singing the words.

"Please, have a seat," Rose said to Father Tony. "What can I get you to drink?"

"I'm fine for now, thanks. You go ahead, I know you have a lot to do." The priest sat with a squeak on the sofa. Another fight Rose lost—her mother had refused to remove the plastic cover.

Aunt Inez took off her purple silk jacket with the mink collar—the animal's head and feet still attached. Underneath she wore a black dress, form fitting and low cut, and red high heels. Rose noticed Father Tony's gaze following her aunt.

Her aunt signaled for Rose to step into the hallway. "You look pretty—that dress came out nice."

"Thanks to you," Rose said.

"Are you nervous?" Aunt Inez whispered.

Rose nodded. "I just want everything to go well. I want them to like him."

"Don't worry, *cara*. Deep breaths. All right, I have to say hello to your mother." Aunt Inez said, heading for the kitchen. "*Ciao*, Filomena. Where's Frank?"

"Your guess is as good as mine," Rose's mother replied. She turned her cheek and Aunt Inez gave her an air kiss. Rose saw the flash of judgment in her mother's eyes as she looked over Aunt Inez' outfit.

Rose could hear Marie and her mother coming up the back stairs, laughing at some joke between them. Rose couldn't remember the last time she'd laughed with her mother like that, if ever. Marie came through the kitchen door with a big wooden bowl full of salad. "*Ciao a tutti!*"

"*Buona sera,* Filomena," Mrs. Leonardi said. "We brought the *insalata*. We just have to add the dressing and anchovies."

Rose's mother had her back turned. "That's great, Joanna. *Grazie.*"

Marie's mother touched Rose's arm. "Don't worry, baby," she whispered. "It's going to be fine."

Rose squeezed her hand. The doorbell rang; she felt her stomach tighten. "That's them. Come with me," she said, grabbing Marie's arm.

"Slow down, Rose. Don't trip in those shoes. *Madonna,* you're a bundle of nerves."

Rose paused in the dark of the stairwell. "Truthfully, I can't wait until this is over."

"Relax. If things go well, this will be the first of many Sunday dinners with these boys."

Marie went ahead and opened the gate at the end of the alley. Vincenzo grabbed her up immediately and planted a kiss on her neck.

"Vinny, knock it off!" Marie giggled. "There are parents upstairs, and a priest."

Their escort, Captain Joseph "Giuseppe" Forzani, held two bottles of red wine. "*Ciao,* Rose, Marie. I can already tell this dinner is going to be tough duty." Rose recognized him from the barracks. Forzani was an Italian-American soldier from Boston.

From what Sal said, he was more friend than jailor. The men called him *Capitano Pepino,* short for Giuseppe.

Sal looked at Rose and she felt her heart race. He looked so handsome in his neatly pressed uniform. "Beautiful dress," he said. "*Pronto?*"

She stood on her toes and kissed him on the cheek. "Ready as I'll ever be." She took his hand, guiding him up the narrow back stairs and into the kitchen.

Her mother wiped her hands on her apron and managed a smile. "*Piacere.* It's nice to meet you at last."

Sal shook her mother's hand with a little bow. "*Piacere, Signora.*"

The rest of the men crowded into the kitchen, shaking hands, and introducing themselves in a mixture of English and Italian. Rose's mother said her hellos then shooed everyone into the parlor, where she'd set out olives, cheese, and crackers on the coffee table. Rose was touched her mother was making such an effort. Father Tony had a small glass of an amber-colored drink in his hand. Whiskey? Rose wondered where it had come from.

"Make yourselves at home," Rose said. "We'll be eating dinner soon. *Capitano,* would you mind opening that wine you brought? There's a corkscrew on the sideboard." She worried about where her father was—he would usually be the one to open the wine.

Pepino opened the bottles and poured wine for the men. Meanwhile, Rose's eyes lingered on Sal. He seemed to be taking in every detail of the room. It felt so strange to see him here, in her private world. He blessed himself before the small votive that flickered in front of Giovanni's picture.

Rose went back to the kitchen where Marie's mother was tossing the salad and adding anchovies from a tin. Aunt Inez transferred the *cucuzza* from the skillet into a serving bowl.

"Rose, put the trivet down," her mother said as she pulled a huge glass baking dish out of the oven, her hands wrapped in dishtowels against the heat. Rose put a big terracotta tile on the kitchen table and her mother set the lasagna on it, the mozzarella still bubbling on top.

"Well?" Rose said.

"Well, what? I saw him before, at the barracks, remember? Joanna, you like this Vincenzo? He's good enough for your only daughter?"

"I do. He's a good boy." Mrs. Leonardi added some pepperoncini to the salad. "Treats her like a queen."

"As he should," Aunt Inez piped up. Rose's mother had her back turned, and Aunt Inez held up her thumb and forefinger to Rose, about an inch apart. Little by little.

At last, Rose's father came in through the back door, carrying a bag of bread loaves. "About time," her mother muttered.

"Are they here already?" he asked in a loud whisper.

"Yes, Papa. In the parlor," Rose said. "Where have you been?"

"I ran into some friends. Lost track of time."

"For heaven's sake, put the bread down and go say hello," her mother ordered.

He put the bag on the counter and stood up straight. He wore his good black shirt; Rose could see he'd cleaned up special for the dinner, though she smelled the faint scent of whiskey mixed with his aftershave. Taking his hand, she led him into the parlor, where the men all stood to greet him. Father Tony introduced Vincenzo and Pepino, then looked at Rose.

She took a deep breath. "Papa, this is Salvatore. Sal, this is my father, Frank."

"*Piacere,*" Sal said, shaking hands firmly with Rose's father.

"*Piacere, Salvatore. Come stai?*" her father said. "Rose tells me you're a boxer. You like the heavyweights?"

Rose thought her father sounded nervous, which surprised her. She wanted so much for him to love Sal as she did.

184

Sal hesitated. "Well, this may be the wrong answer, but I'm not a big guy so I like the middleweights. Jake Lamotta, Sullivan Giordano—I think you call him Young Corbet the third."

Rose's father narrowed his eyes, then clapped Sal on the shoulder. He was smiling. "You've done your homework. OK, Rose, he can stay."

Sal pretended to wipe his brow in relief and laughed. Meanwhile, Rose looked from her father's face to Sal's and exhaled.

"Looks like you boys are ahead of me," her father said. "Where's the wine?" They all chuckled, and Sal moved to pour him a glass.

Rose's mother, Aunt Inez, and Mrs. Leonardi brought all the platters and bowls into the parlor at once. "*Tutti si siedono*, everyone. Sit, please. Dinner is served," Rose's mother said.

The women sat first, leaving space for Vin to sit next to Marie and Sal next to Rose. Rose noticed Pepino held out the chair for Aunt Inez before taking the seat next to her. Father Tony sat at one end of the table and Rose's father at the other, Sal to his right.

"Father, would you please say grace?" Rose's mother asked as she lit the candles. Her face looked softer in the glow of the flames. For a moment, Rose could imagine the young woman her mother had once been.

"Of course," Father Tony said, standing. Everyone bowed, hands folded. "Let us pray. Heavenly father, we ask you to bless the food we are about to eat and the hands that made it. Thank you for bringing us together. We also take a moment to remember those who are not with us. Laura, that the Lord might keep her safe and bring her back to her family soon."

Rose so wished Laura could be at the table today. She needed an ally; Marie would be preoccupied with Vinny. Even Aunt Inez was turning her attention to Pepino.

Father Tony cleared his throat and took a sip of water, holding up one finger. Rose felt her father jiggling his leg under the table. "*Mi scusi,*" the priest continued. "And of course, we pray for dear Giovanni, who is always in our hearts, and for all the souls of the faithful departed. In the light of your everlasting grace, dear Lord, we give thanks. Amen. Now, let's eat!"

"Amen," everyone answered, hands flashing the sign of the cross as they began reaching for the food.

"Wait, *aspetta!*" Rose's father said. He pushed his chair back and stood, raising his wine glass. "A toast to our special guests: Vincenzo, Salvatore, and you too, Pepino." He looked at each of them in turn. "We are all Italians, after all. You are welcome in our home. *Saluti.*" He raised his glass, clinked it with Sal's first, then reached around him to Rose, winking at her.

"*Saluti!*" They all touched their glasses together.

"*Now*, let's eat," Rose's father said.

Rose's mother smiled as the men complimented her food and Rose breathed a little sigh of relief; she'd feel calmer if her mother stayed happy. Sal fell into conversation with Rose's father, a mix of Italian and English as they spoke of boxing, cooking, music, and art. "What do you think you'll do after this is all over?" her father asked.

"I daydream about that all the time," Sal said. Rose looked down at her food. "I love to cook. I think I'd like to open my own restaurant."

Rose looked at him—this was news to her. Was Sal just trying to curry favor with her father? He knew how important food was to her family.

"You mean in Italy or here?" her father asked.

"I guess that depends on some things that are out of my control," Sal said, glancing at Rose.

Rose could feel the heat rising to her cheeks but kept quiet. She knew Sal meant her as much as he meant the Army's plans. Her father started talking about the new restaurants opening in the French Quarter and how popular Italian cooking had become with the Americans. Rose ate a forkful of lasagna and sipped her wine. She turned to find Pepino deep in conversation with Aunt Inez, their voices low. She thought they might be about the same age; Pepino wasn't wearing a wedding ring.

He leaned back, taking notice of Rose. "You should both come up to Boston and visit," he said. Rose thought of Laura's doctor; he was from up north somewhere too. Maybe Boston as well. "In the summer, though," Pepino added. "I don't think you Southern ladies would like the winters up there. You're such delicate blossoms."

"Hah!" Aunt Inez said. "If you only knew how fiercely things grow here. Rose, be a dear and get some more wine for us while I explain a few things to the captain."

Rose went to the wine rack for another bottle. As she was pulling the cork, she saw Father Tony at the other end of the table, telling a story to Marie, her mother, and Vinny. She couldn't make out what he was saying, but they all laughed. Vinny's plate was already clean. He had his arm on the back of Marie's chair, his fingers lightly caressing the nape of her neck. Marie's mother didn't seem to mind, and it occurred to Rose that Vin might somehow have found a way to spend more time at Marie's house than she knew.

Marie caught Rose's eye, tossed her head in Sal's direction. Rose's mother was filling Sal's plate with a second helping of lasagna. She looked younger, more alive than she had in a long while. Rose saw her father gazing at her mother, a small smile on his lips, and she remembered his words in the store. *She was the most beautiful girl I'd ever seen.*

The room felt full of life and chatter, the table complete, like it had been before the war, when Giovanni would bring his friends home for supper. Her mother would complain about the extra

187

work, but Rose knew she loved few things more than fussing over hungry young men, laughing and telling stories at her dinner table. Rose refilled a few more wine glasses. It was good to see her parents so happy. She'd made that happen by bringing Sal here.

As the dinner wound down and people started to push back from the table, Sal stood and raised his glass. Rose felt a tightness in her chest, not knowing what he was about to say.

"One more toast," he said in his best English. "To America. And to Signore e Signora Marino. We are grateful for your hospitality and a taste of home. *Mille grazie.*" Another round of glass-clinking.

Rose squeezed Sal's leg under the table when he sat back down. "That was perfect," she whispered in his ear. She was grateful he was making such an effort.

After coffee and dessert, Aunt Inez and Marie's mother cleared the table while Rose's father led the men down to the courtyard for a cigar. Father Tony declined and said his goodbyes. "Filomena, could you walk me out?" he asked Rose's mother. Marie shot Rose a look.

Her mother took off her apron and smoothed her dress. "Rose, you and Marie start on the dishes," she said, handing Rose a damp *mapine.* "I'll be right back."

Rose washed the dishes while Marie dried. Through the open window above the sink, they could hear the men's conversation and laughter wafting up with the cigar smoke. She looked down into the courtyard and saw Sal, Vin, and Pepino standing around her father. He was telling one of his old jokes—the one about the talking donkey—no doubt happy for a new audience.

"I think your parents like Sal, don't you?" Marie asked.

"Yes, I think so," Rose said, her hands deep in the soapy water as Aunt Inez and Marie's mother brought in more plates.

"What's not to like?" Mrs. Leonardi said.

"Seems like he'll fit right into the family," Aunt Inez said. "How about some music?" She turned on the kitchen radio and the Andrews Sisters sang "Don't Sit Under the Apple Tree" as the women worked.

Rose splashed some water on her apron as she pulled a big pot out of the sink. She took a deep breath. Sal *would* fit right into the family. It was almost too easy. She handed the pot to Marie to dry and had an image of doing this exact thing, at this sink, ten years from now, with Marie's children and hers running around the apartment, her parents spoiling them with treats. She knew that should make her happy, but it just made the little kitchen feel even smaller and hotter.

Rose's mother came back just as they were finishing up. "Can you girls handle things in here? I need to lie down for a few minutes."

"You OK, Ma?" Rose asked. Her mother looked pale, and Rose wondered what Father Tony had said to her. She'd been seemed so happy just a little while ago.

"Yes, dear. I think all the excitement just got to me." Her smile looked forced. "Your young man is lovely. A good eater too." High praise.

It was the first time in months her mother had spoken to her so kindly, and Rose gave her mother a hug. "Dinner was great, Ma. You were right to make the lasagna. Thanks for everything. You go rest."

"I will," Rose's mother said. "Marie, Joanna, thanks for all your help. You too, Inez."

The women said their goodbyes. Rose put away the candlesticks and pulled the tablecloth off to go in the wash. All she had wanted from this dinner was for her parents to like Sal, and for him to feel comfortable with them. *Seems like he'll fit right into the family,* Aunt Inez had said. Like a puzzle piece, Rose thought. She thought about all the times her mother and father had laughed tonight. They'd never stop missing Giovanni, but Sal could help fill the hole in their hearts. Rose didn't realize until tonight how much she'd needed that too. Now she had the power to keep it this way—as long as Sal was in her life.

CHAPTER

# NINETEEN

*May 1945*
*Germany*

*Dear Rose,*
*Thanks for your last letter, which finally got to me this week. We've moved around so much over the last couple of months the Army post office has a hard time keeping up. I loved hearing all about your fella Sal. Sounds like he's become a regular part of the family.*

*So much has happened since the last time I wrote, I don't even know where to begin. The best part (besides Nicholas—I'll get to him in a minute) was V-E Day, last week. We stayed up most of the night listening to the radio. Someone dug up a bottle of schnapps and we celebrated, though it was bittersweet. Everyone's happy about the war ending over here, but we're still sad about President Roosevelt, and can't help thinking about all those we've lost—friends, patients, colleagues. I cried myself to sleep just as the sun was coming up, thinking about Giovanni and all the boys who came into our wards and never made it out. And they're still at it in the Pacific, of course.*

*I don't know how much news you're getting over there about what the Germans did. The fighting, bombing, wounded men—all of it was hell. But none of that prepared us for what we saw in April.*

*The scene was so gruesome, I don't even want to describe it to you. Thousands of human beings, starving and sick. Thousands more dead, just in this one camp. I'm sorry to burden you with this, Rose, but people need to know the truth. I expect pictures and footage will make their way to you. Prepare yourself, Rose. Pure evil. The whole experience makes me wonder how God could let this happen to so many innocent people, just because they were Jewish. Jesus was a Jew himself, after all.*

*We were all pretty shaken up afterward, so the Army gave us four days of R&R. Nicholas borrowed a jeep so we could drive to Paris. We did all the touristy things—the outdoor cafés, the Champs Elysees, and of course the Eiffel Tower you see behind us in the picture. The language and the food reminded me of New Orleans. Finally, a chance to try out my high school French. It was so lovely— flowers blooming, peace at last—even if it felt a little empty still. A lot of Parisians haven't yet returned from wherever they fled during the war.*

*Meanwhile, a lot of my friends got their points (how we earn time off or discharge) and shipped out for home. Nurse McCarthy's back in New York and my friend Frances took an assignment in the Pacific. Her strength inspires me. I miss her already. Tomorrow I have school, believe it or not. A crash course in tropical medicine Nicholas and I both signed up for. I have enough points to come home, but I just can't give up now, especially after what we saw at Buchenwald. They need us in Asia, and we want to see this thing through. If Japan doesn't give up soon, we'll be shipping out to Hawaii in July. I've written to Mama and Papa to let them know, so you can act surprised when the V-mail comes. Nicholas and I hope to get a posting together, though that's usually just for married couples. Who knows—we might just have to elope!*

*It's lights-out, so I'll sign off. Give Aunt Inez a hug for me, and scratch Jake behind the ears. Be good to yourself, Rose.*

*Ti amo,*
*Laura*

Irma wheeled her cart into the mailroom and smiled. "Good morning, Rose."

Rose looked up from Laura's letter, slid the picture back into the envelope and put it in her purse. "Good morning, Irma. How're you doing?" She tried to shake off all the news in Laura's letter: the horrors of the death camps, her sister's growing romance with Nicholas. It was like this every time she received a letter—so much to take in at once.

"Can't complain, I guess. Got any plans for the weekend?" Irma asked, as she sorted mail from a large canvas bag. Her hands worked swiftly, her eyes flitting from Rose to the letters and packages, and back again. She held out a stack of envelopes. "For Mr. Sullivan."

"Thanks. Actually, I do. A bunch of us girls are going to Pontchartrain Beach. I hope I'm brave enough to go on the new Zephyr." No need to mention the POWs, Rose thought. The fewer people who knew, the better.

"That sounds like fun," Irma said. She shook the gray bag out, and one more letter dropped onto her lap. She snapped it up, looked at it briefly, and filed it in the proper slot. "I used to take Alfred to Lincoln Beach when he was a boy. He couldn't get enough of those rides. Of course, they weren't anything like what you folks have at Pontchartrain, but he loved them anyway."

Rose didn't know much about Lincoln Beach. It had always been there, of course, but now that she thought about it, it didn't make sense that there were two separate amusement parks. Irma worked at Higgins, just like her. Her son was fighting the same war as Giovanni and Laura. It made Rose angry to think that Irma and her family had to settle for less. "Any word from Alfred?" she asked.

"We had a V-mail last week. He never says too much. Misses my red beans."

"Giovanni was the same way."

"But I don't care, as long as I hear from him. I keep thinking about your brother, God rest his soul. I count my blessings every day."

Rose turned so Irma wouldn't see the sudden tears that welled up in her eyes. It had been over ten months now, but every time she thought the grief was behind her, something reminded her that Giovanni was never coming back, and she was right back in it. "I'll say an extra prayer for Alfred at Mass on Sunday," she said.

Rose walked through the factory floor, which was still humming along. V-E Day was a month ago, but the war still raged in the Pacific. Some days, it felt like it would go on forever, especially now that President Roosevelt had died. They'd had another big order from the Navy, and they were so busy the Industrial Canal plant had to take the overflow. She waved to coworkers she knew by name now; so many had lost a loved one too. She wondered how they got through their days, how often they thought about their husbands, brothers, fathers. She tried to put her grief away, like she did with Laura's letters, in a box in her heart.

Back at her desk, she took the little black-and-white snapshot from the envelope and held it under her desk lamp. Laura and Nicholas in front of the Eiffel Tower. Her sister looked thinner, but so pretty. Her hair was longer now, and wind-blown. She looked directly into the camera, a little blur where her hand was moving into the pocket of her trousers. She wore a buttoned blouse and a jaunty scarf at her throat. Nicholas wore an

194

Eisenhower jacket and a crew cut. He looked smitten, his head turned slightly, his eyes on Laura's face. Her sister looked confident, strong, unafraid. Laura was making her own way, choosing marriage, but also her work. With Nicholas she could have both. Rose wondered whether she and Sal could ever be like that—partners in love and in life.

Sunday morning dawned bright and sunny, a perfect day for the beach. Rose had gone to early Mass by herself and was changing into a yellow-and-white seersucker dress. She tucked her swimsuit and a towel into a satchel and studied her face in the mirror. Her skin was clear, her hair shining. Her dark curls were a little unruly, as usual, and she caught them up in a white kerchief. She didn't want to put on a lot of makeup; it would only run off in the water and she'd look a mess. Just a little pink lipstick. She felt a small shiver, knowing Sal would be kissing those lips later.

The men were technically still prisoners, but the Army had eased restrictions enough to allow an outing to Pontchartrain Beach today. Her parents had invited Sal, Vincenzo, and other POWs over several times for dinner; Rose could see they were getting attached to Sal, her father in particular.

Rose walked up Dauphine Street, excited to finally go on a date with Sal, like a normal couple. Until now, they'd only seen each other at Jackson Barracks and at her house for dinner. She told herself to relax and have fun, to let go of her worries about work, her parents, the war.

Marie greeted her at the corner of Esplanade with a wave. Her friend wore a sleeveless red-and-white-striped wrap dress that accentuated her curves. "It's a great day for a great day!"

"Beautiful," said Rose. "It's been so long since I've been to the beach."

They walked two blocks to the Italian Hall. The women were gathering on the sidewalk, their purses and sweaters hanging from the ears of the stone lions that guarded the front steps. Rose scanned the crowd. The four Battaglia sisters stood together in their lovely matching dresses. Meanwhile, Marguerite Graffagnini stood with her clipboard, her bright red hair up in a topknot. Marguerite ran the Ladies Auxiliary at the Italian Hall and had organized the outing. She was dating one of the POWs too, a shy boy named Mario.

Of course, there was Gilda and her gang. *They* hadn't spared the makeup and looked like they were on their way to a fancy party. Gilda wore a low-cut orange flowered dress and matching pumps. She looked Rose and Marie up and down and laughed. Rose felt her face flush.

"You look like you've just come from milking the cows, Rose. Your boy Sal must like the down-home look, huh?" Her friends giggled.

Rose felt her face go hot. She glared at Gilda, struggling to find an appropriate comeback, angry with herself that she couldn't.

"Better a farm girl than a *puttana*," Marie snapped.

"Oooohhh," said Gilda's friends in unison.

Gilda stepped up close to Marie, an ugly sneer on her face. "*Really,* Marie? Who's the *puttana?* I saw you at Jackson Barracks last week, mugging it up with that boy Vincenzo." She poked her finger at Marie's chest. "I see you're not leaving anything up to his imagination, as usual."

Rose panicked, thinking Marie might actually slap Gilda. Once, back in high school, she had.

Marguerite interrupted, stepping between the two women with her sign-up sheet. "*Buongiorno*, ladies," Marguerite said in a singsong voice. "Rose, Marie, you both look lovely. I'll just check you off the list. Thanks for coming."

196

Gilda brushed the backs of her fingers under her chin, dismissing Marie with the crude gesture. She looked at Rose and pulled down the skin under her eye. *Watch out.*

Rose tried to pretend the meanness couldn't reach her.

On the bus, a hot breeze came in through the open windows. The green vinyl seat stuck to the back of Rose's legs, and she shifted to straighten out her dress so it wouldn't wrinkle too much. Marie was sitting next to her, unusually quiet and probably plotting some sort of revenge on Gilda. After a drive to the end of Elysian Fields Avenue, the bus rolled through the grand metal archway marking the entrance to Pontchartrain Beach. Rose saw the big lake glittering on the horizon. The parking lot was already filling up with cars full of families with their picnic baskets and beach toys. School was out for the summer, so there were a lot of children. Rose tried to push the unpleasantness with Gilda out of her mind; she was excited to see Sal and finally have the chance to share a fun day at the beach and amusement park. He'd been through so much, and she wanted him to have some joy and relaxation today.

The girls filed into the locker room to change. Rose quickly zipped up her bathing suit. The skirt came almost to her knees and as usual the blousy top was too large for her. If her seersucker dress was "down-home," the old swimsuit was flat-out ugly. Across the room Gilda was wearing a white form-fitting one-piece with a ruffle at the waist. She filled it out in all the right places and stood in her orange pumps, posing like a pin-up model. She caught Rose looking at her and smirked, tossing her long brown hair to one side. In that moment, Rose hated her more than she hated Hitler.

Meanwhile, Marie was stuffing herself into a suit. "Oof! I tried it on at home—I know I can make it work," she said.

Rose reached over and tucked the tag in at the back. "I love that suit. Mine is just awful," Rose whispered. "Sal's going to take one look at me and run away."

"Don't be ridiculous, Rose. You look fine," Marie said. "He'll think you're a modest Catholic girl, someone he can bring home to Mama." Rose wasn't sure whether that was a compliment.

They headed across the footbridge over the amusement park midway and onto the beach. Bright blue-and-white-striped umbrellas dotted the sand, and children dug with pails and shovels. The water lapped at the shore in little wavelets. Everything seemed so peaceful, almost as if the war didn't exist. Rose and Marie laid their towels down and looked around for the men. "Guess they're not here yet," Marie said.

Rose lay back and closed her eyes, letting the sun warm her face. The gulls cawed overhead, and children squealed, playing at the water's edge. Her brother had taught her how to swim in this lake a lifetime ago. She remembered going to West End when she was a little girl, before they built the new beach and moved the amusement park. In her mind's eye, Giovanni and Laura held her hands as they all ran toward the water, their little feet digging into the soft sand, Papa calling after them, *vai piano-piano. Keep an eye on your sisters, son.*

"*Buongiorno, belle signorine!*" Vincenzo's voice boomed, pulling her from the daydream.

Rose looked up, shielding her eyes from the bright sun. Sal stood next to Vincenzo, staring down at her. She sat up and straightened out her bathing suit. Sal reached down his hand to help her stand. Marie struggled to her feet with Vin's help, and he kissed her on the cheek. Sal raised Rose's fingers to his lips.

In their sunglasses and floppy green hats, the men didn't look like prisoners. They looked American. "They brought us in the Army trucks," Sal said. He kept holding her hand, and she felt the calluses on his fingers from his job unloading crates at the port. His palm was warm, soft, and a little sweaty. "It was a rough ride, but we're glad to be here."

"Where are the escorts?" Marie asked.

"Over there somewhere," Sal said, pointing to a group of men further down the beach. "They're not too worried, I guess."

"The last time we were on a beach, someone was shooting at us," Vincenzo said, holding an invisible gun to his shoulder. "This is much better. The water looks beautiful. Let's swim!"

Sal and Vin stripped off their shirts and shoes, placing their sunglasses and hats on the pile. The men, both tanned and fit, wore baggy Army shorts that came to their knees. Marie and Rose exchanged a smile. Sal tugged Rose by the hand, and they ran barefoot across the hot sand. He pulled her close as they splashed into the waves.

Vin gave Marie a little shove, just enough for her to lose her balance and slide under the water for a minute. "My hair!" she cried. "*Sei cattivo!* Mean! You'll pay for that." She splashed water at him, and he dove into the waves and swam away from her. She stood in the knee-deep water and wrung out her red kerchief. Rose and Sal laughed.

Rose spotted Gilda standing with her girlfriends in the ankle-deep water a short distance away. Sal didn't seem to notice. "Ready?" he asked. Rose nodded and sunk down, happy to let the cool water cover her body and the ugly swimsuit. Sal dove under and propelled himself out in front of her. The lake was shallow, but Rose knew she'd quickly be in over her head. She swam with smooth, even strokes, the way her brother had taught her. She lost track of where Sal was, then bumped right into his legs.

"Hey!" he said, catching her under the arms. Her feet couldn't touch bottom, so she was forced to let him hold her up. "You're so light, like a little wet mouse—don't worry, I've got you, my *topolino.*"

Rose flinched at the nickname, but when he looked at her with flecks of gold in those hazel eyes she relaxed. "You're a strong swimmer for a farm boy."

"We had a pond near our house. My brothers and I used to race each other across it. This water is different—very salty. It feels nice, though." He hugged her closer. "Very nice."

A little further out in the waves, Rose saw Vin holding Marie in his lap as they floated, him nuzzling the back of her neck and Marie giggling. She couldn't see their hands, but she could imagine where they were. Rose's face was just inches from Sal's bare chest; she wasn't sure what to do or say. She reached up to touch his shoulder, caressed it gently then squeezed his muscled arm lightly. "*Forte,*" she said. "So strong." She wondered if he could hear her heart thumping over the sound of the waves. He pulled her in even closer. She could feel him stiffen against her, but she didn't try to back away. His eyes closed, he tilted his head back and the sun glinted off his tan face. She leaned into him just a bit more. Except for dancing, she'd never been this close to a man before. And he was half naked. Rose was pretty sure this counted as the "near occasion of sin" she remembered from the *Baltimore Catechism*. She didn't care and kissed his chest lightly. This was worth a few more years in purgatory.

"*È così bello,*" Sal said. "Feels nice." He ran his fingertips down her back, and she shivered. "You're cold," he said.

"*Sì,*" she lied—it wasn't the cold making her shiver. She felt the weight of his body against hers, the water flowing around them as they made a little island together. "I think we'd better get back on land." He let her drop gently back into the water. She could feel his reluctance to turn her loose, and she liked the feeling of being desired. She wanted him too but knew this was about as close as they could get. For now.

Back on the beach, Rose and Marie sat on their blankets watching the men kick a ball around with some children, shouting and laughing, free men for the day. Sal looked graceful, his strong legs pumping as he ran. He had filled out since she first met him. She saw the muscles of the boxer he'd been back home.

"They look like big kids themselves," Marie said. "It's nice to see them so relaxed."

"I know," said Rose. "Like normal men."

"They *are* normal men. And look at Sal, how good he is with those boys. So patient. He'll make a great father."

"Don't you think that's getting a little ahead of things?" Rose asked, even though she'd been thinking the same thing.

"I saw you two lovebirds in the water. He's crazy about you," Marie said. "And your parents love him too. Even your mother."

"We're just dating, Marie. We're not as serious as you and Vin." The words felt false, but she had so little experience with relationships. "Dating" she could handle; "serious" made her nervous.

Marie rolled her eyes. "Say what you want. Everybody can see how you two look at each other. What are you so afraid of?"

"Nothing."

"Could've fooled me. I *know* you Rose, in case you've forgotten."

Rose thought about how Sal's body felt against hers. The physical attraction was undeniable, and they connected in other ways too. He was kind and thoughtful, they shared a love of music and dancing, and he seemed to genuinely enjoy being around her parents. So why did she feel a nagging reluctance too? She loved her life as it was, riding the streetcar to work every day, making a difference at the shipyard, seeing Sal on Sundays. She tried not to think too far ahead about what came next: marriage, working in the store, changing diapers—her mother's life. She knew it was what she was supposed to want, but whenever she tried to picture it, her mind went blank. Maybe there was something wrong with her.

"I don't want to just go from depending on Mama and Papa to depending on some man," Rose said. Of course, she wanted the war to end, and it would. Even more reason to keep working, she told herself, to make the most of her job for the duration, to keep adding as much money to the coffee can as possible, so she'd have options.

"That's where we're different, Rose. I can't *wait* to quit my job and start a family," Marie said. "I guess I shouldn't be surprised—I remember when we were kids, you always looked up to the nuns and those saints of yours, giving up their lives for the poor and whatnot."

What Marie said was true. She'd loved the *Lives of the Saints* stories about the female martyrs—Saint Catherine, Saint Cecilia, Saint Lucy. None of them were married with children.

Marie rolled over to face Rose and propped herself up on her elbow. "My dream would be to have a place big enough for Ma to move in with us, where she could put her feet up and play with the grandbabies."

"You mean here or in Italy?"

Marie fanned herself with her hand. "Oh, here. Vinny's got plans to open his own barber shop. We'd live upstairs with Ma. I think he'd be a good husband and father. I'd be crazy to let him get away."

This was the first Rose was hearing about Vinny's plans. Rose assumed Marie had been telling her everything, but apparently not. Or maybe she just hadn't been paying attention, too caught up in her own life.

"What does your mother think of all this?" Rose asked.

"Ma loves Vinny as much as I do. She wants me to be happy."

"She doesn't think you're too young?"

"No. She was my age when she married my father," Marie said, brushing sand off her arm.

"I'm glad for you, but—"

"Look at him, Rose," Marie pointed her chin toward Sal. "You really think you're going to do better than that?"

The question didn't fit into Rose's thinking. Was she really looking for a "better" man? "I wish I could meet him ten years from now."

"Ten years! I thought you were supposed to be good at math," Marie said, sitting up. "You'll be an old maid by then! I thought we were gonna have our kids grow up together, our husbands be best friends. This is our chance, Rose. Don't blow it!"

Rose smiled, trying to lighten the mood. But Marie looked serious and upset. Rose looked out at Sal, now back in the water playing catch with Vincenzo and the kids. Maybe Marie was right. Sal was a fine man; he could have his pick and had chosen her from among all the girls. If she didn't jump at the chance now, would she regret it later? Would she end up a lonely old spinster, or worse, married to some *cafone* from the neighborhood, a leftover that nobody else wanted?

"Here comes trouble," Marie said. Rose looked toward the lake. Gilda was strolling by with two of her henchwomen. They stopped at the water's edge. A ball came flying out of the surf and Gilda bent to pick it up—slowly and deliberately so Sal and Vin could get a good look at her backside—then threw the ball back to them. Rose panicked a little, remembering Gilda's hand on Sal's shoulder at that first dance.

"A good man like that won't be alone for long," Marie said. "Think about it, Rose. You can't have it both ways."

Rose and Marie changed back into their dresses in the bathhouse and met Sal and Vin on the Midway. Except for the green oval *ITALY* patch on their sleeves, they looked like any other servicemen on R&R with their girls. A few passers-by even said, "God bless you, boys," and "Thank you for your service." They ordered hot dogs and beer, which Rose and Marie insisted on paying for. The men started to protest, though they didn't have much money. The army only paid them $15 per month for their work at the Port of Embarkation, loading and unloading cargo.

"I'm embarrassed," Sal said. "We can barely afford cigarettes." Rose knew Sal sent most of his money home to his parents; she didn't mind paying.

"It's OK—you'll just owe us," Marie winked.

"Let's try the rides," Vincenzo said. "We never had anything like this back home."

They walked through the Cockeyed Circus, a fun house Rose didn't find all that fun, with its mirror maze, moving floors, and the air jets that blew up the ladies' skirts as they exited. She held down her dress. Marie, of course, got a big kick out of it and stood laughing over the grate, her red bloomers shining out from under her skirt. Rose watched Vincenzo—he couldn't take his eyes off her friend.

On the carousel, Rose spotted Gilda, sitting behind one of the other POWs on his horse, pressing her big bust against his back. As they got off the ride, he pinched her bottom. She giggled and gave him a playful slap on the arm, wagging her finger at him. Rose felt a little nauseated.

"OK, enough of this baby stuff," Marie said, climbing down from her own horse. "Time for the Zephyr!"

"Oh, I don't know . . ." Rose stammered. As a girl, she had always shied away from the thrill rides at the old park. She'd watch as Giovanni and Laura climbed on and were swept so high up in the air, wishing she were brave like them.

Sal looked at her and cocked his head. "Don't be afraid, *topolino*," he said. "I won't let anything happen to you."

She took a deep breath and nodded once, taking his hand as they walked toward the giant wooden roller coaster. He seemed so sure of himself, so strong.

As the coaster car click-clacked slowly up the steep slope, Rose gripped the safety bar and held her breath. Sal put his arm around her, and she leaned into him. The car paused at the top. Except for the bridge over the Industrial Canal, there were no real hills in New Orleans, so she had never seen the city from this perspective. On the right were the giant lake and the cypress marshes to the east. On the left were the pastureland of Gentilly and the mighty Mississippi River shining beyond. A whole world waited over that horizon.

The car lurched forward and zoomed down the hill, so fast Rose's stomach dropped. Sal pulled her closer and she buried her face in his shoulder. A few more ups and downs, then it was over. As they rolled into the offloading area, Rose opened her eyes. Sal was smiling at her, and she tried to muster a smile back. She was a little queasy, but relieved to be back on the ground, and grateful for his strong arms around her.

"I told you I would protect you, *topolino*," Sal whispered. He kissed the top of her head, just like her father always did.

The sun was low and a cooling breeze off the lake riffled Rose's dress as they made their way out of the park. She and Sal walked arm in arm, following Marie and Vin toward the parking lot. Several of the other women were saying goodbye to POWs and soldiers, and the chaperones were milling around, trying to herd the girls onto the buses and the men to the Army trucks. Rose spotted Gilda with one of the other POWs. He took a silver flask from his pocket and handed it to her. She took a swig, then leaned over and kissed the man hard on the lips.

Marguerite clapped her hands, trying to get the women on the bus. The Army truck drivers were blowing their horns now. Sal pulled Rose close in a tight hug. "This has been one of the best days of my life, *mio topolino*," he said into her ear. "*Grazie.*"

It was the longest they had spent together. It had been wonderful for her too. She was reluctant to let him go, and pulled him a little closer, hoping Gilda was watching. "It was fun, like normal people."

"That's what I want," Sal said. "To be normal people. A family, a home. Simple things. That all seems so far away, except when I'm with you."

Rose felt thrilled yet a little scared, like she had when he was pressed up against her in the water—the same queasiness she'd experienced on the roller coaster. He kissed her lips gently, gave her hands a final squeeze, and she watched him walk off. He looked at her one last time over his shoulder before he got on the truck.

Rose spotted Gilda near the bus, watching Sal as well. She leaned over to whisper something to her friend. It made Rose want him even more. Marie was right; she couldn't have it both ways. She would have to decide. And soon.

CHAPTER

# TWENTY

Monday morning in her office, Rose still felt the glow from the outing to Pontchartrain Beach: Sal's hands on her body, his lips brushing her neck. She looked at the figures in front of her for the fourth time. Scraps of their conversation kept interrupting her attempts to add up the column on the monthly inventory report. *I want to be normal people. A family, a home.*

"Rose."

She dropped her pencil and looked at Mr. Sullivan across the short distance between their desks. He peered at her over the rim of his reading glasses, sweat beading on his forehead and an unlit cigarette tucked behind one ear. "Sorry to interrupt, but I've had some news this morning." He mopped his brow with a handkerchief.

It was hot in the office, but she wondered if he was also upset about something. She'd seen Rocco's parents at Mass the previous Sunday and heard her cousin was on his way home from France. She was happy he'd survived the war in one piece but wondered how long it would be before he reclaimed his job. Her job. Mr. Sullivan was patting his pockets. Rose opened a desk drawer where she kept a spare book of matches and tossed them to him.

"Thanks," he said and lit his cigarette. He pointed vaguely in the direction of the new plant. "They're almost finished building the expansion over at the Industrial Canal."

"That was awfully fast." The Higgins workers were so good at building boats that the Air Force had taken note, and now wanted cargo planes for the Pacific.

"Mr. Higgins himself called me this morning. He wants me to take over their procurement office for the duration."

Rose tried to read his face while she processed the thought of losing Mr. Sullivan as her supervisor. He was a handful sometimes, but he treated her with respect, and they worked well together. The thought of breaking in a new boss felt a little daunting. But better that, she figured, than losing her job.

He took a drag. "I said yes, of course. But I also said I would need you to step up and take over some of my duties here. He asked me if you could handle it, and I told him I was certain you could."

Rose wasn't sure she was hearing him right. "You want me to do *your* job?"

"Why not? You see everything I do here. Heck, you're better with the numbers than I am anyway." He tapped the cigarette in the ashtray. "I'm talking about a *promotion*, Rose."

She let the word sink in. "Well, I'm flattered, but I don't know if I can do everything you do."

"If I didn't think you could, I wouldn't suggest it. Besides, I'll just be a phone call away. I'll come back over here at least once a week until you get your feet under you. And we're going to add five cents an hour to your pay."

Rose quickly did the math in her head; the raise would bring her up to $32 a week. More money for her coffee can, her own place within reach. She knew Mr. Sullivan made much more than she would, even with the raise. But he had a lot more experience, and a family to provide for. Still, the five cents felt a little short.

208

She told herself not to appear too eager, to sound calm. Mature. "Well, I'm certainly flattered. But what about my cousin Rocco? He'll be home soon. He's got a fiancé waiting. My aunt and uncle would never forgive me for taking his place."

"When I move over to the other plant, you'll basically be doing two jobs. I can't imagine Rocco—with all due respect—stepping back in and taking over. I need you here. More to the point, the company needs you here. The war's still on." He took off his reading glasses, pinching the bridge of his nose. "Don't worry. We won't leave Rocco stranded. We need another bookkeeper at the Industrial Canal plant. I'll just move him over there."

Rose was thrilled but tried not to get ahead of herself. "I know they're starting to lay people off. How long do you think they'll keep us?"

"Depends on how long things drag out in the Pacific," he said. "They won't need all the workers on the line, but they'll still need us, at least for a while. Mr. Higgins doesn't want to cause any domestic problems, so we're sending the married women home as their husbands come back."

Rose thought about Marie, so eager to quit working and marry Vin. But she also wondered whether all those other married women would want to be sent home with no more Higgins paychecks.

"Since you're not married, you can stay," Mr. Sullivan said. "If that's what you want. I know you've got a sweetheart—I don't want to pry—but we'll keep you on as long as we can."

Rose struggled to keep her voice steady. "The situation with him is . . . complicated." She didn't know how much she should share with her boss. She heard Aunt Inez' voice in her head. *It's just business, Rose.* "We don't know what's going to happen to them once the war is over. They'll probably be sent back to Italy. I mean, I want to stay here, to work as long as I can."

"Grand." He smiled, stubbed out his cigarette butt, and pushed his chair back from the desk. "I'll start thinking about what I need to tell you that you don't already know. But it probably won't be too much." He stood to leave. "I have to head over to the other plant for a bit. I'll be back after lunch. We can sort out the details then."

"Sounds good. See you later." She didn't remember saying "yes" to the terms of the promotion, but Mr. Sullivan clearly assumed she had. She picked up her spreadsheet, totaled up one of the columns and entered the sum into a report. Rivets. Steel. Lumber. Labor. The numbers swam before her eyes.

She put the paper down and looked over at Mr. Sullivan's big mahogany desk. She could barely see it beneath the mess of papers, overflowing ashtrays, and dirty coffee mugs. She shut the office door and walked over to his chair. She hesitated a moment, then sat. The view from her own desk was through a grimy interior window, looking down over the factory floor. Meanwhile, his window looked over at the bayou and leafy oak trees. A snow-white egret took flight. Somewhere beyond to the east, she knew, lay Jackson Barracks. She wondered what Sal would think of her sitting here, at her boss' desk, of it becoming *her* desk. She smiled just knowing he was out there, thinking of her, rooting for her, loving her.


Rose headed downstairs to meet Marie for lunch. It was late June, stifling hot inside the factory and out. At least there was a slight breeze off the bayou. Nearby, giant cranes were lifting metal-clad boats onto the train tracks with a clang. They sat close together so they wouldn't have to shout over the noise.

Marie pulled a fan out of her purse and waved it at her face, then at Rose. "I thought it would slow down after V-E Day, but we're working even faster now. I'm exhausted."

Rose unpacked her lunch, pouring zucchini with tomato sauce from a glass jar into a metal bowl. "I heard on the radio our guys are attacking Tokyo." She did her best to follow the news but didn't always understand it. Japan was so small. Did Hirohito really think they'd take over America?

"It's crazy," Marie said. "I wish they'd give up already. What's the point?"

"They can't hold out forever," she said, taking a bite of the squash. She had no idea if that were true or not. The Japanese seemed willing to fight to the last man. In theory it sounded honorable; in practice it just meant thousands more dead. She knew she should blame the leaders, not the people, just like Mussolini had forced good men like Sal and Vin to fight. Jesus said to turn the other cheek, but she couldn't forgive. Not after they took Giovanni, not after hearing about the camps.

"Hey, I have some news," she said, not wanting to dwell. "Mr. Sullivan offered me a promotion this morning. He's moving to a new job over at the Industrial Canal plant, and he wants me to take over most of his duties."

"Good for you! Will they be hiring someone to take over your work? Because I know Marguerite is looking—"

"No, no. I'd do both jobs," Rose said. She didn't mention the part about staying after the war was over. That would only open a whole other can of worms.

"That's swell, Rose," Marie said. She took a sip of milk. "Are they paying you both salaries?"

Rose sat back. "No. But there's a raise. Two dollars more a week."

"If it was me, I'd ask for double that." Marie pointed her sandwich at Rose. "Consider."

"Double? That'd be more than you make." Rose saw the books. Marie made more than she did—$1.45 an hour, same as the men.

211

She'd always thought of her job as easier than Marie's, not as valuable. "I just work the books."

"What are you talking about? I couldn't do your job, keeping all those numbers straight. I'm no businesswoman, but if it was me, I'd ask. All they can say is no. But I bet they won't. They need you. It's called *leverage*, Rose."

Rose moved the zucchini around the bowl with her fork, suddenly no longer hungry. She envied Marie's certainty, always knowing what she wanted, never wavering. "You don't think that's greedy? It is a war job, after all."

"Greedy? No. It's called earning what you're worth. Plus, the war's almost over. Who knows how much longer we'll have the chance to earn this kind of money? Don't be a sucker, Rose. Sometimes I wish you'd stand up for yourself a little more."

"I do stand up for myself," Rose protested. She shoved down a forkful of zucchini and finished her milk. She knew Marie was right—five cents more an hour wasn't enough. She'd known it from the moment Mr. Sullivan had spoken of it. Even so, she'd said nothing.

"If you don't believe me, ask your Aunt Inez," Marie said. "She's a businesswoman, right?"

Rose was pretty sure Aunt Inez would ask for more money. More than pretty sure.

A loud *BANG* came from the rail spur, a group of men worked to tie down a boat to a flat rolling car. "So, on another topic, the guys had a lot of fun at the beach yesterday, don't you think?" Marie asked.

"Sal said it was one of the best days of his life."

Marie patted her lips with a napkin. "Nice. The only fly in the ointment was that *puttana* Gilda. I saw her giving you the *malocchio* when Sal kissed you goodbye. That made my day. Almost as much as sweet Vinny. *Madonna mia!*" Marie said with a sly smile. "I think maybe he's going to pop the question soon."

Rose put down her fork and pushed a damp curl off her forehead. "How do you know?"

"My mother's acting funny. I think Vinny's been in touch with her somehow. She keeps asking questions about him and me. I know her too well. She's hiding something."

Rose wasn't really surprised. Still, it made her a little nervous to hear that Marie's engagement might be happening soon. Maybe Sal would feel pressured to do the same? She wasn't ready for that, even if her father was.

"I wonder how he's going to do it. Do you think he'll get a ring somehow?" Rose asked.

"I can't imagine how he'd get ahold of a ring," Marie said. "They pay those guys peanuts. But I don't care."

*She must really be in love*, Rose thought. She remembered when Marie had cut a photo out of a movie magazine—Lana Turner wearing a giant diamond in the movie *Slightly Dangerous*. "Do you think the Army will let them get married before the end of the war?"

"No idea. I don't care about that either. As long as I know I'm his," Marie said, melodramatically holding her hand to her heart.

*His.* Rose flinched but didn't want to rain on Marie's parade. "I'm happy for you, Marie. He's a good man." It was true. She did like Vincenzo. He was funny, kind, and crazy about Marie. She never saw him look at another girl—unlike poor old Louie. It occurred to her that Sal shared most of those same qualities, even if he was quieter about it. And that quietness, she liked that too.

"Not to jump the gun, but you'll be my maid of honor, right?" Marie asked.

Rose smiled. She thought about Laura, who'd asked the same thing. But nobody knew about that yet. "Of course. As long as you don't make me wear a hideous dress."

"Who knows, maybe we'll have a double wedding. Maybe Sal will—"

"No," Rose said, stopping her. "I mean, I wouldn't want to take away from your special day."

"Who knows when we'll even be able to do it. Might have to be in Italy for all I know," Marie said. She swept her hand at the factory. "Even if the money's good, I just want all this to be over."

Much as Rose wanted the war to end, she didn't like thinking about what would happen afterward. Now with the promotion, she hoped she could stay after war production transitioned to civilian work.

Rose wrapped her lunch things in a dishtowel and tucked them into her bag. "Aren't you nervous at all?"

"Nervous about what?"

"Getting married. It's the biggest decision of your life. There's no going back."

"That's the whole point, isn't it?" Marie said, raising her eyebrows. "Real life, Rose. Finally. I thought you'd be happy for me. You know this is what I've always wanted, more than anything."

Rose felt a pang of selfishness. Marie had grown up without a father, without siblings. Having a family would mean everything to her. She grabbed Marie by the elbow to stop her from leaving. "I *am* happy for you!" Rose said. "Really, I am. I can't wait to see how Vinnie pulls it off!"

Marie smiled and gave Rose a hug. "Me too!"

Rose walked slowly back to her office. Sparks flew and workers climbed around hulls, motors, and ramps. The giant machines hummed and clanged, pistons pumping, torches and hammers fastening wood and steel. Pre-assemblies were ready for ships' galleys, with cabin doorknobs and even cooking equipment. There was talk of transitioning into pleasure boats and travel trailers, but for now it was still about the landing craft and PT boats bound for the Pacific. One wall was lined with trays of components she remembered ordering—spools of wire and hundreds of parts she could now name, right down to the nuts and bolts.

*This* is *my real life*, Rose thought. And she loved it.

Mr. Sullivan was talking on the phone at his desk when Rose came up from lunch. She stowed her purse in her bottom drawer and tucked her hair behind her ears. *Leverage*, she reminded herself. If she waited, she'd lose her nerve.

"Good. I'll get back to you on that," he said, hanging up the phone.

She stood up as straight as she could. "Mr. Sullivan, I had a question about…the promotion."

"I hope you haven't reconsidered!" he said, laughing.

"No, but I was wondering, I mean, the new job will certainly mean more responsibility, right?"

"It will. You know most of what I do, and how I'm always rushing around. You're more organized than I am, so maybe you'll handle the workload better."

She smiled but was wary of the compliment. Marie's voice rang in her head: *Don't be a sucker.* "I was thinking that responsibility might be worth a little more per hour than what you mentioned." She stopped, looking him in the eye.

He tapped his fingers on the desk. "You know we're trying to keep a lid on overhead—you see the numbers. The margins on the last two contracts were paper thin. I thought you'd be pleased."

"I am," she said. "But you said you're not planning to replace me, so I'd essentially be doing your job *and* mine. That's a big savings, at least for this plant. I'm not asking to make as much as you do, of course…"

He chuckled. "I should hope not."

She didn't flinch. "I'm thinking maybe $34 a week would be fair." Ten cents more per hour.

He looked up at the ceiling, and she worried she'd overstepped. She could feel her face getting hot and knew she must look ridiculous, a young girl demanding a full four dollars more per week. *Don't cry.*

He stood, pushing his chair back. "Well, you drive a hard bargain, Rose." He smiled. "I like that. Tell you what, let's split the difference. Three dollars more a week. Deal?"

Rose considered it—that extra three dollars could go straight into the coffee can. Good enough. "Deal."

Mr. Sullivan stuck out his hand and she shook it firmly, just as her father had taught her.

That afternoon, Rose watched the familiar scenes out the window of the streetcar home. Toward the end of the ride, the summer sun washed the stucco storefronts, wrought iron balconies, and brick sidewalks on the business end of Canal Street with a pale glow. The Maison Blanche department store's windows displayed red-white-and-blue clothes and flags, getting ready for the July 4th holiday. She wondered if they'd at last be out from under this war by Independence Day next year.

Everywhere she looked, women emerged from office buildings, walking alone or in groups, wearing skirts and pumps or factory overalls. She remembered when she'd first started at Higgins, how strange it had felt to think of herself as a working girl. Now she'd gotten an award and a promotion. She couldn't wait to tell Aunt Inez, especially the part about asking for more money. She felt connected to all the women working in the city, in the country— even to Laura working in the war thousands of miles away. It was like all that energy had been bottled up in the kitchens and nurseries until the war needed them. Over and over, she heard the phrase *for the duration.* But she couldn't imagine going back to the way things were before, and didn't want to.

Walking down Rampart Street, she stopped at the flower pushcart on the corner of Dumaine. She'd walked by the old peddler every day on her way home from Higgins but had never stopped. "*Buona sera, signorina,*" he said. His face was weathered, his smile missing a few teeth. He wore a battered brown *coppola* cap and a worn tweed vest over a grimy white shirt.

"*Buona sera, signor,*" she said. "*Per favore,*" she pointed to a bouquet of lilies, ginger, and gardenias. She gave him a few coins from her purse.

He wrapped the flowers in a paper cone and handed them to her with a little nod. "*Bei fiori per una bella ragazza.*"

"*Grazie,*" she said. A small extravagance, but the flowers made her smile. Anyway, she could afford them now.

# TWENTY-ONE

Rose's mother put the chicken and a bowl of roasted potatoes on the table and sat down. "*Mangia*," she said. "While it's hot. What's with the flowers?" Rose had place her bouquet in a vase at the center of the table.

"Aren't they pretty? I'm celebrating," Rose said. "I got a promotion at work today."

"A promotion? Congratulations. Tell us more about it, *cara*," her father said, forking the food onto his plate.

"My boss Mr. Sullivan—you remember meeting him at the award ceremony." Her father nodded, cutting up his chicken. "He's going to be working at one of the other Higgins factories, at the Industrial Canal. So, he's asked me to fill in for him. They're giving me a little raise too." She didn't volunteer how much more, thinking about her coffee can.

"What about Rocco?" her mother asked. "He'll need that job back when he comes home." Rose felt anger welling up inside her. Just once, she wished her mother would be on her side.

"Who knows when that'll happen, Fil?" Her father chimed in. "This isn't about Rocco. It's about the Higgins people recognizing when they have a good worker. She knows she'll step aside when the boys come back. For now, keep making that money, Rose. I'm proud of you."

Rose was grateful for her father's support, though frustrated that everyone assumed her work life would come to an end as soon as the war did. "Rocco will be fine," she said. "I asked about him, of course—they'll need him at the Industrial Canal plant."

Her mother grunted but kept her eyes on her plate. Rose tried not to be offended. She ate her dinner quickly, anxious to get out of there. "Just a reminder—Marie and I are going to the movies with the boys tonight," she said.

"Good. Ask Sal if he still wants to come to the truck farm next Sunday," her father said. At dinner the week before, Rose's father and Sal had cooked up a plan for a trip across the lake. Captain Pepino was game to be their escort. "I want to show him more about the business, where the produce comes from."

Rose was glad to see her father so happy—Sal could easily fit into the business, just as her father had planned for Giovanni. They were growing close; they'd even talked about opening a restaurant together some day. But sometimes when her father spoke, it felt like the walls were closing in, binding Rose closer and closer to Sal, but also to her family and the store.

*"Good evening, ladies and gentlemen of North America and all the ships at sea."*

The radio announcer Walter Winchell's rat-a-tat voice interrupted the music.

"What now?" her father said.

*"An important news bulletin from the White House in Washington. Here's the President of the United States."* He reached over to turn up the volume.

*"My fellow Americans. The British, Chinese and United States governments have given the Japanese people adequate warning of what is in store for them.*

*"The world will note that the first atomic bomb was dropped on Hiroshima, an important Japanese army base. That bomb had more power than twenty thousand tons of T.N.T. It is a harnessing of the basic power of the universe. The force from which the sun draws its power has been loosed against those who brought war to the Far East.*

*"If Japan does not surrender, bombs will have to be dropped on her war industries, and unfortunately thousands of civilian lives will be lost. I urge Japanese civilians to leave industrial cities immediately and save themselves."*

"Twenty thousand tons of T.N.T." Rose tried to understand. She'd seen the newsreels and photos in *Life* magazine of the field of the dead at Normandy, London after the Blitz, heart-breaking pictures of Rome after the bombing there. This sounded much bigger. Impossible to fathom.

"I'm glad we got the atom bomb before they did." Rose's father said, spearing a piece of potato with his fork.

"They deserve everything they get," Rose's mother said. "I'm just sorry they didn't do this sooner. Maybe we'd have Giovanni back."

Rose's father held up a hand for silence. The president was still speaking.

221

*"I shall recommend that the Congress of the United States consider promptly the establishment of an appropriate commission to control the production and use of atomic power as a powerful and forceful influence toward the maintenance of world peace."*

The radio station switched back to music. Rose stood and brought her plate to the sink. It was too much to take in: one minute they were hearing about massive destruction, the next minute Perry Como was singing about love and springtime. She thought about her own relatives in Sicily, who'd written to them about surviving without running water and electricity, somehow living among piles of rubble and food shortages. It pained her to think of the kind of devastation and suffering the president was talking about. She touched the scapular, thinking of Laura, glad the war in Europe was over.

She looked at the clock, dried her dish and put it in the cabinet. "They have to surrender now, don't they?" she asked. Surely the Japanese couldn't go on much longer. If they surrendered, she knew it would change her own life too—the military orders would drop off at Higgins, Sal would be sent back to Italy. Even so, she truly wanted the war to end, regardless of the consequences for her personally.

"We'll see. They are a stubborn people, the Japanese," her father said. "But I think this will change the war. It's too big not to."

"I hope so," Rose said. "I need to get ready now." She felt strange saying something so mundane after hearing about the giant bomb. She pushed the thought into a dresser drawer in her mind. She supposed it was the only way human beings could go on: balancing the trivial details of life and the grand scale of the war, somehow navigating both.

In her room, she put on a blue cotton dress she knew Sal liked. She applied a little lipstick and powder, checked her hair in the mirror, and grabbed her purse. As she passed through the kitchen, her parents were still at the table. The music played softly now— Billie Holiday singing with the Duke Ellington orchestra. Her mother and father ate without speaking, looking lost in their private thoughts. She could almost see the wall between them and wondered what it would be like for them when she wasn't in the house anymore. Would they talk to each other at all?

"What movie are you seeing?" her father asked as Rose reached down to adjust the strap on her shoe.

"*Anchors Aweigh* at the Dreamland. Gene Kelly and Frank Sinatra." She knew her father would be happy that Sinatra was in the film.

"*Bene.* Remember the songs so you can sing them to us later. You'll be home by ten?"

"Yes, Papa." The fact that she still had a curfew at almost twenty-one years old grated on her, but it wasn't worth fighting over now. It was just a habit her parents clung to; they all knew there wouldn't be any real consequences if she was a little late. It was more habit for her parents to try to impose their rules than any restrictions she actually lived by.

"*Vai piano-piano,*" he called as she closed the door behind her.

Rose walked quickly down St. Philip Street and took a left on Decatur. Small geckos skittered out of her way into cracks in the sidewalk. Neighbors were out on their stoops, and she could hear them talking about the president's message as she passed by. She looked up at the sky: hazy blue with a few white puffy clouds, thunder clouds on the horizon. Had the people on the ground in Hiroshima seen the giant bomb coming? She pushed the thought away. She wanted Sal near, his body close, to hold his hand in the dark theater. Arriving at Marie's house, she knocked on the front door.

223

"Come on in," she heard Marie's mother call.

Rose passed through the front rooms. She found Mrs. Leonardi in Marie's room, sitting on her daughter's bed. Meanwhile, Marie primped in front of the vanity mirror. "*Ciao,* Mrs. L," Rose said.

"They're not here yet?"

"No, thank God. I'm not ready," Marie answered. She was powdering her cleavage with a makeup brush—something that would never cross Rose's mind.

"You heard about the bomb?" Rose asked.

"We just listened to the president on the radio," Marie's mother said. "It sounds awful, but the Japs had it coming, God forgive me. What they did to your brother, may he rest in peace." She blessed herself.

"I just hope they'll finally surrender, so we can all get on with our lives," Marie said.

"Enough of that. I wish I could go with you to the movie," her mother said. "I love that Gene Kelly. So dapper."

"You can come, Mrs. L—," Rose started to answer, but Marie met her eyes in the mirror and cut her off with a look.

"Oh, no dear. You girls go and have a good time. You don't need an old fifth wheel around. Besides, I might catch the matinee with some of the ladies from the diner on Monday."

Rose felt sorry for Mrs. Leonardi—having to work all the time, never having a sweetheart to cuddle with at a movie. It occurred to Rose that might this be her same life if she didn't have Sal.

"Let me look at you," Mrs. Leonardi said as Marie stood in front of her for inspection. She lifted Marie's chin with a forefinger and gently brushed a lock of hair off her daughter's cheek. Rose's throat tightened; she couldn't remember the last time her own mother had touched her with such tenderness.

"*Bella,*" Marie's mother said, smiling. "Ah, to be young again."

A knock sounded at the door. "There they are!" Marie's mother sang.

"I'll get it," Rose said on her way to the front room.

"*Buona sera!*" Vincenzo's voice boomed as Rose opened the door. Sal was right behind him, holding his Army cap in his hands. They were both in uniform, freshly shaven and smiling.

"*Ciao,* Rose," Sal kissed her on the cheek. He smelled clean and spicy. She rubbed the back of her hand across his smooth cheek, and he smiled.

Marie and her mother came into the parlor. Vin gave Marie a hug, then kissed Marie's mother on both cheeks. "You look beautiful, *signora,*" he said, even though Mrs. Leonardi was wearing an old house dress. "Every time I see you, I know where Marie gets her good looks."

"Oh *Vincenzo*. Stop that," Marie's mother blushed, patting her chest.

"Did you get the bus OK?" Rose asked. She knew they'd had to bribe their way out of the camp to avoid having to get a pass—and an escort.

"Well, we were going to," Vincenzo said. "We got out under the fence. At the bus stop, a car pulled over and a man offered us a ride, thinking we were American soldiers." He turned to show the faded spot on his sleeve where the ITALY patch had been. "Our friend Nunzio the tailor took off our patches—just for the night."

"Wasn't the driver curious about your accents?" Marie asked.

"What accents?" Vincenzo said.

"We told him we were from Puerto Rico!" Sal said.

They all laughed, and Marie smacked Vin on the arm playfully. "*Andiamo,*" she said, grabbing her purse and kissing her mother's cheek. "See you later, Ma."


After the movie, Vincenzo danced Marie down the sidewalk, crooning a song from the film in his thickly accented English.

"I appreciate the sentiment, Vinny," Marie laughed, "but Sinatra's got nothing to worry about."

They crossed Esplanade Avenue from the Marigny neighborhood into the French Quarter. Above them, giant live oak trees formed an archway across the wide road. The night air was soft, and it was a little cooler; it had rained while they were in the theater. The damp streets reflected the flickering of the gas lanterns. The blackouts had ended, so the lights were back on. Rose noticed more American soldiers in uniform now, some with girls on their arms. One of them nodded to Sal as if he was one of their own. Not long ago, the streets would have been filled mostly with women and old men. The war was almost over. *I should be happy,* Rose thought. *This is what I've prayed for.*

"*È una serata così bella,*" Vincenzo said. "It's a beautiful night. Let's get some gelato and eat it down by the river."

Sal took Rose's arm and they walked along the narrow brick sidewalks down Royal Street to Ursulines, where Brocato's was still busy. Rose ordered *stracciatella*, her favorite, and they ate their cups of gelato with small wooden spoons as they made their way to Jackson Square.

"*Scusi.* We're going to take a little stroll through the park," Vincenzo said, pulling Marie along with him as they wandered away.

Rose started to follow, but Sal held her elbow and pulled her back gently. "*Aspetta,*" he said. "Give them a minute. Let's sit." He pointed to a bench in front of the cathedral. He took out his handkerchief to wipe off the damp before they sat.

A street musician was playing a violin somewhere in the dark— an old Italian love song Rose couldn't quite place. Her father would know. Her mind was overflowing: the bomb, the war about to end, Sal's arm around her shoulders. She wished she could slow things down, just appreciate the beautiful night out with her friends. Her eyes kept wanting to spy on Marie and Vin; instead, she looked up at the ornate wrought iron balconies wrapped around the nearby brick buildings. "You know these buildings, and the park, were all built by a woman?" she said, pointing to the grand Pontalba apartments. "A baroness." Aunt Inez had been to a party in one of the fancy apartments and had told Rose the story.

Rose had fantasized about living there herself one day.

"She must have been a working girl, like you," Sal said, poking her gently with his elbow.

"I'm pretty sure it was her father's money, but it was her project," Rose said. "Speaking of work, I got some good news today. They want me to take over my boss' job." She looked at him and tried to read his expression in the dim light. "It's a promotion."

"That's nice," he said. "Too bad you have to do more, though. You work so hard already."

"I love my work," Rose said, more sharply than she intended. She watched his face. He wasn't smiling. "And they're paying me extra too. They even told me I might be able to keep the job once the war is over."

"That's silly," Sal said. "Once the war is over, the men will come back to the factory, *si*? It's a man's job to work, to take care of his family."

Rose felt anger rising in her throat. She needed to make him understand. "But things are changing now," she started to protest.

"Shh. *Guarda*," he interrupted, lacing his fingers through hers. "Watch." He pointed his chin toward where Marie and Vin sat kissing on a bench at the edge of the park. Then Vin stood up and took something out of his pants pocket. He bent down on one knee. Rose tried to catch her breath. It was happening.

"Is that a ring?" she asked. "How did he get it?"

"Marie's mother got it for him at the pawn shop. He's been saving up. I hope she says yes," Sal said.

"She will." Rose's heart beat a little faster. It had all seemed abstract up until now.

They watched, though they couldn't hear the words. Marie put her hands over her chest, nodding. Vin put the ring on her finger, and she hugged him to her. Still on his knees, Vin buried his head in Marie's lap, and she ran her hands through his hair. Rose felt tears come to her eyes. It was so romantic, like a scene from a movie. She told herself to be happy—this is what Marie had always wanted—but part of her felt the loss of her friend already. Sal squeezed her hand and she turned to face him, his beautiful eyes smiling down at her. She tried to picture herself in Marie's position, out in public like this at such an important moment: Sal proposing on bended knee, choosing her. She turned away, wiping tears from her eyes.

Marie and Vin walked toward them, arm in arm. Marie held her left hand out. A tiny diamond glinted from the ring. Rose stood up and gave her a long hug.

"Say hello to Mrs. Vincenzo Faroldi!" Marie gushed.

Rose flinched. Marie wasn't Marie anymore but someone with a different name. They'd been best friends forever; now Vincenzo would be the most important person in Marie's life. She pushed away the thought. "Oh, Marie. I'm so happy for you! Let's see that ring again."

"Someday when I have my own barber shop, I'll replace it with a big rock, like a movie star," Vincenzo said.

"I don't want a big rock," Marie said. Rose knew it was a lie to make him feel better. "I love this ring, and I love this guy." She kissed Vin on the cheek. Marie pulled a handkerchief out of her purse and dabbed at the mascara running from her eyes. Sal and Vin shook hands, laughing and cuffing each other on their shoulders.

Then Vin grabbed Rose and hugged her too. "Thank you for making Marie come to the barracks that first time. If not for you, none of this would be." The violinist came out of the shadows and started playing "Here Comes the Bride." Marie and Rose held one another and twirled; Sal and Vin looked confused. Rose explained the song as she took a coin out of her purse and dropped it in the musician's hat.

"I'm the luckiest man in America tonight!" Vincenzo yelled.

The cathedral clock chimed ten times. "We'll have to celebrate soon, but if we don't catch the last bus, we'll be in the brig," Sal said. They walked Rose home first. Marie and Vin hung back.

At Rose's gate, Sal kissed her passionately, then hugged her close. Her face was buried in his chest, and she could hear his heart beating. "*Buona notte, topolino*," he said. "Someday I hope we never have to say goodnight."

"I'll see you Sunday, silly." She leaned back to look at his face. His brow was knitted, his mouth in a slight pout. She tried to read his expression. Love? Expectation? Sadness?

"You'd better go," she said. "You don't want to miss your bus."

He kissed her gently on the lips, which sent a shiver of pleasure through her. "*Si, arrivederci.*" He brushed his lips against her ear, "*Ti amo.*"

"*Anch'io ti amo,*" she said. Did she really love him? Or was she just saying it back?

She blew a kiss to Marie and Vincenzo then opened the gate and latched it shut from the inside. She leaned against the cool bricks of the wall, closing her eyes until she could no longer hear their footsteps. As she stood there, Kathryn Grayson's song from the movie floated into her head: *All of a sudden, my heart sings.* She looked up, relieved to see her parents' bedroom window was dark.

She walked up the back stairs to the apartment, trying to step quietly so as not to wake her parents. She wanted to hold onto this feeling: loving Sal, being loved. This is what she and Marie used to daydream about, laying on her bed as teenagers, reading movie magazines. But that look Sal gave her, the grip of his hands on her arms. Was he planning to propose too? *It's a man's job to work.* He'd called her silly for wanting to keep her job after the war. She thought about Laura and Nicholas, working together like equals, training for their next assignment, maybe even eloping. Her father's words came back to her. *Just be sure, Rose.* Her future was coming at her fast. If she didn't take control of it, it would take control of her.

# TWENTY-TWO

Rose sat at her desk, scanning the latest layoff list for names she knew. Since the end of the war in Europe, they'd started shutting down some production lines. Marie was scheduled to leave at the end of September. So many men were back now—they almost outnumbered the women. Halfway down the list, she saw Irma Jones' name—this would be her last week.

Rose made it a point to visit the mail room that afternoon. Irma was sorting a pile of envelopes and packages on the counter. "I'm sorry," Rose said. "I heard the news. We're losing so many good people these days."

"It's OK," Irma told her. "My cousin got me an interview over at the post office, and I think I have a good chance. The pay's not as good as here, but it's steady."

Rose knew Irma would be stuck in the back at the post office. Meanwhile, Irma had done a great job working the counter in the Higgins mail room for over four years. It wasn't fair. "I'll certainly miss you around here."

"I'll miss you too," Irma said. "This was a good job. But nothing can make me sad now that Alfred's home, safe and sound. He's already back at his old job, even got himself a girlfriend." Irma smiled and shook her head. "I'll miss hearing your sister's reports. I'm sure she'll be home soon too."

"I hope so," Rose said.

"Give my best to your Mama and Papa for me too," Irma said. "Good people, your parents."

"I will," Rose said. She was sad to think she might not see Irma much anymore, even though she lived just a few blocks away. Rose never had much reason to cross Rampart Street into Irma's Treme neighborhood. The war had brought them closer for a time; now it was ending.

Back in the office—all hers now—she sat down in Mr. Sullivan's old swivel chair; it was too big for her, but she loved it anyway. She'd cleaned out his desk and polished the wood surface. A bouquet of fragrant gardenias bloomed in the old china vase she'd brought in from home. Since her promotion, she bought fresh flowers from the old man on the corner every week. Today's newspaper sat on her desk; *ATOMIC BOMB HITS NAGASAKI*, the headline blared. The Japanese were sure to give up soon.

She pulled out the report she had typed up. Government orders were still coming in slowly, but the company needed to shift gears into new areas if they were going to make it in peacetime. Mr. Sullivan had asked her to look at different production scenarios— parts, equipment, and materials required for products like travel trailers and fishing boats. She also started identifying new suppliers and analyzing the mix of skills they'd need from their labor force.

"Knock knock," Mr. Sullivan said, standing in the doorframe. He looked harried as usual: no jacket and an ink stain on the pocket of his white shirt. He held two steaming cups of coffee in thick white mugs and handed one to Rose. "Look at this place. Am I in the right office?"

"Oh, hello! Thanks," she said, taking the coffee. "I hope you don't mind. I tidied up a bit."

"More than a bit! It looks like a different world in here. Even smells better."

She almost got up to let him have his old spot, but he quickly sat in the side chair. She took a clean ashtray out of her drawer for him. He fumbled with a lighter for a moment, then lit his cigarette as she sipped her coffee. Still the bitter taste of chicory, and no sugar, but at least it was fresh.

She handed him the report; he leafed through the pages. "What did you find, Rosie?"

"I think there's a profitable path forward if we can shift to commercial customers more quickly," she said. "We'll have to talk to our suppliers and see how fast they can make the transition. We won't need the giant rivets and boat parts anymore. They'll have to scale down."

Mr. Sullivan ran his finger down the column of numbers. "Good, good. Yes. Very good. This is excellent work, Rose. This is the kind of thinking we're going to need. What about labor?"

"We'll need to adjust the mix. We'll either need to get different people or retrain the people we have."

He took a drag from his cigarette and blew out a cloud of smoke. "You know I have a big strategy meeting coming up with Mr. Higgins and his top men. We can use some of this for sure, and maybe you could do some more research—the university library has some resources we can use. Government reports and such. Mr. Higgins always wants data—facts to back up the figures."

They talked for a while longer, tossing ideas back and forth. Maybe they could work with the unions on retraining, so some of the best workers could stay on when they changed over the production lines. They probably needed to beef up marketing if they were going to sell more directly to consumers instead of just the government. Mr. Sullivan asked her tough questions, and listened to her opinions, taking notes in the margins of her report.

Rose felt a surge of pride. She was excited and eager to dive into the project, but nervous at the same time. Before the war, it had been day in, day out, week after week the same customers at the grocery, the same tasks. Now Mr. Sullivan was trusting her with a critical company assignment for Mr. Higgins.

The following Tuesday, Rose and Mr. Sullivan were huddled at her desk, looking over the numbers she'd put together showing the types of skilled labor they'd need for the proposed new product lines: travel trailers, fishing boats, and modular homes. Mr. Sullivan had just asked about the government data she found on housing projections when the loudspeaker in the corner of the office ceiling clicked on.

"Testing one-two-three. Attention all hands. We have some important news to share." It was Mr. Higgins' son, Andrew Jr., who had recently come back from the front and was helping to manage the company. He cleared his throat. "We have just been informed that the Japanese have surrendered. I repeat, the Empire of Japan has surrendered unconditionally. The war is over!"

The hum from the machinery downstairs came to a stop, and for a moment there was complete silence. Rose was pinned to her seat, looking at Mr. Sullivan. Tears welled up in his eyes and he reached for her hands, grasping them tightly.

"In light of this momentous news, we are declaring the rest of the day a holiday. Please join your loved ones at home and be careful as you leave the building. God Bless America!"

A roar went up downstairs on the factory floor. Mr. Sullivan took a handkerchief out of his pocket. "It's over, Rose. It's finally over," he said quietly. "Everything we've been working for. Victory. They're all coming home." He blew his nose loudly into his handkerchief, his eyes red.

"Thank God," She made the sign of the cross, fighting back her own tears. Giovanni would not be coming home. But Laura would. She stood and looked through the interior window, down to the factory floor. People were climbing out of their workstations, hugging each other and yelling. Some were on their knees, hands covering their faces or praying, or both. Outside, church bells began to ring out and car horns blared.

"This can all wait," Mr. Sullivan said, pointing to the paperwork on the desk. "Go home and be with your family."

"Thanks," Rose said, grabbing her purse. "I'll see you tomorrow!"

She flew down the stairs, searching for Marie among the throngs of celebrating workers. When she couldn't find her, Rose ran out of the building to the corner where they usually met for lunch. Her mind was racing; she felt for the scapular under her blouse. *Laura will be coming home.* After a few minutes, Marie came out arm in arm with a couple of other women from the welding shop.

"Rose! Rose! It's over! We did it!" Marie ripped her off red kerchief and waved it in the air, then ran to Rose and grabbed her, lifting her off her feet and twirling her around. "Let's get out of here. I need to get to my Ma."

On the streetcar, Marie leaned her upper half out the window. Rose kneeled on her seat and put her hand on Marie's shoulder, craning her neck to see better. People were streaming out of office buildings, flashing the V for Victory sign. Paper streamers and bits of confetti drifted through the air from the upper floors, and firecrackers popped.

"It's like Mardi Gras and Fourth of July all rolled into one!" Marie shouted, pushing herself back into her seat. "I wonder if they're celebrating at Jackson Barracks."

As they got closer to the French Quarter, they saw people crowding Canal Street. Traffic was stopped and cars were stuck on the tracks making it impossible to pass. The driver opened the door, and everyone piled out. Rose and Marie made their way down the sidewalk toward Rampart Street, where every door was open—restaurants, stores, houses. Groups of people danced in impromptu parades, some with horns and drums. Newsboys yelled *"Extra! Extra!"* and held up copies of the paper, headlines reading *PEACE*. It all felt like a dream.

Before Rose turned down her street toward home, Marie stopped and took both her hands. "I'm going to walk down to the diner and meet my Ma," Marie said. "I'll catch up with you later." She gave Rose a big hug, her stiff coveralls digging into Rose's arms. "This is it, Rose. The rest of our lives about to begin. Batten down the hatches!"

Rose walked the last few blocks to her house, her heart pounding. New Orleans had prematurely celebrated the end of the war three times before, after false news reports. But now, the war was really over. *Over.* No more air raid drills, no more nightmares about U-boats in the Gulf or kamikaze planes diving into the French Quarter. Neighbors waved and shouted to Rose from their balconies, music blared out from radios, little kids rushed past her on the sidewalk, waving miniature American flags. The boats on the river were sounding their horns; she could her the bells at Immaculate Conception ringing incessantly. On the corner of Dauphine and St. Philip, the door to the grocery store stood open, and her father held out a bottle of wine, pouring short glasses for a crowd of neighbors. "Rose!" he cried when he saw her.

"Papa! It's over!" Rose hugged him around the waist. "What are you doing?"

"They closed all the bars in the Quarter—afraid people will get out of hand. So, I guess we'll just have to give it away!" He handed Rose a glass of wine, toasted with her, then clinked glasses with neighbors. "God bless America! The greatest country in the world," he said. "*A saluti!*" He downed his wine in one gulp.

"*Saluti!* To President Truman! To our troops!" The neighbors toasted each other. Jake was leashed to the leg of a chair, barking and howling, his tail wagging furiously. Rose crouched down and hugged the dog's neck. *To Giovanni*, she thought.

"Let's have some music," her father said. He ducked back into the store and carried the radio out to the sidewalk, running a long cord out the door. The Andrews Sisters were singing "The Victory Polka."

Rose's mother came outside, her eyes red, as if she had been crying. Rose hugged her; for once, her mother didn't resist. Rose poured her a glass of wine. "To Giovanni," Rose said, clinking glasses with her mother.

"To Giovanni," her mother said, fresh tears springing to her eyes.

"To Laura," Rose added.

"To Laura." Rose's father took her mother's wine glass, setting it on one of the café tables, and held out his arms. She relaxed and leaned into him as they swayed to the music. For all their troubles, they still had a special bond, Rose thought. Life would never be the same, but maybe they could get past the grief and heal after all. Together. It was the only way.

People started dancing on the street. Even Cousin Carmine looked happy and offered his hand. Rose danced with him, then held hands in a circle with Mrs. Fabucci and her little boy. Meanwhile, cars drove slowly down Dauphine Street honking their horns to move the crowd out of the way, with people filling the streets again as they'd pass. Rose was thinking of Sal, how much she wanted him here. She was desperate to talk to him and find out what was going on at Jackson Barracks, but they wouldn't see one another until Sunday.

Aunt Inez came up the sidewalk, dodging the dancers. "I thought I might find a party down here." Rose saw her mother kiss Aunt Inez on the cheek. Aunt Inez tightly embraced Rose. Rose poured her a glass of wine and they clinked rims. "I'm proud of you, Rose. Of all you girls—Marie, Laura. You all did your part." Rose's father called to his sister, and they danced off, dodging a mule-drawn cart decorated with American flags and overflowing with celebrating riders.

Rose dabbed at her forehead and throat with a napkin, suddenly overcome. The heat, the wine, and the crowds were making her a little lightheaded. She slipped into the store and up the back stairs to the apartment, closing her bedroom door and shutting the window to quiet the sounds from in the street. Her palms were sweating, and she was out of breath. She sat on her sister's bed, feeling a little dizzy, like the earth was wobbling on its axis. Life would be different from here on out. Everything had changed: Giovanni wasn't coming back, Laura would soon be married, off on her own. And Rose would never be the same either.

# TWENTY-THREE

Rose smiled at herself in the mirror, turning left and right. Her new dress looked sophisticated: black rayon, with sheer netting over the collar bone and a keyhole neckline. Side ruching and a narrow black patent leather belt defined her petite waistline. She wore white gloves, a smart little hat and had even sprung for a new pair of silk stockings with a seam up the back. After V-J Day a few weeks ago, she had taken some money from her coffee can and splurged on a shopping trip to Maison Blanche with Marie. She thought about the dresses she'd worn in the past—to that first dance at Jackson Barracks, to the church hall. Girl dresses. A lifetime ago.

She usually didn't like being the center of attention, but it was her birthday, and she was excited about a night of dancing at - Segretto's. She grabbed her purse and headed downstairs, where her father was already waiting on the sidewalk. When he saw her, he let out a low whistle. He wore his old black suit, a little tight at the waist now. Rose knew he hated wearing formal clothes and was touched he'd put on a tie for her. She noticed he'd polished his shoes and put some pomade in his hair.

"Thanks for doing this, Papa," Rose said. "I wish Mama was coming." Her mother had pleaded a headache but promised she'd have a birthday cake ready when they got home. Rose was hurt, although not surprised. Her mother still had her ups and downs.

"I wouldn't miss this for the world," her father said. "It's not every day my baby turns twenty-one! Plus, Louis Prima's playing, so that's an added treat for me." No mention of her mother.

She had to take two steps to her father's one as they picked their way along the brick sidewalks through the French Quarter. The city was livelier now that the war was over. The sidewalks were crowded with people stepping out on a lovely Friday evening, heading to bars, restaurants, and nightclubs. So many families were throwing parties to welcome their soldiers home. Her own family hadn't had much to celebrate until tonight.

"I wish Laura could be here," Rose said. She hadn't heard from her sister since V-J Day, when Laura sent a telegram to the family from Honolulu. She almost mentioned Giovanni but didn't want to make her father sad.

"*Si,*" he said. "She'll be home soon, God willing." He walked with his hands jammed into his pants pockets.

"I hope Mama will be kind when Laura gets back. I can't imagine what she's been through over there," Rose said. She chose her words carefully, since she didn't really have to imagine—she knew a lot from Laura's letters.

"I'm sure she will," her father said. He didn't sound very sure. "I guess we'll all have to learn how to live together again."

Rose knew it was unlikely Laura would be living under their roof for long, but she kept that to herself. She wondered where Laura was at this moment, whether she and Nicholas had eloped after all. She pushed the thoughts away, telling herself to just relax and have fun tonight. It was her birthday, after all. Twenty-one. The year she'd be striking out on her own.

They turned left onto St. Louis Street. She saw Sal standing with Marie and Vincenzo outside the door to the club and felt a flutter in her stomach. They'd been a couple for more than a year now, but she still felt the same electric connection she had the first time she saw him. She reminded herself how lucky she was to have found him.

"There's the birthday girl!" Marie said, hugging Rose. She smelled like talcum and rosewater and looked beautiful in her new purple chiffon dress and matching hat. "Might as well spend it while I've got it," she'd said on their shopping trip. The little diamond chip in her engagement ring glinted on her hand.

"*Ciao!*" Sal said. He shook Rose's father's hand and kissed Rose on the cheek. "*Sei bellissima,*" he whispered in her ear.

"Happy birthday, Rose! *Così elegante.*" Vincenzo squeezed Rose's arm lightly.

"I got a little something for you," Marie said, putting a small box into Rose's gloved hand. "For tonight—go ahead, open it."

Rose took off her gloves and opened the box. Silver shoe clips with small rhinestones—restrained, for Marie. Her friend knew her well. "Oh, thank you! These are beautiful!"

"Put 'em on," Marie said. Rose reached for her father's arm to steady herself.

"Allow me," Sal said, and Rose's father stepped back. She held onto Sal's arm as she fastened the buckles to her black dancing shoes. She lifted one foot, tilting it this way and that. She liked the way they sparkled.

Marie clapped her hands. "*Bella!* Now you're ready for dancing."

Rose gave her a hug. "They're swell, Marie. I love them. Thank you."

Pepino walked up with Aunt Inez on his arm. They looked good together, but Rose knew she was keeping him at bay. She'd told Rose she was having fun with him but didn't want to get too attached. There was no telling when he'd get his discharge papers and head back to Boston, now that things were winding down.

Aunt Inez gave Rose a hug. "Let me look at you," she said. "I can't believe you're the same little girl I used to take to Monkey Hill at the zoo."

Rose blushed, a little overwhelmed by the thought. She couldn't pinpoint when she'd crossed over from girl to woman, but tonight felt like a marker. Finally.

"Let's head in—the show starts soon," her aunt said. The doorman opened the mahogany door. The room was bustling with waiters and cigarette girls moving through the crowd. Plush red leather booths lined platforms along both sides of the high-ceilinged room. There were dozens of tables on the lower level, and a parquet dance floor in front of the stage. A giant American flag hung from the rafters. The band members were warming up, testing their instruments, and straightening out sheet music behind gleaming white band shells. A black musical note with the initials LP inside it was printed on the front of the kick drum.

Rose took it all in—it was her first time in a real nightclub. She felt grown-up, nervous with anticipation, but in a good way.

Marie leaned over. "Beats the heck out of the Immaculate Conception gym!"

"And dances with the nuns, bless their hearts," Rose said.

The maître d', an older man with slicked-back silver hair and a perfect smile, greeted Aunt Inez with a little bow and brought the group to a reserved booth large enough for all of them, just to the right of the stage. A sign on the table held a card that said, *Happy Birthday, Rose Marino*, next to a bottle of champagne in a silver bucket.

Rose slipped the card out of the holder and tucked it into her purse as a memento. "I feel like a V.I.P.," she said.

"You *are* a V.I.P. Happy birthday, honey." Aunt Inez gave her arm a squeeze, and Rose slid into the booth. Sal sat next to her, and the others crowded in. A white-gloved waiter appeared and popped the champagne cork, then filled the glasses. Inez took two cubes from the sugar bowl and dropped one into her glass and one into Rose's. "For luck," she said.

Rose made the sign of the cross—to keep the devil away—and took a tiny sip of the champagne, the sweet sugar and bubbles tingling her lips. She knew it must have been an expensive bottle, saved from before the war, and wanted to savor it.

Aunt Inez tapped on the side of her glass with her ebony cigarette holder. "Before the music starts, I want to propose a toast. To our girl Rose, now a young woman. Happy Birthday! *Cento anni!* May you live a hundred years!"

"*Cento anni! Saluti!*" They all touched glasses. Pepino lit Aunt Inez' cigarette for her. People waved to her as they passed by, and she fluttered her fingers and blew kisses to them like she was a celebrity. If she ever got lonely without a husband, Rose didn't see it. Meanwhile, Sal put his arm around Rose, pulling her close.

Her father was excited, pointing out musicians he recognized in the band. Vincenzo and Marie were across the table, gazing into each other's eyes. *Mrs. Vincenzo Faroldi.* Rose missed her friend already. She wondered if she'd ever feel comfortable as Mrs. Salvatore Dilisio, her own name made invisible.

Louis Prima took the stage, wearing a tan suit, blue tie, and white pocket square. "Play pretty for the people!" he shouted to his band, and they launched into "Felicia No Capicia." Rose's father sang along, much to Rose's embarrassment. Sal was laughing.

"He's pretty good, Louis Prima!" Sal said in Rose's ear.

"You like this? It's an awful song. I like his love songs better than when he makes fun of Italians."

"He's Sicilian himself, no?"

"*Si.*"

"So, he's allowed. The people seem to love it."

He had a point—Rose looked around and everyone who wasn't dancing was clapping along. Pepino stood and put out his hand to Aunt Inez, then they wove through the tables to the dance floor. Rose sat back and sipped her champagne. She wished she could be like Aunt Inez. So sure of herself, keeping her emotions in check. Living on her own terms. Free.

The next song was a fast number, "Sing, Sing, Sing." Sal grabbed her hand and they melted into the crowd. Sal moved her around the dance floor, smooth and certain, spinning and dipping her like they'd been together forever. Rose remembered the first time they danced at Jackson Barracks. How new everything was then, when it felt like the war would never end. Knowing him as she did now, she was even more attracted to him—his warmth, his kindness, his spirit.

Her father tapped Sal's shoulder as the next song started. "May I have this dance, *signorina*?" he asked, his big brown eyes pleading. His formal tone made Rose laugh. Sal stepped back with a bow, and her father took Rose's hand.

Louis Prima stepped up to the microphone. "Ladies and gentlemen, please give a warm welcome to Miss Lily Ann Carol for "Sentimental Journey!"

Rose's father led her smoothly around the dance floor. "We haven't danced like this since Cousin Marianna's wedding," Rose said. She'd been sixteen then. Giovanni had danced with Laura, knocking into them on purpose, horsing around. She'd been irritated at the time, but she'd give anything to have her brother here tonight to see her in her new dress, drinking champagne. He would have liked Sal, made fast friends with Vincenzo. She told herself he was there in spirit, looking down from above.

"Seems like a million years ago," her father said. Sam Butera's tenor saxophone wound through a solo. "This is good practice, though."

"Practice for what?" Rose asked, though she knew the answer.

"The father-daughter dance, when you and Sal get married."

She backed away and gave him a stern look, but he held onto her hands. She thought about Vin's plotting with Marie's mother, how her father ceded his arm to Sal's on the sidewalk. "Has he said something to you?"

"My lips are sealed," he said. He pulled her toward him again, then spun her around gently. "He's a good boy, Rose, a hard worker. A good-looking man. I'd be happy to have him as a son-in-law. And I've seen the way you are together. You love each other. Am I wrong?"

"You're not wrong, Papa. But . . ." Rose didn't want to be having this conversation. Not now, not tonight. She saw Vin and Marie dancing nearby, their bodies practically fused together. Marie had one hand on his shoulder, and the other hooked in his waistband. Vin's eyes were closed, his fingers lightly caressing Marie's bare skin at the V on the back of her dress.

"But what?" her father said. He leaned back enough to look at her, his lower lip sticking out in a mock pout.

"It's complicated," Rose said into his ear. "We don't even know if they'll be allowed to stay here."

"Love shouldn't be complicated. If you have to marry him in Italy and bring him back, we'll find a way to pay for it. Don't worry," he said, as if that were the problem. He twirled her effortlessly. "They can't keep those boys locked up much longer."

She looked over at the table; Sal was sitting back, always so at ease in his body, watching her dance with her father, a big smile on his face. So earnest, so true. "I can't just leave my job. You know they gave me that big promotion. I thought you were proud of me," she said.

"Sure, *cara*. But the war's over."

"They're still counting on me. It's an important time for the business," she shouted over the music. "The company wants to keep going."

"Things are bound to change soon. A good man like Sal—you don't want to lose him."

Rose felt a little lump in her throat. It was the same thing Marie had said to her that day on Pontchartrain Beach. Gilda was back with her old boyfriend, now returned from the war, but there were dozens of other girls out there who would jump at the chance to be with Sal. Rose knew she should count her blessings; she might never find as good a man. But she also knew Sal would want her home, not out working. If Higgins would even keep a married woman on—possible only if Mr. Sullivan would fight for her. Everything felt like it was coming to a head.

The band took a break, and her father went to find the men's room. Back at the table, Sal poured more champagne for Rose. He clinked his glass to hers again and smiled. She wished she could freeze this happy moment, and not have to think about what would happen tomorrow, or next week.

"Let's go out to the courtyard. I need some air," Sal said. They slid out of the booth, and he took her hand, leading her through the club to the back door. The night air was mild and silky. Couples talked quietly at small wrought iron tables, the courtyard twinkling with candles. Sal pulled her over to sit down. "*Che bella notte*," he said. "A perfect night for your special birthday."

He reached into his pocket and for a moment Rose panicked. But the box was long and narrow, not small and square.

"For you, *mi piccola topolino*."

"What's this?" she asked.

"Just a little birthday present. I'm sorry it can't be more."

She opened the box and lifted out a thin gold bracelet. She was so relieved. "It's lovely, Sal. How did you get this?"

"Marie helped me," he said.

"It's perfect." Sal fastened the bracelet on her slender wrist. She held her hand out and the gold glinted in the candlelight. Simple, just her taste. She looked at Sal and thought about her father's words. *A good man like that—you don't want to lose him.* Surely, he was right.

"*Grazie*, Sal." She leaned over and kissed him on the lips. He pulled her toward him with his other hand, kissing her passionately. They separated and Rose looked around, self-conscious. But the other couples were involved in their own stories.

"We'll have more news from the Army soon," Sal said.

"About?" Rose asked.

"What they're going to do with us. We should sit with your parents, make some plans."

She leaned back. "What do you mean?"

He raised his eyebrows. "You know what I mean. Like Vincenzo and Marie."

"We'll talk about it soon." She looked down at the bracelet. "I promise."

"When?" he asked. His face was full of expectation, his eyes locked on hers, his mouth in a slight smile.

"Sal, I—I don't know . . . Let's go back inside and enjoy the music."

"I want to do this right. I'll talk with your father, ask his permission first. I'll get a ring. I'll get on my knees like Vincenzo did—not in public, though. I know you wouldn't like that."

*Permission.* "Sal," she said, too loudly. She wanted him to stop. "I'm sorry. I don't care about a ring. I love you very much, Sal. But I don't know if I want to be married. Not now."

His face shifted, his lips in a straight line and his forehead creased. "Not now? You want to wait? That's OK. I'd marry you today, but I know there are a lot of questions—the trip back to Italy, the paperwork. But we can get engaged now."

She squirmed in her seat. "We've talked about this, about my work. I don't know if it would be fair to you. You deserve a girl who'll make you happy."

He reached for her hands, squeezed them. "What are you talking about? *You* make me happy. *You* are that girl."

She pressed her hand to her forehead, suddenly feeling hot. "You need someone who'll give you a family, like you want. You're going to be such a great father, Sal."

"And you will make a great mother. We'll have beautiful children, you and me." He squeezed her hands again, tears in his eyes. "I know you don't want to live on a farm. That's all right. We could live here, in New Orleans. I can work with your father, open that restaurant like we talked about. I want us to make a life here in America."

Her heart ached; she knew he'd been dreaming of their life together. But she hated the thought of others—Sal, her father— negotiating one of the biggest decisions of her life. She didn't want to hurt Sal, but she also felt frustrated, pressured.

"You and my father have it all planned out." She looked down at the ground. "But it's still my decision, isn't it?"

He tipped her chin up with the tip of a finger. "Is there someone else?" Sal asked, his voice quivering. The look in his eyes was past hurt, beyond disappointment. Anger, maybe.

"What? No, of course not." She reached for him, brushed the side of his face with her fingertips. "Only you."

"Then promise me you'll think about it. *Per favore.*"
She nodded.

"*Ti amo,*" he said and kissed her again.

"*Anch'io ti amo,*" she said. "Let's keep this to ourselves for now, OK?"

They heard Louis Prima's voice from inside. Sal grabbed Rose's hand. "OK. Whatever you want. The band is back. *Andiamo!*" he said, and they headed inside and straight to the crowded dance floor.

Louis Prima spoke into the microphone. "Here's one for all our lovebirds out there. It's called 'How Deep is the Ocean.'" The drummer counted off the song and Lily Ann Carol stepped to the microphone.

Rose felt light as a feather in Sal's arms. She looked over his shoulder and saw Aunt Inez dancing with Pepino. He was nuzzling her neck as she whispered in his ear. Across the room Vin and Marie swayed to their own beat. Her father was dancing with a woman she recognized from the Italian Hall—not too close, but she was glad to see him having fun. She hadn't seen him look so relaxed in a long time, since before they'd heard about Giovanni. At moments like these, Rose thought she'd do anything to keep him this happy. She pressed herself closer to Sal, breathing him in.

# TWENTY-FOUR

At the end of the evening, Sal, Vincenzo, and Pepino said their goodbyes on the sidewalk before they headed to Rampart for the last streetcar back to Jackson Barracks. Sal kissed Rose on the cheek—her father was watching. She smiled at him, thanked him for the bracelet.

"We'll see you next weekend, then? Work on that ice box?" her father asked Sal, shaking his hand.

"*Si,* of course." Sal said. "*Arrivederci.*"

*Thick as thieves,* Rose thought. It was like Sal was already a member of the family.

Aunt Inez flagged down a horse and carriage. Rose leaned against her father in the front seat as they clip-clopped through the streets of the French Quarter, Marie and Aunt Inez behind them. They passed by dark storefronts and quiet houses; most of the neighborhood was asleep by now. A few drunk-looking soldiers staggered their way toward Bourbon Street. She heard the streetcar rumbling by on Royal, bound for Desire.

At Dauphine Street, Aunt Inez got out with Rose and her father, and sent the carriage on to drop off Marie, who waved from the back seat. "I feel like a princess!" she shouted. "*Grazie! Buona notte!* Happy Birthday, Rose!"

Rose followed her father and aunt through the side gate. She was still slightly dizzy from the champagne. They were laughing as they went up the stairs; her father was doing his Louis Prima impression. "Filomen-a! Where's the cake-a?" he shouted, a little tipsy himself.

When they came into the kitchen, Rose's mother was there, at the table, no cake in sight. Her hair looked wild, like she'd been through a windstorm. In front of her, thin blue pages from airmail letters were scattered—Rose immediately spotted Laura's precise penmanship. A few of Sal's drawings lay littered on the floor, and the red Community Coffee can was on its side, money spilling out. Rose felt heat rising to her face.

"What's all this?" her father said.

"You ungrateful *cagna*," her mother spat. She had one of Laura's letters in her hand. "Keeping all these secrets from us."

"Give me that," Rose grabbed for the letter; her mother pulled back, crumpling it. "You went through my things?"

"And your sister with this doctor. *Puttana!*"

"Fil, please," Aunt Inez said. "Calm down. You don't mean that."

"Don't call her that!" Rose cried. "Laura's a hero."

"Hero, *pphh*," she flipped her hand at Rose. "Putting bandages on people. Emptying bedpans. Your *brother* was the hero."

Rose's father backed away, leaning against the doorframe with his hands behind his back.

Rose reached for the letters. "These letters are between my sister and me," Rose said. "Private."

"She's right, Fil. Not your business," Aunt Inez said.

"*Sta zitta*, Inez. It's *all* my business," her mother sneered. "This is *my* house and I found this—this nest of *sin* under the bed. My daughters—always thinking of themselves. *Disgraziato.* Selfish and ungrateful."

Rose looked at her father; all the color had drained from his face. He turned and left the room. "Where are you going?" Rose shouted after him. "Papa! Say something!" She started to walk after him, but he was already headed down the back stairs.

"She's a grown woman, Filomena," Inez was saying. "Twenty-one today, not that you noticed."

"You keep out of this, Inez. What kind of godmother are you? All the men you keep around. Your dead husband spinning in his grave."

Inez raised her palm. "Don't start with *me*, Filomena."

"Carousing around the Quarter at all hours. You think I don't know? No wonder my daughter is a liar, with you for an example."

"What are you talking about?" Rose was distraught, her mind racing. "Leave Aunt Inez alone. And I didn't lie about *anything*. Why can't my own sister write to me?

"Secret letters. You think I'm a fool."

"Nobody thinks you're a fool, Ma," Rose sputtered. She struggled to keep up with her mother's tirade. It was always like this, shifting sands. Answer one point and she'd move onto another.

"And keeping all this money instead of helping out more around here? For what?" her mother said. "Fancy dresses and lipstick."

"I earned that money. Every penny. I pay my own way here," Rose said.

"Rose works hard, Fil," Aunt Inez said. Rose could hear the anger in her aunt's voice. "Why can't she buy herself a few nice things?"

253

"A few nice things? Look at all this money. No, no. She's up to something."

"If you must know, I'm moving out. Getting my own place." As soon as the words were out of her mouth, Rose regretted them. It wasn't how she wanted her parents to learn of her plan.

"Moving out? Before you're married? *Puttana.* Just like your sister." Her mother's face was blotchy, her mouth twisted.

"You're out of line, Fil," Aunt Inez said. She pulled a cigarette out of the pack on the table and lit it. "I won't have you talking to Rose like this. She's a good kid. You should be thanking your lucky stars."

"This is unbelievable," Rose said. She felt like she was going to be sick. "Why are you this way? Ever since Giovanni died, you've been impossible." The words caught in her throat, and she felt tears welling in her eyes. "Laura and I are your daughters—do you even love us at all?"

"Love? You don't know anything about love."

Aunt Inez took a drag. "You know I love you Fil, but you're a hypocrite. Accusing Rose of keeping secrets when you've kept the biggest secret of them all."

"Don't," her mother warned, waving her finger at Aunt Inez.

"What are you talking about?" Rose asked, turning to her aunt.

Aunt Inez put her hand on Rose's mother's arm. "It's time she knows, Fil."

"Shut up, Inez," Rose's mother said, pulling her arm away.

"If you don't tell her, I will. My brother paid the price, and I've been keeping your secrets for 25 years. *Basta.* Enough."

Rose didn't understand. She saw fury in her mother's eyes. But also, something else: Fear? Sadness? Bitterness?

"Stay out of it, Inez," her mother snapped.

Aunt Inez pointed her cigarette at Rose's mother. "Tell her or I will."

"Tell me *what?*" Rose said. "What the hell is going on?"

"Watch your mouth," her mother said. Rose just stared at her. Aunt Inez took a puff of her cigarette and tapped the ashes.

"Your choice, Fil."

Rose's mother motioned with two fingers to Aunt Inez. "Give me one of those." Aunt Inez handed her a cigarette and lit it for her. Rose watched her mother take a deep drag of the cigarette, then another. She stood and walked toward the sink, looking out the window with her back to them.

"It's about your brother," Rose's mother said, blowing out a cloud of smoke.

Rose started to tear up again. "Did you hear something more from the war department? Do you know how he was killed?"

"It's not that," her mother said, waving the smoke away. "Something else."

Rose stood there, feeling stupid. She put her hands on her hips, looking from her aunt to her mother's back, waiting.

"*Aspetta.*" Aunt Inez held her hand up to Rose.

"Giovanni had a different father from you and Laura." Her mother exhaled. "Happy now, Inez?"

Rose couldn't process what her mother was saying. She felt a pounding in her ears. "What do you mean a different father? Who?"

"It was an impossible situation," her mother said. She turned to face them, covering her eyes with her hand. "Dammit. I swore I would go to my grave with this."

"Who? Ma, for the love of God, who was it?" It felt like her mother wanted to punish her, to bludgeon her with this information.

"Father Tony," she said. She clapped her hand over her mouth and started to cry.

Rose felt like the floor was moving out from underneath her. She gripped the edge of the table to steady herself. "What are you talking about? Father Tony?"

255

"We were selfish. Fools."

"What about Papa?"

"He stepped up," Aunt Inez said. "He loved Giovanni as if he was his own son. It was the only way."

Her mother drew a handkerchief from her pocket. "I—I can't do this now." She blew her nose. She extinguished the cigarette in the sink.

"Wait, Ma." Rose opened her mouth but had a hard time forming words. She was as much enraged as she was confused. She reached out her hand, but her mother pushed it away.

"And now Giovanni's gone. This is what happens when you think only of yourself. When you forget about family, about God. He doesn't forget." Her mother walked off down the hall to Giovanni's room, slamming the door behind her.

"I'm so sorry, Rose," Aunt Inez said, putting her hand on Rose's shoulder. "I wish there'd been a better way to tell you, and I wish it wasn't on your birthday."

Rose was pacing in tight circles around the cramped kitchen. "It's unbelievable," she said again.

"It's been quite a day. We'll talk more tomorrow. I'll tell you whatever you want to know." Aunt Inez gathered her purse and jacket. "Go easy on her, if you can. You have no idea what it was like back then. How frightened she would have been. You have choices she never did."

After her aunt left, Rose sat at the kitchen table, feeling more alone than she ever had in her life. She felt suddenly exhausted, hollowed out. Too upset and confused even to muster up tears. She stood and walked into the parlor. The votive candle flickered in front of Giovanni's photo. She lifted the picture and looked closely at her brother's face. Her *half brother*. She saw something of Father Tony's dark good looks in him—the sultry eyes, the perfect smile. Had Giovanni known the truth? Memories started to wash over her, unexplained events clicking into place. The math about her parents' anniversary and Giovanni's birthday—she had never thought much of it, sure her parents were just fooling around before the wedding. Father Tony and her mother on the floor the day they got the news about Giovanni. The tender way he'd brushed her mother's hair from her forehead. Her father's impatience with the priest. She returned the picture to its shelf and blew out the candle. She desperately wished she could talk to Laura. How could her parents have kept this from them?

She went back to the kitchen and gathered up the scattered letters, smoothing out the pages her mother had crumpled. The pleasant buzz from the birthday champagne was long gone and her head ached. She poured a glass of water from the sink and looked through the open window down to the courtyard. A slight breeze cooled her face as she sipped the water. The tip of her father's cigar glowed in the darkness. They'd been loud; he must have heard everything. What was he thinking?

She stuffed the letters back into their box, then picked up the money and returned it to the coffee can. She stood there, unsure of what to do next, then heard her father coming up the stairs. He came through the kitchen door. His tie was undone and his hair—so elegantly pomaded just a few hours ago—mussed up. His eyes looked so tired. Pouchy and worn. Old.

"Why didn't you tell us?" Rose said, tears rolling down her face.

"I'm so sorry, *cara*," he said. "When you were little, you wouldn't have understood. Then when you girls got older, it seemed not to matter anymore."

"How could it not matter? We went to Mass every Sunday and Father Tony was there. He spent time in this house. How did you stand it?"

"I did what I had to do."

"And when Giovanni was killed . . ."

"Your mother's been punishing herself since Giovanni's death. She thought it was payback for her sin."

Rose could never have imagined this was the explanation for her mother's wild grief. Her father understood her mother in a way she never would. "Did Giovanni know?"

Her father shook his head. "No. We didn't want him to think he was any different from you and your sister. Now he's gone, though. It doesn't seem to matter so much. Except to Father Tony probably." His voice was quavering.

She went to him and hugged him tightly, weeping. "Papa, I can't believe you married Mama knowing she was carrying another man's baby. A priest, of all people!"

"I did it for her. I loved her, don't forget that, *cara*. I still love her." He kept his grip on her, and Rose could feel him breathing hard, shaking a little. "And I loved your brother every bit as much as I love you and Laura. Giovanni was my son. Don't ever let anyone tell you otherwise."

Rose stepped back, wiping her eyes with the back of her hand. "We need to tell Laura."

"When she gets home," he said, handing her his handkerchief. "When the time is right."

"I can't believe it."

"Things happen. Things that can change your life forever," he said.

"Do you regret it?" Rose asked. "Now, I mean."

He was quiet for a long moment. "I love my family. I'd do the same thing again, even knowing how it would turn out. Listen to your heart, *cara*. You don't get to go back."

# TWENTY-FIVE

A few days later, Rose pulled open the heavy cypress doors of Immaculate Conception Church and entered the hush of the sanctuary. She stopped for a minute to let her eyes adjust and breathed in the sweet smell of incense. Her footsteps echoed as she made her way toward the bank of offertory candles up front. Two nickels clanged in the metal box, and she lit the wicks with a long taper: one for Giovanni, one for Laura. Kneeling, she blessed herself, and looked up at the statue of Saint Joseph. *San Giuseppe, may Giovanni rest in peace. Please, keep my sister safe and bring her back to us soon,* she prayed silently. Saint Joseph had married Mary even though she was already pregnant and brought up Jesus as his own son. Rose's heart ached for her father, who'd made the same sacrifice.

The green light was on above the ornately carved confessional booth. She remembered her mother dragging Giovanni, Laura, and her to confession every week as youngsters. They'd made up little kid sins, so they'd have something to say. *I fought with my sister. I fibbed to my father. I didn't share my toys.* How innocent they were. It crossed her mind now that their frequent visits to Immaculate Conception might have had something to do with Father Tony—a chance for her mother to see him, for the priest to see his son. She took a deep breath, steeling herself for this conversation.

She climbed inside the confessional box and knelt, drawing the heavy purple velvet drape closed behind her. A small candle inside a red glass glowed on a high shelf. She could hear the priest shuffling around on his side of the booth. The little wooden door slid open to expose the lattice panel between the two sides. She knew she was visible, but the priest was only a silhouette. She smelled tobacco and spearmint gum. Father Tony.

"Bless me father, for I have sinned. It has been a month since my last confession," she began.

"That's a long time, Rose." His voice triggered images: Giovanni's photograph, her mother at the kitchen table surrounded by Laura's letters, Father Tony and her mother on the floor the day they got the terrible news. He cleared his throat. "I hear you had a talk with your mother."

So, he knew the secret was out. "Yes, Father."

"Are you OK?" he asked.

The question took her by surprise. Why wouldn't she be OK? She felt awkward talking to him through the little screen, but she was grateful she didn't have to look at him directly. "I'm fine. But I have so many questions."

"Let's do the confession, then we can talk," he said.

"I took the name of the Lord in vain twice and I had impure thoughts . . . a few times." Rose felt a little ridiculous, confessing her small sins in the face of what she knew about this man. *Her brother's father.*

"Anything else?" he asked.

"Not really. I'm trying not to be a disappointment to everyone, but I guess that's not really a sin." She hadn't expected to say any such thing, but once she said it, she knew it was true. The situation with Sal had been weighing on her mind.

"I'm sure you could never be a disappointment, Rose. Do you want to talk about it?"

"No, I want to talk about my brother," she said, struggling to keep her voice at a whisper. *Your son*, she wanted to scream and realized she was furious with Father Tony. "I want to talk about how my parents could have kept such a secret from him, from us, all these years. How my mother . . . and *you* . . . and my father could have . . . I don't know."

His shadow form adjusted itself in the chair. "It's a lot to take in. I understand."

"Do you? Because I *don't* understand. Maybe you can explain it to me, father." She wasn't used to talking to priests this way. It wasn't how she was raised. But the rage she'd been feeling the last few days was bubbling up. Her parents seemed to want to sweep the whole thing under the rug, never to speak of it again. She had no place to put her anger. "You all went on like nothing happened? Giovanni made his First Holy Communion, his Confirmation in this church. With *you*."

"I felt lucky just to be near him," Father Tony said. "To watch him grow up into such a fine young man, thanks to your mother and father. I never thought I'd get that chance."

"Priests aren't supposed to get that chance," Rose said. She knew it sounded bitter, but along with everything else, he had shattered her sacred notion of what it meant to be a priest.

"I know it was wrong, what your mother and I did," he continued. "We were so young. I was still in the seminary. We tried to make the best of it, did what we thought was right."

"Wouldn't it have been right to stand by my mother?" Rose asked. She'd been trying to think about what Aunt Inez had said, how her mother would have been younger than Rose was now— afraid, vulnerable, and in love.

His shadow nodded, then went quiet for a moment. "I made a promise to God, Rose. I had to follow my vows, not my heart," he said, his voice cracking. "I know you're angry, and I don't blame you. There was no rule book. Your father stepped up, and we all decided. And after a while, it was just . . . life. I pray for Giovanni every day, still." She saw his shadow reach a hand to his eyes.

"I miss him so much," Rose said, tears welling in her throat. She could see Giovanni's face: his fine, straight nose, strong jaw, beautiful smile. "It was bad enough when he was away at war, but knowing I'll never see him again is so hard. No goodbye, no nothing."

She heard Father Tony shifting, the sound of paper rustling, perhaps a bible. "I think we all feel that way," he said, his voice just above a whisper. "He's left an unfillable hole in our hearts." His voice trailed off.

She could feel his pain sifting through the lattice between them, and it tempered her anger. He'd loved her brother too, of course, and had to grieve for him alone. He'd made mistakes, but even if he was a priest, he was just a man, after all. A father who'd had to watch another man raise his son, marry the woman he loved.

"It's hard enough losing a brother. I feel like I've lost my mother too." Rose hadn't even realized the truth of it until she said it out loud.

She heard him take in a deep breath, then let it out slowly. "In a different way, I lost her too, all those years ago. But I've stopped asking myself the 'what if' question. Regrets don't help anyone."

Rose thought about the conversation with her father. *You don't get to go back.*

Father Tony sat up in his chair. "I don't know what else to say, Rose. I know I'm the one who's supposed to comfort people, but I don't think I have any words that will help you right now." Outside the confessional, the heavy church door creaked open and banged shut. "For your penance: three Hail Marys, two Our Fathers, and an Act of Contrition. May God the Almighty bless you, in the name of the Father, and of the Son, and of the Holy Ghost." The silhouette of his hand made a sign of the cross. "Go and sin no more. Amen."

"Amen," she said, touching her forehead, heart, left and right shoulders. She gripped her purse, started to stand up.

"Rose, I want you to know something. I've put in for a transfer," he said. "It's too much for me here. I need a fresh start, away from everything. It's only fair, for your mother too. For all of you."

"You'll be missed," she said. She knew the words were inadequate, but she wasn't sorry he'd be gone. She couldn't imagine having to take communion from him every Sunday at Mass, knowing what she knew. She wondered if her mother would be better off or not, if she'd ever gotten over him.

Rose left the confessional and knelt in a pew before the statue of Mary to say her assigned prayers. She fingered the bracelet Sal had given her, glancing up into the Virgin's porcelain gaze. She felt more alone than ever. She prayed for her parents, for Aunt Inez, and Laura. There were no magic answers here in the church—or anywhere else. She thought about her mother's decision all those years ago, driven by other people's expectations, motivated by shame and guilt. That decision had changed her life.

The next day, Rose sat against the wall of the conference room, her knees pressed together and her toes barely touching the floor. She was nervous to be in the board room with all the bosses. Mr. Sullivan sat at the long wooden table with the other men; he gave her a wink when he caught her eye. She took a deep breath and rearranged her notebook, pen, and folder of reports on her lap.

Mr. Higgins came in with his entourage, the stub of an unlit cigar in the corner of his mouth. He was red in the face, yelling at one of the men following him. "I don't care what he says. The man's a damned idiot!" He looked around the room and spotted Rose. "Pardon my language."

Rose wondered who the idiot was today. "No problem, sir," she said with a smile. Mr. Higgins was irritable every time she saw him lately, which made her nervous. Mr. Sullivan had assured her that her job was safe, though; they'd all be working for the new peacetime Higgins, Incorporated. The meeting started with a few long speeches—Mr. Higgins went on a rant about the unions, with his son, Andrew Jr., egging his father on. The plant manager Mr. Haddock only poured fuel on the fire by bringing up the costs they were still carrying on inventory for ships they'd never build now that the war was over.

Rose kept quiet during the tirades. She felt invisible until Mr. Sullivan met her gaze and rolled his eyes. After about twenty minutes, Mr. Higgins smacked his palm on the table. "Enough! This meeting is supposed to be about the future, and I haven't heard one goddamned idea about what's next for this company."

"Perhaps this would be a good time to discuss our report," Mr. Sullivan said, his voice as steady as Rose had ever heard it.

"By all means, Michael." Mr. Higgins scowled at the other men. "Save us from ourselves."

Rose watched as Mr. Sullivan opened the manila folder in front of him and pulled out her beautifully typed report. He nodded to Rose. She swallowed hard and stood up with her own folder, distributing carbon copies of the report to Mr. Higgins and the other men.

"We've been taking a closer look at the market research about where the country is headed," Mr. Sullivan said. "The returning veterans are going to be getting married, settling down. They'll need houses for new families, and they're going to need them fast. We believe there's a lot of pent-up demand."

"Who's 'we'?" Mr. Higgins asked.

"Myself and Rose, Miss Marino," Mr. Sullivan said. "More importantly, the government economists." Mr. Higgins looked over at Rose, nodded his head. "Now if you look at the first chart on the handout, you'll see the predicted numbers for housing demand." Rose watched Mr. Higgins trace his finger over the graph she'd put together.

At first, she'd struggled to decipher the information she'd found at the university library. Her high school education and one year at Soulé hadn't given her much preparation for analyzing statistics. But as Mr. Sullivan spoke, she realized she knew the material well—certainly better than any of the other men around the table did.

Andrew Jr. raised a hand, interrupting. He looked irritated. "Won't people be more interested in boats than housing? Men will have more leisure time for fishing and so on. Besides we know how to make boats."

Rose and Mr. Sullivan had gone over the answer to this question, but one of the other men chimed in first. "And travel trailers. I read an article about something called the 'interregional highway system' the federal government's planning. If that happens, men will want those travel trailers so they can take their families to see America. They're like boats but on wheels."

"Good points, and eventually, yes," Mr. Sullivan said, and tapped the report. "But in the meantime, they'll need a place to live. Shelter comes first." Rose enjoyed hearing her own words coming out of his mouth. "The trick is to catch the needs of the market at the right time, as they evolve."

Rose's heart was beating fast. It had been hard sifting through all those dry government reports, but she'd bet the data backed her hunch. She knew the returning veterans like Laura and Nicholas, people like Marie and Vin, even her own parents—most longed for security and stability now—and at an affordable price.

"Impressive research but what does it mean for us—specifically?" Mr. Higgins asked.

Mr. Sullivan looked him in the eye. "We should shift our production focus to the modular housing for the near term, like the prefabricated units they're experimenting with over at our Michoud plant."

The room was quiet, and for a moment Rose feared she'd made a huge mistake. Maybe her ideas were crazy. *No*, she thought, pushing away the doubt. The numbers supported her ideas.

"What's the source of this so-called research?" Andrew Jr. asked, sneering.

Mr. Sullivan started to answer. "Well, we looked at the government data . . . Department of Labor, Commerce, Federal Reserve . . ."

Mr. Higgins held up a palm. "Thank you, Michael, but I'd like to hear Rose's take on all this. After all, America's women will be involved in these decisions. I don't know about you men, but I know who really calls the shots in my family when it comes to houses." The men chuckled nervously. "And stand up so we can see you."

Rose felt herself blushing as she rose from the corner. Mr. Sullivan nodded to her. "Well, sir, since the war is over, people all over the country will be getting back to pursuing the American dream. That means homes, children, washing machines. A normal life again, after so much sacrifice. And a house is at the center of all that—a place where every man can be king of his castle."

"Can't the returning veterans just buy from available houses?" Mr. Higgins asked.

"Well, we reviewed housing inventory data, and some surveys that said people want more modern, affordable housing. It's our belief, sir, the men will specifically want a new home, as a reward for all their sacrifice. And women will want more modern conveniences." She looked around at the men and saw scowls—all

266

except Mr. Higgins, who put the summary sheet down and stood up.

He slapped his palm on the table again and everyone jumped. "All the money I pay you people, and our bookkeeper comes up with this?"

Andrew Jr. waved his copy of the report at his father. "These are just numbers, Pop. We should be concerned about profit, not government hoo-ha. What do they know?"

Rose kept her chin level, trying to keep her face expressionless. She hated bullies.

"Evidently more than you. At least they've put the work in, given it some thought," Mr. Higgins said. "Hustle, gumption. We could use some more of it around here. I want to check with some of my friends in real estate, find out what they're seeing out there. Thank you, Michael, Rose." Mr. Higgins took Rose's summary, returned his unlit cigar to his mouth, and walked out. His son and the other men scurried after him, leaving Rose alone with Mr. Sullivan. For a moment, neither said anything. The room felt devoid of air.

"Wow," Mr. Sullivan said. "I think he was impressed."

"The others seemed angry, though," Rose said. "Especially Higgins, Jr."

"Jealous and embarrassed," Mr. Sullivan said. "Don't worry about them. You did good. I'm proud of you."

Rose beamed. "Thank you, sir. I learned a lot." She had enjoyed the research process. It was like exercising muscles she didn't know she had. "Now what?"

"We wait," Mr. Sullivan said.

On her walk home from the streetcar, she decided to take a longer path than her usual route. In her mind, she was going over everything that had happened in the meeting. She thought about her life before Higgins, how her father had responded whenever she'd made recommendations on ways to modernize things at the store. *If it ain't broke, don't fix it.* Now people were listening to her, important people like Mr. Higgins. The work there was real, valuable—not just for the company or for her coffee can, but for getting the country moving again.

A few blocks into the Quarter, old men were sitting at small wooden tables on the sidewalk in front of Cosimo's bar, laughing, drinking, and smoking cigarettes. One of them tipped his hat as she walked by. A family sat on the porch of her favorite house, the white cottage on the corner of Burgundy Street. Across the street was a two-story beige stucco townhouse with beautiful orange and yellow flowers spilling from the planter boxes on the upstairs balcony. A hand-lettered sign was fastened to one of the dark blue shutters covering the windows on the lower floor. *Apartment for rent.* Rose took a small notebook and pencil out of her purse and scribbled down the name and phone number.

# TWENTY-SIX

This was the first time Rose had taken the bus ride to Jackson Barracks alone. Marie was coming later, catching a ride with the Battaglias. Rose told Marie she needed to have this conversation with Sal by herself. As the bus crested the bridge, she saw the sprawling Higgins Industrial Canal plant below. Quiet on a Sunday, now that war production was over, but ready for whatever was to come next.

The bus let her off at the entrance. She waved to the guard as she walked through the gate and up the crushed-stone path. It was a breezy autumn day, sunny and cool. She wore a tan skirt and a forest green short-sleeved cable-knit sweater. She loved the sweater, but her arms were cold, and she hugged herself. There were more US Army soldiers around now, and Rose knew it wouldn't be long until they took over the base again. She took a deep breath, pausing to touch the scapular at her neck, not for Laura or even Giovanni this time, but for herself.

She found Sal playing cards at a table in the back of the training building. His hair had gotten a little longer and curly, and she felt the same flutter in her stomach she always had when she saw him after being away, when she was reminded he was real. He was with Vin and their friends Nunzio and Giuseppe, who was engaged to

Felicia, one the Battaglias' cousins. All four Battaglia sisters had engagement rings and were planning a big trip to Italy to meet their fiancés' families, then to Sicily for a round of weddings at some point. After the men were sent back.

Sal looked up and his eyes met Rose's. He smiled, then looked down at his cards and held up one finger. "*Aspetta,* I'll be right there."

She sat on a sofa and watched the men play cards. She remembered an earlier time, when he'd thrown down his cards and rushed to greet her. He seemed so sure of her now. And she was sure of him too, no longer worried some other girl was going to steal him away.

Sal pushed his chair back. "I'm out," he said.

"Afraid to lose, eh?" Nunzio said.

Sal opened his palms to them. "Look at her—can you blame me?" The men shook their heads. He held Rose by the waist and kissed her on the lips—a little longer than usual, probably to show off for his friends. Rose didn't mind, though she felt herself blushing.

"You're alone?" Vincenzo asked, unable to hide his disappointment.

"Marie had to help her mother with something," Rose lied. "Don't worry, she'll be out later." She tried to smile and stay calm.

"Let's take a walk on the levee," Sal said.

Her stomach clenched. There would be no more postponing the conversation. She squeezed his warm hand and followed him outside and up the grassy slope to the top of the levee. They walked along the dirt path beside the river. Seagulls swooped and rode the wind and small whitecaps swirled on the surface of the water, marking the currents. A red tugboat nosed a barge loaded with giant burlap bags toward the Domino sugar factory, just downriver.

270

"Looks like they're back up and running," Rose said. "I've almost forgotten what it's like to have sugar in my coffee." She tucked her hair behind her ears, but it kept blowing forward. She shivered in the cool breeze. She knew she was stalling and had to get on with it.

"Here, take this," Sal said, draping his jacket over her shoulders.

"Thanks," Rose said. The coat was warm and smelled like Sal—tobacco and aftershave. She closed her eyes briefly to impress his scent in her memory. "Any news?"

"Nothing official. But Pepino told us he saw orders for trains to come for 24 men on October 10, and tickets for boat passage from Norfolk, Virginia to *Napoli*. He showed us on the map. Might be for us, might not."

"That's just two weeks from now!" Rose said. She'd known his departure was inevitable, but it hit her in that moment: soon he'd be an ocean away. "Why don't they tell you more?"

"I think they don't want to get us riled up. They know how so many of us have . . . ties here now."

Rose wrapped his jacket around her more tightly. She took a deep breath. "The river looks beautiful today."

He stopped walking. "Nowhere near as beautiful as you, *topolino*." He wrapped his strong arms around her. Even without his jacket on, he was so warm. "I get sad thinking about leaving. I feel like time is speeding up."

She stepped back from him and felt the chilly wind off the river on her face. "Sal, we need to talk," she said. She tried to keep the quiver out of her voice. "I owe you an answer."

He looked at her, his eyes bright and a small smile at the corners of his mouth.

She held his gaze. Hesitating would only make it worse. "I'm sorry, but I can't marry you."

His brow furrowed. The crooked smile became a grim line. "No, *cara*. You can't mean that. I thought you loved me."

She kept her voice steady, though she couldn't keep the tears at bay. "*Si*, I love you, but I just can't."

He pinched the bridge of his nose with his fingers and stepped back. "Can't—or won't?"

"I'm so sorry, Sal." She reached out to touch his arm, but he pulled away.

"I don't understand," he said. He was red in the face now, looking down at the ground. "The others are all planning trips to Italy. I thought we could travel to my family's farm so you could meet them all, then get married in Sicily with the others. Everyone expects it. Please, Rose. Think about it."

"I don't care what other people expect." She knew it sounded harsh, but she needed him to hear her. "It might be wonderful for a while, but I think I'd regret it—being tied down with a husband, with children."

"Tied down—you say it like it would be so terrible. We're not like your parents," he said.

She hadn't told him the secret about Giovanni, but he knew her parents' marriage wasn't the best. "This has nothing to do with them," she said, though in the back of her mind she knew it did. Her father made the ultimate sacrifice, raising another man's child, even though he got the girl he was in love with. Her mother was forced to give up Father Tony, to settle down and live the life her family expected of her. Rose wanted to chart her own course, not be forced into a decision. "I have other hopes and dreams for myself. Things I have to do."

"What hopes and dreams?" he sounded angrier now. "My only hope is raising a family with you here in America. That's my dream. You are killing it."

"I want to keep working, and I know you wouldn't like that. You'd end up resenting me," she said, though she knew it would

272

more likely be the other way around. "That's no way to start a marriage, a life—with doubts."

He turned to her abruptly. "What am I supposed to do now?"

Rose hated to hear him like this, not the strong man she loved but like a wounded child. "You'll find the right girl. You'll be happy, back with your family."

"*You* are the right girl, *topolino*. I wish you could see it; how happy we could be as a family. You're breaking my heart."

She felt an excruciating pain in the center of her chest. "I know, and I feel awful. I'm so sorry, Sal. You've been nothing but wonderful to me, to my family. It's not your fault. If I wanted the same things as you, I would want them with you."

"So, what happens now? This is it? After everything? We just say goodbye—have a nice life?" He bit his lower lip.

She reached up to touch his face, but he turned away. "We have some time, a couple of weeks anyway. If you don't hate me, I'll come back. We'll see each other before you go."

"I could never hate you," Sal said, softening. "I love you."

She looked up at the gray sky thickening with clouds; she couldn't bear to look at his face right now. "I'm going to get going before the rain comes," she said. "I'll come back before you leave. We'll talk again."

"*Va bene.* I'll walk you out," he said, his words choked.

At the guard shack, she took Sal's jacket off and handed it back to him. She stood on her toes and kissed him lightly on the lips. "*Ciao,*" she said. "See you soon." He held his jacket over his arm, his silence like a knife through her heart.

Rose turned and headed for the bus stop as a light rain began to fall. She could feel his eyes on her back, and knew he'd be humiliated having to explain to Vin and the other men what happened. She felt terrible about causing him so much pain, but she was certain she'd made the right decision. She thought about all the conversations she'd need to have explaining that it was over with Sal. Marie had pretty much guessed the truth already, and Aunt Inez would support her, as always. Most of all, Rose dreaded having to tell her parents, especially her father. He'd come to love Sal and losing him would only bring back the grief of losing Giovanni. She knew they'd never understand. But she did, and in the end that was what mattered.

# TWENTY-SEVEN

Rose took off from work so she could make the final trip to Jackson Barracks with Marie. When they arrived at the training facility, there were no POWs in sight. "Where are they?" Marie asked one of the American soldiers. She sounded worried. "The Italians? Where'd they go?"

"They're already on the train," he said, pointing down the road to the railroad siding that ran into the base property. "You'd better hurry."

They could see men loading luggage trunks, some already leaning out the train windows. "Dammit!" Marie said. "They weren't supposed to leave for another hour." She and Rose took off across the yard.

Vincenzo spotted them and started yelling from the steps of the railroad car. "Marie!" he yelled. "*Vieni qui!* Come here—hurry! They won't let us off." The train engine was already chugging, and men were shoveling coal into a side compartment. Vin was waving frantically, and Marie ran to him. The Battaglias and the Messina girls were blowing kisses to their men. They must have gotten a ride out earlier.

Rose scanned the faces leaning out the windows. She spotted Sal's arm, his sleeve rolled up, a cigarette between his fingers. "Sal!" she yelled as she ran to the side of the rail car.

He looked down at her and smiled. "*Topolino,*" he said, taking a drag of his cigarette and flicking it to the ground. "I didn't think you'd make it."

Rose felt a lump in her throat. Seeing his face framed in the train window, she knew this would likely be the last time she ever saw him. The busted nose, his crooked smile. She wished she could give him one final kiss, if he'd still let her. But he was too far up for her to reach. Pepino stood nearby and she called to him. "Pepino! Lift me up!"

"What? I can't . . ." he said, waving his hands awkwardly as if he wasn't sure where to grab her.

"You can. I'm light. Please. I want to kiss Sal goodbye."

He looked up and Sal nodded. Pepino hoisted Rose up on his broad shoulder and brought her close to the train. She wobbled, holding onto his head until she could grip the window's edge. "I can't believe you're really leaving," she said. It hit her how much she would miss him. When they first met, she'd been just a timid girl. In the time she knew him, she'd become a woman with grown-up emotions. She'd always carry a piece of him with her.

He gave her a passionate kiss. "*Ti amo,*" he whispered in her ear. "I won't forget you, my little mouse."

Pepino shifted his feet and Rose grabbed Sal's arm. She put her other hand on the side of his face and kissed him again. "I'll write to you. Send me some drawings. We'll stay in touch, right?"

"Sure," Sal said.

She wanted to believe him. Hot tears rolled down her cheeks, but she couldn't let go of the window to wipe them away. "*Buon viaggio. Arrivederci,*" she said.

"*Ciao, cara,*" Sal said. He swiped the tears from under her eyes with his thumb, then bent down to kiss her knuckles on the window's edge.

Pepino gently lowered Rose back down on her feet. She saw Marie and Vin on the steps of the train, locked in a hug. A guard was tapping Marie on the back.

"Time to go, miss," he said. She kissed Vin a final time and climbed down from the car.

"See you soon. Be good. *Ti amo!*" Marie called. "*Ciao,* Sal!" Sal waved to her. "See you in Italy!"

Rose felt a pang of sadness at the thought of the three of them celebrating over there, without her. Marie would see Sal again, but Rose never would. A huge part of her life was about to end. Her first love.

"*Arrivederci,* Vincenzo!" Rose called to him through her tears. He blew her a kiss and climbed aboard the train. At least she was pretty sure she'd see him again, when he and Marie returned to America. He could bring her news of Sal.

Marie walked over to Rose, who was trying to stop her tears with a handkerchief. The whistle blew, and the engine roared, puffing black smoke into the air. The women ran alongside, waving and calling to the men as the train slowly chugged away from them.

"*Ciao! Arrivederci! Ti amo!*" The men leaned out the windows for one last look at their *fidanzati.* Sal turned his head and smiled at Rose; she put her hand to her heart.

Pepino came over and hugged Rose and Marie. "I'm shipping out in a couple of days myself," he said. "Inez has my address—I hope you'll come visit me in Boston someday. I'd love to show you ladies around. Bring your aunt, Rose."

Rose kissed him on the cheek. "Thanks, Pepino. For everything," Rose said. She would miss him too.

Marie linked her arm through Rose's. They watched as the train became a speck on the horizon, then disappeared, leaving behind a puff of smoke. Rose looked around at the base. Without the Italian prisoners, it looked like a ghost town—just a few soldiers walking between buildings, no more laundry on the cabin stoops. Empty, like her heart. From a distance, the train gave one more blast of its horn.

"Well, I guess that's it," Marie said.

"I can't believe it's over," Rose said. Her tears refused to stop. "I'll never see him again. The first man I really loved."

"I have a feeling he won't be the last," Marie said. "You'll be OK, Rose. Both of you will be. I'm sad but not for you. You did what you had to do. I'm sad for me because I wanted you to end up with Sal, so I wouldn't lose you. If we married best friends, we'd stay together forever."

Rose felt a lump in her throat. "You'll never lose me." She squeezed Marie's arm.

"You better mean that." Marie wiped tears from her eyes, black smudges on her cheeks. "Uh. My mascara's running," she said, looking at her handkerchief. They started walking toward the gate. "I can't say I'll miss this place, but I miss my Vinny already."

"You'll be with him soon enough," Rose said. "The time will go by fast."

"I hope so."

"Do you mind if we take the streetcar back instead of the bus?" Rose asked.

"Sure. I've got nothing else to do. Maybe we can go get a gelato when we get back to the Quarter."

Rose had always preferred the rhythm of the streetcar to the bus; it took more time, but she needed to think. Marie was quiet for once, lost in her own thoughts. Rose leaned her head against the window, the streetcar gently rocking from side to side as it made its way back into the city. On the sidewalks, people went about their business, in and out of stores. A shoe-shine man was set up on the corner, a dressmaker—back in business now that fabric rationing was over. *Son of Lassie* was billed on the movie theater marquee. Ordinary people, most of them living their lives again with a little less fear, a little more joy than during the war. She'd have to do the same, to find her own life now. Without Sal.

She was exhausted and closed her eyes, holding on to the image of his face framed in the train window. She'd pushed the grief away after Giovanni died, staying busy to keep the pain at bay. This time, she let the sadness in, and it was all right. She had been so full of Sal for so long; his energy and attention had filled her. Now she felt that space opening inside her. The loss was there, for sure, but other feelings fluttered in her heart too: Relief. Hope. Freedom.

CHAPTER

# TWENTY-
# EIGHT

*Three months later—March 19, 1946*

Rose placed a framed photograph of Giovanni on the first tier of the Saint Joseph's altar, next to a small ceramic dish of favas. She took one of the lucky beans and slipped it into her pocket. The store radio played softly in the background—Enrico Caruso on the Italian station, which was finally back up and running. Jake was curled up snoozing on the floor in a pool of sunshine.

"That looks good there," her mother said, putting her hand lightly on Rose's shoulder.

Rose made the sign of the cross and lit a tall glass prayer candle next to her brother's picture. She and her mother had reached a truce of sorts, though they hadn't spoken of the secret since that awful night of Rose's birthday. Father Tony had moved to a church in Lafayette, two hours away, around the same time Sal was sent back to Italy. Rose wondered if her mother missed knowing Father Tony was around the corner—the same way Rose caught herself missing Sal. Now and then she wondered what he was doing, whether he'd met another girl. Her parents had been upset with her at first, calling her selfish, but they had moved on.

Her father and Cousin Carmine had cleared space near the front window the day before and set up the three shelves representing the Holy Trinity. Meanwhile, Rose, her mother, and Aunt Inez had been preparing for weeks: cooking, hauling dusty decorations from the storeroom, planning for the *tupa tupa* pageant later and the meal tonight. Rose had taken the day off from work so they could get everything ready before the store opened. That Saint Joseph's Day would be celebrated in full was one more sign that life was getting back to normal.

Rose's mother fluffed up the palm fronds and tweaked the arrangement of the food, wine, and candles. Some schoolgirls from Immaculate Conception had baked a pastry in the shape of a giant rosary, just as Rose and Laura had done when they were children. Three girls, shy but excited in their plaid uniforms, had delivered the cake this morning. Tomorrow, all this food would be distributed to the poor, but today the altar was on display for all to see.

"I wish Laura had made it home for the feast," Rose said. Her sister was coming home soon, her fiancé Nicholas in tow. They had been stationed in an Army hospital in Hawaii, helping with the last of the wounded men returning from the Pacific and the Americans who'd been held as prisoners by the Japanese.

"Me too. She'll be here for Easter, though," her mother said. "I hope the *fidanzato* likes what we have to eat. He's not Sicilian, after all."

"I'm sure he will, Ma," Rose said. "When has anyone complained about your cooking?"

Her mother smiled and tilted her head. Her hair looked pretty, smoothly swept up in a silver comb. "I'm going to get an eggplant to add to the fruit bowl," she said. "It'll be a nice contrast." She went to the produce section of the store and started picking through the vegetables.

"Good. I'm leaving space on one side for Aunt Inez' cookies," Rose said.

Rose stepped back and admired the display. St. Joseph looked down from the top shelf, holding the infant Jesus in his right arm. The Virgin, in her blue and white cloak, stood on the next tier, just below her husband, her palms facing up. Everyone was right; her mother had a good eye. The altar was a work of art. The bells on the front door jingled and Marie came in with her mother, carrying a tray covered with dishtowels. The Gold Star banner was gone now, replaced by a sign taped to the glass door advertising the St. Joseph's Day events. The Italian flag flapped overhead next to the American flag. Her father had decided it was time.

"*Ciao a tutti!*" Marie called. "We have the *salsa milanese* for tonight." She put the tray down and lifted the dishtowel to show off the big bowl of tomato gravy, brimming with sardines and smelling of anise—the centerpiece of the traditional feast day dinner. Rose's mother had already prepared the stuffed artichokes; there would be *froscia* vegetable omelets as well, and batter-fried *frittura*. The church didn't allow meat during Lent, but with so much delicious food, nobody missed it.

"*Grazie,* Joanna. That looks delicious," Rose's mother said to Mrs. Leonardi. "You're looking nice."

Rose nodded. It was true. "I like that dress, Mrs. L. Is it new?"

"Thanks for noticing," Marie's mother said, her face a little flushed. "As a matter of fact, it is new. A gift." It made Rose happy to see Marie's mother enjoying life a little. Marie had told Rose her mother was dating a bartender from one of the fancy downtown hotels, where she'd gotten a job as a banquet waitress. Marie said her mother's new "friend" Maurice—an older French gentleman—treated her like a queen.

"Marie, are you getting excited for your big trip?" Rose's mother asked.

"I am! Just a few weeks more," Marie said. "I'm just sad Rose won't be there to stand up for me."

Rose wouldn't be making the voyage to Italy. She had too many responsibilities at Higgins, since Mr. Sullivan had been put in charge of the new housing production line and had insisted that Rose continue on as his assistant. She'd suggested Dorothy Messina stand in as Marie's maid of honor. Rose felt a small pain in her heart at the thought of missing the ceremony. She and Marie had planned all their lives to be in each other's weddings. "We'll celebrate when you come back," Rose said. "Something special."

Aunt Inez came in pulling her red wagon, laden with dishes, trays, and bowls. "*Buongiorno,*" she said. "Happy Saint Joseph's Day! Rose, give me a hand with these." They unloaded the wagon and placed the cookies on the altar. *Cuccidati, biscotti regina*, and the *pignolata*—a pyramid of honey-covered pastries, said to represent the pine cones Jesus played with as a child.

"We're off," Marie said, following her mother toward the door. "Ma has to work today, but we'll see you tonight."

"*Che bella,*" Aunt Inez said, inspecting the altar as Rose's mother placed a purple eggplant in with a group of fruits and vegetables. "Spectacular job as usual, Filomena. Always the best in the city."

Rose's mother smiled at the compliment. She wiped her hands on her apron. "*Grazie.* I think we're done. I'm going upstairs to make breakfast."

"I'll be up in a minute to help," Aunt Inez said. "Rose and I will tidy everything up here so Frank can open on time."

As her mother walked away, Rose and her aunt began picking up stray pieces of pastry and wrappings from around the altar. "Have you heard when Laura's getting home?" Aunt Inez asked. "I've been working on a dress for her. I'm guessing she'll need a few new things once she's out of uniform. Maybe for her trousseau too."

"Yes. She should be home by Easter week. I guess we'll have a wedding in the family after all." Rose swept the floor. "I can't wait to have her back."

"Will she sleep in Giovanni's room?"

"For now, yes," Rose said. "But it's pretty small for two people—after the wedding when Nicholas moves in."

"So, where will they stay?"

Rose stopped sweeping and leaned on the broom. She thought of her coffee can stuffed with cash. She hesitated but figured she could trust her godmother. "Don't say anything yet but I'm planning to give them my room. I'll move out, get my own place. I've been saving up. I think I can finally do it. Hopefully I can find something downtown I can afford, not too far from here. Maybe you'll have a vacancy in one of your buildings?"

Aunt Inez smiled. "I saw a beautiful double shotgun in the Marigny the other day. Nice front porch, gingerbread trim, and just across Esplanade so you'd still be close—but not *too* close."

"For rent?" Rose asked. A double would be too much. She remembered the apartment she'd seen all those months ago—it had been way out of her price range. "Sounds pricey. I might have to look further downriver."

"Not for rent, for sale," she said, putting her hands on her hips. "You should invest in some property. You're a businesswoman now, after all."

"*Zia*—I don't have that kind of money. That's crazy talk." She'd fantasized for years about the little white cottage on Burgundy Street, but the thought of actually buying a house seemed impossible.

"But *I* do," Aunt Inez said. "I could front you the down payment, and with your salary at Higgins you'd probably qualify for a mortgage. I'd co-sign it for you if the bank gave you a hard time. You could rent out the other side—it would practically pay for itself."

Rose looked at her aunt. "You're serious?" Once again, Rose was struck by her aunt's clarity and her mind started racing. Her own house? "What would my parents think?"

"Whatever they want. The question is what do *you* think? You're twenty-one years old, not Baby Rose anymore," her aunt said. "Can't hurt to look."

"Maybe Laura and Nicholas could rent the other half of the house?" Rose said. *My house.*

"Now you're catching on," Aunt Inez said, tapping her head. "Thinking like a businesswoman." She pulled some black rosary beads out of her pocket and hung them on the framed photo of her dead husband Roberto. She kissed her fingertips and touched them to the picture. "I'm going up to help your mother with the breakfast. We'll talk more later."

"Yes," Rose said. "I'll be right up."

Jake stirred and wandered over to nuzzle Rose's leg. "What do you think, Jake? My own house?" He wagged his tail. "Yeah. Me too." She reached down to scratch him behind the ears. In her mind's eye, she pictured a cozy parlor—no plastic on the sofa—paintings on the walls, a little backyard where she could plant flowers.

She reached into her purse and took out a small, framed sketch of a lily Sal had sent soon after he returned to Italy. She hadn't heard from him after that, which made her sad for a while. But now she just felt warm, remembering the good feeling she had when she was near him, his kindness, his crooked smile, his kiss. She placed the drawing next to a bowl of red camellias cut from the tree in their courtyard that morning.

Rose heard her father whistling as he came up the sidewalk, carrying a crate from the market. She opened the door for him. "Fresh fish for tonight," he said, setting the box on the counter. He wiped his hands on a cloth, then kissed Rose on the cheek. "*Che bella!*" he said, looking at the altar. "This might be the best one yet. Happy Saint Joseph's Day, *cara.*" He picked up the little framed drawing for a closer look. "Sal's?"

Rose nodded. She knew she'd disappointed him by sending Sal away, and she could tell he was still smarting from the loss. She hoped Laura's Nicholas would help fill the void.

"He's a good man," her father said. He put his arm around her shoulders. "I know you miss him. We do too. *Va bene.* What's meant to be is meant to be." He put the picture down and looked at her. "You did a brave thing."

"How's that?" Rose asked.

"You did what was right for *you*, not anybody else."

Rose had always thought of Aunt Inez as her role model, maybe Laura too. But it occurred to her now how lucky she was to have her father's quiet strength, his courage, his selfless love. "You're a good man too, Papa," Rose said. "Kind of like our own Saint Joseph."

"I am," he said, puffing up his chest. He kissed her on the top of her head. "Well, Saint Frank is hungry."

"Ma's making pancakes."

"Let's go upstairs then. *Andiamo!*"

-THE END-

# AUTHOR'S NOTE

As with most historical fiction, this book is a blend of truth and imagination. Rose and the Marino family are the latter, as are most of the other characters (with the occasional homage to some of the Jackson Barracks POWs and their future wives). Filomena's character is not based on my own mother, just to be clear. Real people who make an appearance in the book include shipbuilder Andrew Jackson Higgins and band leader Louis Prima, but the situations and dialogue are fictional.

This project started with a random conversation in the early 2000s with New Orleans chef Joe Faroldi and his wife Kitsy Adams. Chef Joe told me his father (Giuseppe Faroldi) was a POW at Jackson Barracks, and his mother (Felicia D'Anna) was a local Sicilian-American woman when they met. Like many people, I was unaware that the downriver end of the French Quarter was a thriving Sicilian enclave in the first half of the 20th century—many echoes of which are evident in New Orleans culture and cuisine to this day. I was astonished to hear there were Italian POWs in the US during the war, and that they met and married local women in New Orleans and elsewhere. I thought, "that would make a great setting for a novel."

After leaving my corporate job at the end of 2016, I finally had time to follow up on this idea I'd held at the back of my mind for many years. I connected with scholars, researchers, and others who've been piecing together the little-known stories of some of the 51,000 Italian POWs held in the US from 1943-1945, 1,000 of whom were held at Jackson Barracks in New Orleans' Lower Ninth Ward. I worked with Sal Serio, Curator of the American-Italian Library, and Linda DiMarzio Massicot, the daughter of one of the Jackson Barracks POWs on a treasure hunt for information, artifacts, and people. Together, we identified ten local families who had descended from the Jackson Barracks POWs and the local Sicilian-American women they met and married. Those families have been very generous in sharing their remarkable stories. For more information, visit www.elisamariesperanza.com.

**The Jackson Barracks POW Families**
Lorenzo Nuzzolillo married Eleanor "Noni" Battaglia
Eugenio Chierici married Concetta "Tini" Battaglia
Lorenzo Giancontieri married Marianna "Annie" Battaglia
Giovanni DiStefano married Vergie Battaglia
Giuseppe Faroldi married Felicia D'Anna
Loreto DiGregorio married Mamie Lore
Mario Maranto married Marguerite Graffagnini
Antonio Pezzana married Mary Messina
Ermanno DiMarzio married Dorothy Messina
Giovanni Manfrin married Anna Mae Cassesi

# ACKNOWLEDGEMENTS

I have so many people to thank, each of whom were as essential to bringing this book to life as the Higgins boats were to winning the war. Heartfelt thanks to the DiStefano, Faroldi, DiMarzio, Pezzana, Nuzzolillo, DiGregorio, Maranto, Chierici, and Giancontieri families of the Jackson Barracks POWs and their Sicilian-American sweethearts (please see the Author's Note for more on them).

*Mille Grazie* to Sal Serio, Curator of the American-Italian Research Library at the E. Bank Regional Library in Jefferson Parish, without whom this project might have died on the vine. *Semper Fi.* Many thanks to Linda DiMarzio Massicot for her steadfast support, sleuthing and language skills, and unwavering enthusiasm. I'm also grateful to the many other researchers, historians, documentarians, and archivists I met on my quest, including: Kevin McCaffrey, filmmaker; Heather Green, Historic New Orleans Collection/Williams Research Center; Laura Guccione; Professor Gunther Bischof, University of New Orleans; Kathy Kirkpatrick, GenTracer; authors Flavio Conti & Alan Perry; Bev Boyko, Louisiana Guard & Jackson Barracks Archives; Gus Palumbo; Brian Altobello; Gerald Keller; Anne Marie Reardon; New Orleans Public Library/Cabildo Oral Histories; Professor Boris Teske, Louisiana Tech Libraries/Special Collections; Joe Messore; Dr. Laura Ruberto; Andrew J. Higgins' biographer Jerry Strahan; and Kim Guise at the National World War II Museum.

Special thanks to Marco Nuzzolillo, Octavia Dileo, Ray Pisano, Joe Bruno, Sylvia Giancontieri, Jana Napoli, Charline Provenza, Rita Sudman, Bevin Beaudet, Toni Dilisio, Tom Bonner, and especially John DiStefano and Marguerite Graffagnini Maranto for sharing their time and recollections.

It's one thing to stumble upon an untold true story, it's quite another to learn how to write a novel anyone would want to read. Coach Allison Alsup of the New Orleans Writers Workshop was the book whisperer and I'm forever in her debt for her patience, guidance, and expertise.

So many fellow writers and publishing professionals were generous with their time, advice, and connections. Top of the list is Lalita Tademy, whose voice I heard throughout the process ("Yes, but what's the *story?*"). Also, in no particular order: Alan Brickman, Pamela Rotner Sakamoto, Barbara Ross, Christopher Castellani, Alyson Richman, Kate Lehman, Anne Marie St. Clair, Jim Kurtz, C.E. Hunt, Clea Simon, Tonja Koob, Ann Hagedorn, Tasha Eurich, Michele Mitchell, Vicki Leslie, Charles Jones, the F&S Writing Collective (Kevin Vandever, Valerie Skinkus, and Brenda Horrigan), Felicia Eth, Julia Kingsley, Marcia Heath, fellow New Orleanians Cheryl Gerber, Tom Piazza, Maurice Carlos Ruffin, Ann Boyd Rioux, and Jami Attenberg's #1000wordsofsummer. And thanks to the judges in the 2019 William Faulkner-William Wisdom Writing Competition, who made me feel like a real writer by choosing my book as a novel-in-progress finalist.

To my many early readers, especially: Frances and Kathleen Speranza and Marianne Speranza Hartmann, Rita Kardon, Carolyn Russ, Jeanne LeJeune, Lorraine Downey, Marianne Connolly, Ann Hart, Austen Herlihy, Lalita Tademy, Bob and Marilee Miller, Sal Serio, Linda Massicot, Mickey Levinger, Kate Nathan, Deborah Koch, Dana Eness, Elena Drislane, Joan DiLaura, Mary Devlin, Sue Kaplan, Karen Lustig, Carole Florman,

Ali Webb, Susan Tracy, Alan Roberson, Chuck Hunt, Lisa Henthorne, Kerry Meyer, Karen Lustig, and Gina Wammock. Thanks to Gatekeeper Press and my author manager Kandace Tyler for helping bring my book and Burgundy Bend Press to life.

My first paid job other than babysitting was as a "page" in the Swampscott Public Library when I was 14. I spent so much time there, they just hired me. Librarians have a special place in the heart of this book, as do the English teachers of my formative years, including Scott Webber, Dot Weiner, George O'Har, and Henry Blackwell. I also need to thank the Sisters of St. Chretienne, Saint Joseph, and Saint Dominic for instilling in me the values of noble work, respect, and justice.

Big love to my Italian family (living and deceased) for inspiration, especially Grandma Speranza (whose words and witticisms are sprinkled throughout the book), Nonno, my sisters Marianne Speranza Hartmann and Kathy Speranza (and our dear Laura), Cousin Susan, who loved a good book and a dirty joke, my own "Aunt Inez"—godmother Auntie Jo, keeper of the flame Auntie El and Uncle Den, my Nana Ida, my mother Frances for encouraging my love of reading and independence, and my late father Fred, the hardest working man I ever met. To Bryce and Ruby, and the rest of my family and friends, who cheered me on and grew to know and love my characters as much as I do—thank you from the bottom of my heart.

Finally, to Jon, especially and always. Thank you for your unconditional love and support, and for keeping me well-fed. *Vai piano-piano.*

# ABOUT THE AUTHOR

Elisa M. Speranza is the granddaughter of Irish and Italian immigrants, raised Catholic, and educated by nuns. She's been a writer and book nerd all her life. Her first paid job was in the children's room of her town's public library, and she was a journalist early in her career before spending thirty-plus years in the water and critical infrastructure business. *The Italian Prisoner* is her first novel.

A native Bostonian and die-hard member of Red Sox Nation, Ms. Speranza moved to New Orleans in 2002. She is committed to celebrating and honoring the city's fragile and fascinating culture, environment, and history. She lives with Jon Kardon in New Orleans and Oak Bluffs, Massachusetts.

Learn more at www.elisamariesperanza.com.